# PAST

# HAUNTS

**BOOK TWO OF THE KELSEY'S BURDEN SERIES**

# KAYLIE HUNTER

This book is a work of fiction. All names, characters, places, businesses, incidents, etc., etc. are the imagination of the author, and any resemblance to actual persons or otherwise is coincidental.

## Dedication

I would like to dedicate Book Two of this series to my friends and family whom I have seriously neglected over the past few years as I worked on this series. Most of them didn't even know why I went into my cave and stopped visiting so often, but I am sure they will forgive me.

Love to all.

Special thanks to Megan for the pre-review of books one and two. I appreciate the extra set of eyes and the valuable feedback.

## Kelsey's Burden Series:

LAYERED LIES

PAST HAUNTS

FRIENDS and FOES

BLOOD and TEARS

LOVE and RAGE

# Chapter One

"*Kelsey to Menswear. Kelsey to Menswear,*" the PA system at The Changing Room squawked. That's me, Kelsey Harrison, and The Changing Room is the name of my clothing resale store. Formerly a car dealership, the ample square footage building has been redesigned into a boutique style warehouse, with earth tone walls and chandelier lighting.

I make a bunch of money from the profits of The Changing Room, but the bulk of my fortune is from writing under the pen name of Kaylie Hunter in the erotic romance genre. I started writing as a hobby, and somehow it spiraled into large sums that I have reinvested in multiple corporations and several million still sitting in a checking account. I finally spent some of the recent profits building the new houses, buying the woodlands across the side street from the houses and buying the property across the highway from the store. The woodlands will remain untouched, but on the property across the store, I hope to develop a motel, diner, and bar.

Most of the money though is earmarked for my secret investigation into finding my son Nicholas. While the rest of the world believes he died a few years ago, I know in my gut that he is alive. Katie and Tech are the only ones that know about Nicholas. It's been a long agonizing and frustrating process. Every time we get a lead, the trail vanishes.

I will never give up, though, not ever. I would be out searching the streets of Miami if I could, but the last time I got too close, innocent people died. It's safer for Nicholas if no one knows I am watching. And, in the meantime, I build my contacts, my bank accounts, and try to stay busy. I try to do anything to avoid drowning in my desperation to find him.

"Kelsey to Menswear. Kelsey to Menswear," the PA system squawked again.

I finished cashing out a customer and closed down my register. On my way to Menswear, I saw Goat and his daughter Amanda in my peripheral vision, entering the store.

Goat was one of the club members of the Devil's Players, regular visitors at the store and my home. You would think that my customers would get nervous with dangerous looking, leather and chain clad bikers walking in and out regularly, but if anything, it seems to have improved business. In fact, I think a large number of the women that shop on Saturdays are here primarily because the club works Saturdays as security. The rest are just shopping addicts who know we turn over our inventory weekly and offer unbeatable prices for quality clothes. Okay, so some of them may also come because everyone that works here is a bit off their rocker, but we don't charge extra for the entertainment value.

"Hey, you guys. Is it 3:30 already?" I asked Goat and Amanda as I looked at my watch.

"Nah. Kids have a half day today. Some teacher thing," Goat answered. "I was wondering if you could spare a minute."

"Yes and no. I am on my way to see what's up in Menswear. Follow me until we get a moment. Amanda sweetie, Sara is in my office today. You can let her know that she can take a half day too. Just make sure she tells her mom that I gave her permission."

Amanda took off running, and Goat followed me to Menswear.

"What's up with the Little House on the Prairie dress?" Goat chuckled.

I groaned. Lisa had taken it upon herself to pick out clothes for me to wear, *again*. The floor length cotton dress was simple with little bouquets of white flowers printed on a baby blue background. My shoes were boring baby blue slip-on sandals. My normal attire ranged from street bum to slutty bitch, but I didn't want to hurt Lisa's feelings, so I wore the ugly dress.

"Ahh. Just trying something different today," I answered.

I turned the corner to menswear and struggled not to laugh. Two middle-aged men were playing tug of war with a navy business suit. Katie was leaning against the wall, hand on forehead, eyes closed and appeared to be counting to 1000.

"I saw it first!" yelled the first man.

"No, I had it and set it down for a minute to look at something else. It's my suit. Find your own!" screeched the second man.

"I'm not leaving without this suit," the first man insisted.

"STOP!" I yelled.

Both men turned toward me, still clenching their share of the suit.

"I am Kelsey, the owner. Now give me the suit before you ruin it."

They looked at each other but still held on to their portions.

"NOW!"

Both men released the suit to me, and I passed it over to Katie.

"Both of you get the hell out of my store and don't return until you learn to act like adults." I pointed toward the door, but neither moved. "You walk out on your own, or I call the cops to drag your asses out. It's your choice. You have three seconds."

Both men turned and stomped out of the store.

"You couldn't handle that yourself?" I asked Katie.

"I was going to hit them. And, the last time I hit someone, Donovan made me run six miles on the treadmill, and you made me clean the toilets for a week. I didn't know what else to do. I have no tolerance for this bullshit today," she vented as she dragged a hand roughly through her hair.

She did look a little wild-eyed.

I went to the PA and called Anne to Menswear while Katie leaned back up against the wall and appeared to be counting again.

"What's up?" Anne asked coming in through the back hallway door.

"Do you mind taking over Menswear for the rest of the day? It seems Katie is having anger management issues," I laughed.

Katie mumbled 'bitch' but chuckled as well.

"Love, Love, Love too! Lisa is driving me crazy in Bridal & Gowns talking about different seam lines, Italian lace, pearl buttons, ugh! I know she knows her shit, but that doesn't mean I want to be tutored," Anne said. "Go. I got it. I'm sure you have other stuff to do."

Anne leaned over and picked up some of the fallen clothes. "And Kelsey, you may want to head out back. On my way through, it sounded like Alex and the contractors were arguing again. It was getting pretty loud."

Days like today, it was hard to remember that I started the business in a 750-square foot storefront. Women's wear represents the majority of our business, but our Menswear and Bridal & Gowns departments have been growing fast. If the contractors ever complete the construction, both of these departments would move into adjacent buildings, linked by access hallways to the main store.

I can't take the credit for our success, though. I hired amazing people to help me run the store and within a short period of time, not only did the profit rates soar, but those same employees became family to me.

My new family consisted of Hattie, Alex, Lisa, Katie, Anne, and of course, the ever-endearing little Sara, aka *little-bug*. In my own way, I've adopted them. We're not what most would call normal, but we don't care to be either. We like who we are, and together, we are pretty damn unstoppable.

Anne and Sara were the first to earn their place in my life. Anne is the sensitive and empathetic one of our group and is the single mom to seven-year-old Sara. They had it rough before they came to Michigan. There are things that only I know of their past and for their safety, it needs to stay that way.

Sara attends school online and is most assuredly not like other kids, placing at a middle school education level in most of her studies and computer skills that scare the shit out of me. On the outside, she's all kid with long curly brown hair bouncing behind her as she skips from one end of the store to the other and big brown eyes that sucker us into spoiling her rotten.

Unlike empathetic Anne, Katie is in a class of her own. She's bossy, confrontational, stubborn and a tad bit bitchy. She also has a gentle heart under that thick skin of hers that she tries to keep hidden, but we see it.

She was promoted to store manager and does a fantastic job keeping up with the books, the buildings, and employees.

Alex is our everyday prankster and inventory guru. Without him, we would be lost and run out of clothes to wear, let alone, sell. We never know from day to day if he will be wearing men's or women's clothes or a combination of both, and none of us care. Always present is a big bright white smile and a fake diamond in one ear. And, his taste in shoes is impeccable.

Hattie is our rock. Entering the workforce after she retired, she joined us and took over laundry services. She also helps with purchasing and dress alterations. And, while her work at the store is beyond perfection, it's all the other tasks she does to keep us going that we count on the most. She's the one that will make you chocolate chip cookies when you need cheering up or bring you a fresh cup of coffee at 3:00 a.m. when you are working late.

The lovely Lisa keeps us up to date on the latest styles and fashions. Lisa's real name is Annalyssia Bianchi, and she is the daughter of a crime boss in New Jersey. It's a long scary story how she ended up with us, and even scarier how we successfully kept her with us. We still have the scars of those days, mine are literal, but I wouldn't change a thing.

When the dust settled, Lisa decided to keep her alias and drop the long first name. Her father approves of her staying, but the way things heated up between her and Donovan, my ex-bodyguard, I don't think her father had much of a decision in the matter.

Donovan was hired to be my bodyguard, but truthfully, we agreed he would train us girls and help Katie install security systems and to develop safety protocols for the store. He and I share a passion for shooting, and the constant practice has improved my skill level with my Glock 22 and my sniper rifle. Luckily, he never asked why I own a sniper rifle. I am not sure what line of BS I would have manufactured to explain it.

Donovan also taught me some new kick-ass fighting skills. I have a scary ex-boyfriend out there somewhere that I plan on using as a practice dummy if he ever dares show his face. At the present, the restraining order seems to be keeping him away.

And then, we have the local biker club, the Devil's Players. They have become a permanent fixture in both our work and personal lives. James is the President, a good friend and someone you can count on to lend his shoulder on a bad day. He's funny, charming, and very cute in that surfer-meets-biker kind of way, with his long wavy dirty blond hair and bright blue eyes.

Whiskey is the VP, big and jovial, and currently, seems smitten with Anne. How Anne feels about that is still a mystery.

Their Sergeant is Bones. Bones is sinfully delicious with his deep caramel tinted skin and dark brown, almost black shoulder-length hair. I think he's part

Native American, but I have never asked. There have been moments in the past that I questioned what exactly my relationship with Bones was. When he's around, he is constantly touching me. We've kissed. He even gave me one hell of a clothes-on orgasm once. We have chemistry, but I am leery of putting a label on whatever is between us. And whenever I have felt that it may be an issue, Bones has packed up and left.

Where? I don't know. It seems to be a regular habit of his to leave every month or so. No one has ever said where he goes, and I haven't asked. What I know for sure is that when those deep dark brown eyes lock with mine, I start having hot flashes, *everywhere*.

There are other members of the club too. Chops is my mechanic and has a service garage called Chops' Shop. He gives me good rates on truck repairs, calls them frequent wreckage discounts. I have a habit of running into things while driving in reverse.

His longtime girlfriend Candi serves the role of friend and personal shopper for hire. The shopping role is as much to fulfill her shopping addiction as it is to save me time.

Goat is around a lot. He brings his daughter Amanda to the store and house to play with Sara. And, the prospects Tyler and Sam get assigned to keep an eye on me on occasion. Not that I am in danger most days, but the Players tend to be overprotective.

Then there is Tech. He's the club's computer guy, the store's new head security guy, and he is also subcontracting through Donovan's security company now too, running backgrounds and investigations online. Sometimes his computer work falls into the illegal hacking category, but we have a "don't ask, don't tell" policy.

We built Tech a loft office above the one that Katie and I share at the store. He just moved into it two weeks ago, and so far, he seems to like it up there. He watches our security footage while working his other projects and is close-by if we need him. Not to mention, most of the time he is palling around with little Sara talking computer geek and drinking root beer floats. Sometimes it's hard to remember that Tech's a biker.

As I left menswear, Goat followed me once again and we picked up fallen hangers and clothes on our way toward the back stockroom.

"Goat, it's going to be one of those days. Let's talk while we walk." I grabbed an almost empty rack on my way by and started pulling it with us. "So," I started to say, but the shouting from the backroom was so loud that it captured my full attention.

The large overhead doors were open to the back. Alex and one of the contractors were indeed in each other's faces screaming at each other. I abandoned the rack I was pulling and rushed over to inserted myself in-between them before it turned physical.

"Alex back-off! Zach, you too!"

Both were angry, but each took a half of a step back. I looked out the loading dock door and saw what the problem was. "Zach, why are you blocking off the loading docks?"

"It was the closest location to drop off supplies. If you want this job done timely, then you will have to work around us."

He had a snarky attitude going, and I had had a few run-ins with him already. I also knew he didn't like taking orders from women. I pulled out my cell phone and called Billy, the foreman of the construction company.

"Yeah," Billy sighed answering his phone. He sounded tired, but that wasn't my problem.

"Don't tell me you didn't hear all that yelling. The clock is ticking, $1,000 an hour." I hung up without saying anything further and within seconds, Billy came around the corner of the loading docks.

"Damn it, Zach. This is the last time I am going to tell you – don't block the loading docks! Now move the semi."

"I will as soon as I unload," Zach insisted and stomped off.

Billy's fists clenched.

"Sorry Kelsey. I will fire him and get the keys to move the truck. Give me a minute." Billy stormed off after Zach.

Goat was grinning next to me. "So, the construction project is going well, aye?"

"Some days are better than others," I sighed.

An older pickup truck pulled into the back lot, and I knew it was Henry. He was one of our regular sellers and always had quality clothes. I needed to get the semi moved so Henry could pull up, or he would leave like he did last week.

"Alex - stall Henry."

Alex took off running toward Henry's truck as I ran toward the semi and opened up the door. I was hoping the keys were in it but was disappointed after inspecting the ignition, center console, and above the visor.

"I got this, get out of there," Goat said.

He pulled the panel under the steering wheel and cut two wires. Touching the wires together while pushing in the clutch, the truck started up. I walked alongside the rig over to the other side of the building, as Billy and Zach were walking toward us. Billy was grinning. Zach was livid.

"You can't just go messing with someone's truck. I'm going to have to charge you to get the wires fixed."

"See that man pulling up to our loading docks? That's Henry. His weekly drop-offs make us a profit of anywhere from two to eight grand a week. Last week, you blocked off the ramp, and he drove away. So, I will bill you the minimum two thousand I lost last week because you were an ass, and you can bill me the $12 service charge it will cost to tape the wires back together. How's that sound?"

Zach was still livid, but he managed to keep his mouth shut.

"Now Billy – call your crew over, get this truck unloaded and then I don't want to see Zach on any of my properties again. Is that understood?"

Billy nodded and whistled his crew over to unload.

# Chapter Two

Goat and I went back inside. My flower printed dress wasn't warm enough to be running around outside in December, and the cold seeped into my bones. I put on my visual blinders, ignoring all the other chaos around me and made a bee-line for the break room.

"Coffee?" I asked Goat.

"If you can spare the time, sure," he answered.

"I will make the time. I need to recharge."

What I desperately needed was five minutes without anyone yelling, myself included. I poured us both a cup, and we each commandeered a stool at the table.

"So what's up?"

"I need a job. And, I know that, except for Alex, you hire women, but thought maybe you would know of something available at least?"

"I don't hire just women. I just don't get many men applying to sell women's clothes," I smirked. "We have openings, but my concern is the understanding of what we pay. So, let me just lay it out there. I pay a few dollars above minimum wage to most employees. Those that have formal titles are on salary, and make a lot more money because they make me money. Alex, for example, started at $12 an hour. When his contribution to the business increased our revenues by about $30,000 a month, then yes, I put him on salary. But that's not typical. For the other employees, the job is just a lot of hard work for an average hourly pay. And all employees are required to work Saturdays. That means that you would have to exclude yourself from the security gig that you have through the Players for Saturdays."

"I don't have an issue with any of that. I can still make some money through the club on other side jobs if needed. I just need something a little settled in the scheduling end of things. Marcy took off again and when Amanda called and said she was alone, I was out of town on a job. It was a mess. Luckily Bridget stepped in and watched her until I could get back. I need to be able to stay closer to home for my daughter's sake."

Bridget was a club girl, but one that I approved of. She had helped me out on a pickpocket job last summer, which turned out looking like a skit from I Love Lucy, but produced the results I needed.

But, Marcy, Goat's wife, I didn't have anything nice to say about that bitch. Goat and Marcy had lived separate lives for years and she was a lousy mother to Amanda.

I tried to imagine Goat working at the store. Of all the bikers, Goat appeared to be the oldest, with an almost gentleman like demeanor. He was tall, good looking with just a hint of grey forming at his temples.

But on a personal level, I didn't know him as well as some of the other club members. And, I was clueless at what kind of side jobs Goat had been doing over the years for the club. I have intentionally made sure club business did not get discussed with my family or me.

"I have a record," Goat admitted.

"Yeah, I guessed that a long time ago. I figure that's what Marcy holds over you so you can't divorce her ass and pursue sole custody."

"It would be a gamble if things went that way," he said.

"So fess up. What will I see on your background check?"

"Miscellaneous. There is an assault charge, but it was minor. Few small drug charges stuck, and then later I got caught with a firearm after the State had told me I was no longer allowed to have one. I served a couple short stints in county. I've been out of trouble for three years now, though."

"You mean you haven't been caught in three years," I grinned at him. We both knew he still carried a firearm most of the time. "I'll admit, if a stranger walked in with that background, I probably wouldn't hire him. But I trust you. You can let Katie know that I gave you the green light. We will float you around a bit and see what fits. When do you want to start?"

The door to the break room opened and in sauntered Bones. Upon spotting me, he grinned wickedly as he slowly approached and leaned down to kiss the side of my neck.

"Hi" was all he said as he continued to smile.

I was a little surprised to see him. He had been out of town a lot lately.

"Hi," I said while nudging Bones with my elbow and pointing toward Goat, "Goat and I were just in the middle of a business conversation."

"What business conversation?" he asked.

"As in, it is *my* business, not *your* business, type of conversation," I said, poking him with a finger in the chest.

Goat laughed. Members of the club have told me many times that they think it's strange that I will go toe-to-toe with Bones. The Players just do whatever he wants because he intimidates the hell out of them.

"You know, that smart mouth of yours sounds strange coming from a person wearing a pilgrim's dress," he smirked looking my outfit over.

I rolled my eyes but didn't comment on the ugly dress.

Alex stepped into the room, just staring at me, hands on hips.

"What now?" I asked frustrated.

"Are you in one of those moods where you're likely to kill the messenger?" Alex asked with a smirk.

"Not yet, but if you don't get to the point, I might be soon," I smirked back.

"Contractors just broke the main water line and shut the water off to the buildings. They are saying it won't be back up until tomorrow sometime. Oh, and that dress is butt ugly. I wouldn't have even allowed it to be on a sales rack, let alone wear it." Alex spun on one heel and left the room.

"Damn it," I thumped my head twice on the table before I got up to hunt down the contractors.

Goat and Bones followed me, whether to help or for the entertainment value, I wasn't sure. I found Billy in the main room of the future Bridal & Gowns building.

"What's up with the water, Billy?"

"Hylo-lift ran into the main, but we got the water shut off before there was any water damage. The plumber is going to go ahead and run the new piping in the morning since it's already shut off."

I was at my limit. I didn't know how many more times I could explain that our contract was specific that there were to be no interruptions to the main business services. I just stood there fuming. I was too angry to speak. I glared at Billy. I felt rather than saw, Bones and Goat step up and look at me. Then Bones placed his hands on my arms and pushed me back two steps. I just continued to glare at Billy, *the foreman from hell.*

"I think the point that Kelsey has tried to drive home, is that while she expects the construction projects completed on time, you have a contractual agreement that the main building is not disrupted from being open," Goat said. "She has another week and a half before they close for the holidays, and you need to get that water back on, now, not tomorrow. Call the plumber over so we can sort this out."

"What difference does it make if the water is running? They sell clothes," Billy said rolling his eyes.

"Yes, they sell clothes, a lot of clothes. And, right now none of the bathrooms are working which is a city, county, and State violation. Additionally, none of the laundry is getting done, which means that they are getting further and further away from having inventory ready for this weekend. Have you seen how busy Saturdays are? They sell out of inventory as it is, and often have to close early. So, get the *damn-plumber-over-here*."

Billy called the plumber.

When the plumber arrived, he explained that he didn't have the parts to fix the main until the morning. He showed Goat where the line break was, and Goat started digging through the supplies. He found some metal connector thing and started running the piping. Bones picked up on whatever he was doing and stepped in to help. Fifteen minutes later, Goat turned the water back on. Billy and the plumber both just stood there.

I stepped up to Billy.

"One more excuse, one more interruption to business and we are done. *Done!*" I growled.

With that, I walked away. I re-entered the store through the loading dock doors and retrieved my coffee from the break room. I was walking back out as Bones and Goat entered through the backdoor.

"Goat, don't forget to check in with Katie," I said as I walked passed them.

"*Kelsey to Menswear. Kelsey to Menswear.*"

"*Assistance to Registers.*"

"*Hattie to Bridal. Hattie to Bridal.*"

The PA system was getting a workout today.

"*Kelsey to Menswear - Code Black!*" Anne squealed over the PA.

Running now, I threw my coffee cup in the general direction of the trashcan. I didn't stop to see if it had made it. I ran through the swinging door that led to the employee-only hallway. It was the quickest access to the Menswear department. I heard someone running behind me and knew it was Alex.

"I got your back," he confirmed as I flew through the swinging door into the Menswear department.

The two men that were fighting earlier over the suit were now in a full knock-down-drag-out fight. One had a bloody nose, and the other's eye was already starting to swell. Clothes littered the floor. A hanging rack and a chair were overturned.

I swept the legs out from under the guy closest to me and pinned the second guy's arm behind his back, smashing his face against the wall.

"You have got to be kidding me!" I yelled.

I turned and confirmed that Alex had the other guy pinned on the ground.

"What the *hell* is going on, Kelsey?" a male voice asked.

I knew that voice. I turned to find both Dave and Steve, friends and local cops, were standing in the Menswear doorway, hands on their utility belts, absorbing the scene.

"Hey, guys. How's it going?" I smiled while still smashing the man's face into the wall.

"A call came in that you needed some people escorted out. Nothing was said about blood and violence," Steve said as he picked the first guy off the floor and cuffed him. Dave came over and relieved me of the second guy, cuffing him as well.

"That's my fault," Tech said as he walked in and handed Steve a flash drive. I was sure the flash drive contained the video footage of idiot #1 and idiot #2. "I saw them come back into the store and called it in. I didn't think they would take it this far over a damn suit, though." He looked bewildered at the two idiots. "It's just been a wild day around here," he shrugged and left.

# Chapter Three

After Dave and Steve had hauled the idiots out of the store, I went to the check-out lanes to see if they still needed assistance. Katie was already there, running an extra lane. I opened up the last register to help clear the backlog.

An hour later, I was closing my lane back down when Sara and Amanda came running up.

"Can we play on the playground?" Sara asked.

Having been cooped up all day, she needed some fresh air. We had built a playground for her and the other kids behind the store in the field. It was within view of the main house as well, so served both locations. I looked around the store. It was getting busier by the minute.

"I don't think anyone has time to watch you guys right now. What's Tech up to?"

"He has a big project he is working on for one of Donovan's partners. He said he doesn't have time today," Sara pouted.

I saw Bridget, my favorite club girl, enter through the front door, and I waved her over. She skipped over, full of energy, her spikey pixie-like black hair bouncing before she abruptly stopped with a quick jump. I shook my head and chuckled.

"Hey Bridget, what brings you here today?"

"I'm bored. All the guys are out doing something. The clubhouse is clean. Laundry is washed. I even gave myself a pedicure. I decided to come here to window shop."

This was what I was hoping to hear. I opened the drawer under the register and pulled out two vouchers, both worth twenty dollars for in-store credit.

I held the vouchers out in front of her so she could see them. "Take the girls out back and keep an eye on them so they can play for a while?" I asked wafting the vouchers back and forth in front of her.

"Deal! Oh, this is my lucky day!" She snatched the vouchers, stuffing them in her bra. "Well, let's go, little monsters! Coats and mittens required. Hustle, Hustle, Hustle."

The girls went running off, giggling, with Bridget and her spiked pixie hair running after them.

Large, strong arms wrapped around me, and one hand laid flat on my lower stomach. I didn't have to turn to know it was Bones. He pulled me tight against him and nuzzled through my hair into the side of my neck. "I need to take off for a week or so. If you need anything, reach out to James, okay?"

I almost asked where he was going, but stopped myself in time. He had his secrets, and I had mine. I wasn't willing to share mine with him. And, I wasn't sure I wanted to know what his were.

Bones swept my hair back over my other shoulder and kissed up my neck to the back of my ear. He was warm all over, and my body was reacting to his touch.

"I'll be back soon. Will you miss me?" he asked.

"Mmmmm. You already told me to see James if I need anything, so I guess if I miss you, James can fill in."

I giggled as he playfully pulled me out of the register area and proceeded to drag me into Menswear. Anne and I were both laughing as he pushed me along, straight into the menswear dressing room. He pulled the curtain shut and turned me around to face him. He pulled the skirt on my dress up slowly to thigh height, before picking me up by my ass. My legs wrapped naturally around his lean hips. He held me tight to the wall with his rock-hard body, as he kissed me deeply. His tongue was ruthless. He deepened the kiss even more until a moan escaped my lips.

"Take it back," he growled, turning to kiss down my neck.

"I take it back," I panted. *Gone was all willpower.*

"Good," he chuckled and lowered me back to the floor, slowly dragging my body against his in the process.

"Now behave while I am away, or else," he said smacking me on the ass.

With a smirk and another quick kiss, he abandoned me, leaving me a hormonal mess in the dressing room. By the time I had calmed my breathing and straightened my hair and clothes, Anne, Katie, and Goat were standing in Menswear waiting for me.

"What?"

"So, how's the latest porn book coming? Feeling inspired?" Katie teased.

"Shush Katie. Someone might hear you," I laughed.

"I need your sign-off on Goat's paperwork and the contract for the new blinds when you get a chance," Katie said transitioning back into her managerial role. "The folders are under the phone in the office," she grinned and sashayed off.

I turned to Anne. "Next?"

"We are low on men's socks and underwear. I can run and buy them tomorrow morning before I come in or I can order online tonight. It's cheaper online, but I don't know if we will have them by Saturday."

"Both. Pick up enough to cover Saturday and then order a two-month supply online."

Anne took off toward the office. That left Goat.

"Walk with me. I need to check the registers." Moving toward the front of the store, Goat followed. "Did you get everything squared away with Katie?"

"Yeah. She said to work out the schedule with you."

"When can you start?"

"I am available for when you need me," Goat shrugged. "I can start now if you want."

"*Darling!*" We were interrupted by a woman I knew well: Dallas.

Like a gale forced wind, she blew into the store and headed my way. Dallas was Dave's mom, but he didn't always claim her, especially when he was in uniform. She was beyond adventurous, and never gave a damn about what other people thought.

"My dear, it has been way too long since you stopped and visited. I decided I would swing in and steal you away. We can go to the saloon and consume numerous shots and then call Dave to drive us home in the cruiser. Maybe he will even run the lights and siren this time. Wouldn't that be fun?"

She leaned forward and presented both my cheeks with air kisses before continuing. "Life has just been way too dull, and- *oh my, holy hell…., what are you wearing?*" she screeched loud enough that everyone turned to look our way. "Have you lost your mind? Are you sick in the head? That dress is the most hideous thing that I have seen in decades! You can't run a clothing store wearing that! Go! Take that thing off!" Dallas started to push me toward the backroom as I broke out laughing.

"Hi, Dallas. Good to see you too. Stop pushing me!" I continued laughing. "Goat, meet Dallas, Dallas this is Goat."

"Well *Hello, Sexy!* My, my, my, you are at your prime. Mmmmm." She circled him taking a good look. "And that ass, it's so tight."

I believe she pinched said ass, by the way Goat jumped forward.

"Now dear, you must have this fine specimen join us for a drink. It would make a great afternoon, truly memorable."

"No. I can't get a drink. I have to work, Dallas. Look around, it's busy."

"Well, what time do you get done, because *I* am *thirsty*."

"You'll have to wait until tomorrow night. I will go out with you then. How about 7:30 at the saloon?"

"Fine. I will find something else to occupy my time until then. Now, what's the story with this one?" she asked indicating with a pointed finger toward Goat, who was standing right there listening and grinning.

"He's married and has a nine-year-old daughter."

"Happily?" She asked turning to him.

"Happily married? No. Happy about my daughter? Yes," Goat answered with a grin.

"We can work with that," she nodded openly ogling him. "Now, I must find Alex. That man promised me a pair of those slutty boots like what you normally wear."

She gave another look of disgust to my outfit and sneered when she saw my sandals. "I just don't know what has come over you. You used to be such a badass."

She shook her head and walked off in search of Alex.

"What the hell?" Goat laughed.

"That is the best damn thing since tequila. Hell, she probably invented tequila," I laughed.

"*Assistance to the construction site before I shoot someone!*" Alex broadcasted over the PA.

And, I tumbled down from the happy high that Dallas had left me in.

"I got it," Goat laughed and jogged that way.

"Feel free to fire their asses!" I yelled loud enough for everyone on the sales floor to hear. If the customers didn't appreciate swearing, they shouldn't come to my store. We even put up a sign saying as much at the front entrance.

Seeing that the cashiers were backed up again, I opened the end checkout lane. The first customer asked the question that always dumbfounded me.

"Do you have this blouse in red?"

I looked up at the clock, four more long hours until closing.

# Chapter Four

It was quitting time and on Wednesdays, we didn't care what the store looked like, we just locked up and went to the main house. As I exited out the back door, I saw Goat and Amanda and invited them to join us. Amanda and Sara expressed their excitement in squeals and giggles, and the offer of a cold beer sealed the deal for Goat.

Hattie, Katie, Anne, and Sara live in the main house with me, and while you would think it would be crowded, the house is plenty big enough for all of us. My room is on the first floor at the end of the hall and not only offers a private bathroom but opens to an atrium with an exterior exit. I use the room for writing mostly, but on a rare occasion, I sit in the peaceful room just to relax.

Everyone else is on the second floor. Hattie has the bedroom above the kitchen with a built-in alcove that overlooks the back field and a small staircase to the kitchen. Anne and Sara's rooms are separated by a safe-room that they both can access if needed, that also provides an escape access to the first floor and out of the house. Katie's room is the one across the hall from Anne's and doesn't offer anything quite so fancy. I didn't plan on her living in the main house long, so I spent most of my energy planning her next residence.

Lisa and Donovan live in the house next door. And, Alex lives in the house after that, stating he needed some space from all the estrogen, but I often wonder what Alex does with all that privacy.

Our three houses are the only buildings on the side street around the corner from the store. During nice weather, we often walk to work by crossing the back field, which I also own. Being December in Michigan, 'tis the season to drive the short distance, though.

All in all, we get along like most American families. We love each other, work hard and enjoy each other's company, *most days*. Okay, so we fight daily and tend to throw things on occasion, but as I said, we are like a family.

Hattie pulled two lasagnas out of the oven as we walked in and handed us each our preferred beverage. I took my cocktail and downed half of it.

"Sorry Hattie. The lasagna smells great, but I think I'm dehydrated and need some more liquids."

"Way ahead of you, my dear," she clinked our glasses together. "I was glad to get the hell out of there at five. I can't imagine it got much better."

She fixed plates for the kids at the kitchen table while the rest of us moved to the dining room. Some of the adults fixed plates while others decided to wait.

"I invited Goat. Not sure if everyone heard the news or not, but as of today, Goat is officially an hourly employee with us."

Everyone clapped, cheered or thumped the table happily at this announcement.

"Goat, normally you wouldn't be part of this meeting, but I think it will give you a better idea of what's going on and how we run things. We meet Wednesday nights and go over business informally. This way we can eat, drink, yell, throw things, whatever. So be prepared. This sometimes gets ugly."

Several people nodded in agreement and looked at Katie.

Hattie brought me another mixed drink, and I pulled out chairs for us both.

"Thank you, Hattie."

"You're welcome, Sunshine."

"So let's get started – Work assignments. Who's happy? Who's not? Where do you want to shuffle too?"

"I think Lisa has a good handle on Bridal & Gowns and is a better fit for that department. If she is willing, I would like to turn it over to her to run," Anne stated.

I knew this already but needed Anne to bring it up first.

"Lisa – you game?" I asked.

"If Anne is sure she wants to leave, then yes. But she started the department, so I don't want to push her out."

"Actually, I started Bridal," I grinned, "and Anne warned me against it."

"I hate all those frou-frou dresses," Anne said.

"Anne, where to?" I asked.

"Wherever I am needed is fine," Anne said.

"Oh suck it up," Katie said. "If none of us worked there, and you could pick any job you wanted, what would it be?"

"Menswear," Anne said. "I used to have fun there."

"Yes! That's the answer I was hoping you would say," Katie laughed. "I am all for Anne taking Menswear over. Those idiots fighting today were my last straw."

Katie refilled her wine glass, and we grinned at each other.

"For those of you that don't know, Anne is great in Menswear. Anne is the one that got it off the ground in the first place. I was thinking of ending the line when she came onboard and drummed up the referrals. She even ran a coupon promo for the women to drop off their husbands and boyfriends with us. It was a huge success. I still see those same men coming in with their friends. I think it will be great to get Anne back in Menswear before the launch of the new building."

"Any other re-assignments?" I asked.

"I'm tired," Hattie sighed.

We all turned to give Hattie our full attention.

"My hands hurt from the sewing. My back hurts from doing so much laundry. And there are too many drop-off sales for me to keep up with anymore. I feel like I am letting you all down, but I am tired," she sighed again. "I don't think I can keep working full-time."

"Then be our house mom," I said.

Everyone but Hattie turned and smiled at me. Hattie seemed confused.

"What the hell is that?" she asked.

"Basically, keep taking care of us. Help us out when our personal lives fall apart. Keep doing Wednesday night dinners and setting up Saturday night potlucks. Run Sara to her dentist appointments. Keep reminding us if we were supposed to do something, like eat. Make sure we have groceries in the fridge and liquor in the cabinet. Just be, -our Hattie. And, if, on some random day here and there, you feel like working at the store, fine, but it's not necessary. Don't think for a second we are letting you leave us, though. You're family."

She nodded and smiled. "I don't know how I got this lucky in life."

"We are the lucky ones," Alex said seriously, which was out of character for him. He got up and hugged Hattie, who was tearing up.

"So, are tears normal for your weekly meetings?" Goat laughed while several of us wiped our faces.

"Anne is usually the only one that cries," Katie said.

The funny part was that it was true which made the rest of us laugh.

"Bitch," Anne said throwing a piece of garlic bread at Katie.

I caught it before it hit Katie, and took a bite.

"Don't waste the garlic bread. It's my favorite," I said.

"Construction updates?" I said moving on to the next topic.

"Billy is driving me nuts. I can't take much more of this. You or Katie need to be on him more," Alex vented.

"I agree. The construction projects need more supervision. With Anne in Menswear, this will give Katie more time, but it's not enough. I'm thinking Goat did great today handling them. And if nobody has any issues with it, I want it to be part of his job to deal with the day to day of the project."

Everybody around the table agreed.

"Goat, are you good with that? You'll have other duties in the store, but the contractors would be your priority when shit falls apart like today. Katie and I will back you up with authority when needed."

"Whatever you guys decide, is fine with me. I will be glad to take care of the contractors. They do seem to be a little out-of-control. I can see where it's a problem."

"Zach was the third contractor under Billy that Kelsey kicked off the site. Good luck man," Alex said saluting his beer to Goat before downing half of it.

"Inventory. Where are we on stock for Saturday?"

"Under. *Way under*," Alex answered. "If we don't pull a rabbit out of our hat in the next two days, we will be sold out by noon. I need everyone on inventory, ordering, laundry, stocking the floor, all of it. We are further behind than we have ever been." Alex provided this bleak update, followed by downing the rest of his beer. "I'm sorry. I have just been pulled in too many directions with the construction craziness. We just don't have what we need. If we can't get stocked up by Friday, I recommend we close for the weekend. And, that will hurt our reputation for all the out-of-town shoppers that make the long drive."

"Well, folks, there it is. Up bright and early tomorrow. Everyone on the phones and computers getting restocks drummed up. We will re-group tomorrow and see where we are at. We need some big buys. I would rather pay a little more for inventory and keep our doors open on Saturday than the other way around. Hattie, can you call the laundry mat and see if they will play catch-up for what we currently have sitting waiting for cleaning?"

Hattie nodded and made a note on her pad.

"Sara!" I hollered toward the kitchen.

Sara skipped in with Amanda on her heels.

"We are short on stock for the weekend. Can you do a search of any businesses closing down or offseason moving sales?"

"I'm on it." Sara grabbed Amanda's hand, and they went tearing up the stairs to her room.

"I might have a lead on a business going under," Alex added. "I'm watching and waiting. IRS is coming after the owner. This isn't our normal. This guy's stuff is all new, but he's being boxed in quick. He might have to liquidate fast before the IRS does it for him. If it goes down, we will have to jump. But there are a lot of variables at the moment."

"If it does come through, what volume are we talking?" I asked.

"I'm guessing about one and a half our sales floor in volume. It would go on a Saturday sale for sure. But we would also gain stock for Bridal and the future shoes and handbags section if it pans out."

"Keep me informed," I said. "Let's move on for the moment and circle back if needed. Budgets and profit sharing?" I asked Katie.

She opened a red folder. "We are up another 12% this month which is incredible. I have everyone's profit sharing checks in my bag, so be sure to get them from me. Expenses for everything are down, except for the construction expenses. They are already running at budget and about to break their contract. I have the list of items they are saying impacted their estimate."

She handed me the list, and I scanned it briefly before passing it to Goat to review.

"Can you get Goat a copy of the construction contracts?"

"Here," Katie slid a blue folder down the table at him. "These are all the documents and invoices. I can make a copy of everything before you leave. Kelsey also has spare blueprints that you can steal from her home office."

Goat glanced through the list and then looked in the folder, pulling out several invoices. "At first glance, it looks like they are screwing you over. I will go through everything and let you know what I find. Have you paid them for the additional billing yet?"

"No. You'll see in the contract that they are paid in four installments based on work progress. We haven't made the third installment. It's due sometime next week after the rough plumbing and electrical are finished."

"Good. Gives me some leverage. I will take care of this," Goat said.

We all grinned.

While we were all capable of handling it, we didn't want to. Our interests were more focused on clothes and killer shoes. And, the contractors I had hired were very sexist. We had to fight off their bias every time a situation arose.

Tech arrived and went straight to the kitchen for a plate of food. Hattie got him a glass of milk, and he joined our meeting.

"Any new business items?" I asked.

Looking around the table, everyone looked as exhausted as I felt.

"This is a band-aid you guys. We need to fix this. We are understaffed and overworked. I used to enjoy running the store, but it's no fun anymore. And, if everyone else feels the same, then what are we doing? Are we doing this for the money? I can find other ways for all of you to make money. And I make more money on my books and other investments than the store profits anyway. Should I burn the plans for across the street and sell that property? I don't know how to get ahead of this anymore."

"Hire more people," Goat said.

Everyone groaned and took another drink.

"Sorry if I am speaking out of turn, but everything I have heard tonight and everything I saw today indicated that you are at half the staff you need. And, today was a Wednesday. Kelsey explained that the reason you as a group make so much more money is because you each have skills that increase the store's profits. But you are so busy doing the menial tasks that you're not doing the things that make the store so successful. You need at least ten more employees."

Several people grinned and looked down at the table.

Katie pierced dagger eyes his way.

"You have three days then. Good luck," I said and got up.

As I walked into the kitchen, I heard Tech say, "Don't forget to get the applications to me to run backgrounds before you make an offer."

I waited just around the corner so I could hear the rest of the conversation.

"What are you talking about? And, what does Kelsey mean I have three days?" Goat asked.

"To hire ten people- you have three days. You said we needed ten, she gave you a deadline. That's how these meetings work," Lisa answered him.

"And keep in mind that if Kelsey thinks they suck, she will fire them, and you will have to turn around and find the replacements," Katie warned.

"Don't hire anyone that has issues with swearing in the workplace. That doesn't work out well for most of us," Anne offered as advice.

"Fuck me," Goat said.

Everyone laughed.

I fixed myself a plate of lasagna and went back to the dining room.

"Meeting's adjourned. Thanks, everybody."

Katie filled up her wine glass and stole Tech's garlic bread. Goat grabbed a second helping of dinner and sulked as he read through the construction contract. Anne reviewed the online sales that Sara had printed.

Alex got on the den computer. And Lisa sighed when she looked at her phone.

"No word from Donovan yet?" I asked Lisa.

Donovan was back to work at his security firm and traveled out of state for several days a week.

"No. I left a couple messages today. If I call again, I will just sound needy," Lisa said.

"Bullshit," I said, pulling out my phone and calling Donovan.

After a few rings, his voicemail picked up. "Your girl doesn't want to call you again and sound needy, but I think you need to make the time to call her back. She looks in desperate need of phone sex," I laughed and disconnected the call.

Hattie and Katie chuckled as Lisa threw a piece of garlic bread at me. I caught it and took a bite.

"I can't believe you just did that!" Lisa laughed.

Her phone started ringing as she looked at the display and blushed. She answered it as she ran out of the room. Go Lisa. At least someone gets to have an orgasm.

"I have a personal thing I wanted to talk to you about," Katie whispered, leaning over closer to me. I picked up my plate and nodded toward the kitchen.

"What's up?" I asked.

"I don't want to upset you, or anyone else, but I think I need to move out," Katie admitted. "I love living so close to everyone. I just think I need a little more privacy. I'm so used to being alone that it feels crowded here."

I set my plate down and opened the pantry cabinet, fishing out a set of keys. "See if this works better for you," I said, handing her the keys.

"What are these to?" Katie asked, confused.

"You made it in the main house longer than I thought. Hattie and I were betting you would stay a month. Those are the keys to the apartment above the garage that I had built for you if you are interested."

"I thought that was just a storage area up there. Is that why there is a staircase out behind the garage?"

"Yup. Go check it out. If you don't like it, someone else I'm sure will take it," I said.

She started squealing and jumping up and down which brought Tech and Goat running into the kitchen.

Katie went running out the door. Tech and Goat followed.

Hattie entered the kitchen with a grin plastered on her face. "I take it she confessed that she wanted to move out?"

"Yup. Think she will like the apartment?" I asked.

"I have no doubt. You built and furnished that suite just for her. She's going to love it. I've already stocked the cupboards, but I will get her refrigerator stocked tomorrow."

"Sounds like a plan," I smiled.

Anne, Alex and I cleared the dishes and cleaned up the kitchen. Katie came back and declared the apartment perfect and went upstairs to start moving some of her clothes. Goat went upstairs to check on the girls, and Tech went back to the dining room to finish his dinner. I heard my phone ringing from the dining room and went to retrieve it. The display said unknown caller, but I answered it anyway.

"Kelsey."

"Is this Kelsey Harrison?" The voice was an older male and very abrupt.

"It is. Who may I ask is calling?" I said.

"Stay away from my son if you know what's good for you."

"What the hell are you talking about?"

"Listen, Bitch, I won't tolerate a whore like you being in his life. Just stay away, or else."

"Kiss my lily-white ass!" I said as I hung up on him.

Everyone at the table paused from their various activities, staring at me.

"Who was that?" Alex asked.

"I have no idea," I shrugged and slid the phone to Tech.

He started fiddling with it, and I went to refill my cocktail. I wasn't concerned about whoever it was on the phone, but it wouldn't hurt to have Tech see if he could find out.

I had to make some calls yet tonight to multiple private investigators that I had hired so I moved to the basement to work in the War Room. Two hours later, my calls completed, I stared at the map of Miami-Dade County pinned up to the cork board. *Nicholas – where are you?*

# Chapter Five

Thursday morning, my alarm went off at 6:00 a.m., and I was on a dead run from there. I showered, threw on comfortable sweats and a sweatshirt to work restock, deciding I would change later. I had stayed up long past midnight working in the War Room. Unfortunately, I was no further ahead in my search for my son or those responsible for taking him away from me.

Entering the kitchen, I was happy to see that Hattie had prepped a to-go coffee and a breakfast sandwich for me. I decided to walk to the store, but half way there, I wished I hadn't, as the teen temps stole the breath from my lungs. I jogged the rest of the way to the loading dock and entered my security code, slipping inside.

Turning on the lights as I walked through, I caught a scent of something. Paint? Yup. It smells like paint. Must be the contractors had painted something yesterday and I was too busy to notice. I continued forward and opened the overhead service doors to the sales room, flipping on the lights.

I immediately reached for my gun, except I wasn't wearing it this morning. *Shit.*

Someone had been in the store. And they had spray painted, *everywhere*. And, I wasn't sure if that same someone was still here.

I hurried back to the employee lockers, retrieving a spare glock. While checking the safety and the magazine, I heard something fall over in the main sales area, followed by the bells on the front door. As much as I wanted to check it out, I knew my friends would start trickling in the back door soon. I didn't want them caught in the middle.

My cell started to ring as I moved back to the dock entrance and answered. I knew it was Tech, calling about the alarm. It wouldn't have been the first time I had set it off by accident, but this time was different.

"Call the police" was all I said before disconnecting the line and calling the main house.

Anne answered the phone on the second ring. "This better be good. I had at least one more fight with the snooze button planned this morning," she groaned.

"Get a hold of everyone and keep them away from the store until you hear back from me."

"I'm on it. Don't do anything stupid," she said as she disconnected.

Within minutes, I heard several sirens approaching. I stayed at the back door until my phone rang again. The display confirmed it was Dave, my friend from the local PD and I answered. "I'm inside, at the back door, armed. I think whoever was inside left through the front door, but I don't have a visual from here."

"Stay where you are. We will come to the back door." Dave was already shouting orders as he hung up. Four officers entered the back door, courtesy of the security passcodes that Dave and Steve had. Steve stayed with me as the other three moved forward. I heard more officers enter through the front.

It didn't take them long to sweep the store and call the all clear. I unloaded my glock and locked it back up, before heading up front.

I heard motorcycles pulling up, and I called the main house to let them know I was safe, but to stay put for a while. I walked around the front sales room and tried to mentally absorb all the damage.

Black spray paint accented the walls and floors with pleasant one-word messages such as slut, whore, and bitch. Clothes racks had been knocked over, and the clothes painted. Luckily, we hadn't restocked the night before, so the majority of our inventory was untouched in the back room. The registers and counters also had paint in some spots, but the registers were bolted down so no other damage was done. The overhead doors to Bridal and Menswear were closed and locked, so those areas also appeared to be undamaged.

"What the hell? How did someone get in here without the alarm going off?" I yelled.

I checked the office for damage and was relieved to see that Katie had locked it up tight, and everything was as it should be. I saw Tech come in, heading to his loft office. Steve and I followed. Tech started booting up computers to get to the security feed.

Dave and James joined us a few minutes later, and Dave filled us in on what he knew. "Looks like someone broke one of the showroom windows to gain access. The windows aren't monitored by the alarm, and they never tried to access any of the doors until you spooked them and they left through the front door. I would guess by the damage, it was just one person, no more than two, in some type of a rant."

"That's one hell of a temper-tantrum out there," I snapped, pointing out the large window looking down on the sales floor.

I sat because I didn't know what else to do. I was mad that I didn't catch the creep. I was mad that someone I cared about could have gotten hurt. And, I was mad because this was going to cause even more work for all of us, and I was already too tired to deal with a normal day.

"Shit," Tech said never looking up from his computer. "One guy, wearing a mask entered about 4:30 a.m. I don't have a visual on the vehicle. It looks like he parked behind the construction semis and came in from the new East drive. We don't have any video out there yet." Tech didn't get pissed very often so when he launched his stapler across the room at the wall, it made us all jump. "Fuck. This is my fault. I should have gotten new cameras hooked up on the new East and West buildings."

I snorted.

As much as I wanted to point the finger and blame someone, Tech didn't come close to being on the list. "Would this be the buildings without any electricity to hook cameras up to?" I asked. "Hell, you can't even take a piss in those buildings yet without aiming for a drain hole."

"You talking from experience, Kel?" Steve laughed.

I shrugged. "Katie and I might have gotten a little snookered in the new East building and needed to go," I smirked.

Tech calmed a bit, returning back to the task of copying the files. I got up to watch the scene play out on the monitor. On the video, I watched as a man moved about the sales floor spray painting his artwork. He had a ski mask on and was wearing all black clothes. With all the lights off, it was hard to make out anything other than his general movements on the video.

"So, we can't ID the guy, but do you know who it is?" Dave asked me. "Does anything about him catch your attention?"

I shook my head. "Could be just about anyone, Brett, a pissed off customer, an ex of one of the other girls, an employee I fired, one of the contractors, who knows," I sighed.

"What about your mysterious phone call last night?" Tech asked.

I shook my head. "He didn't seem the type," I answered.

I could be wrong, but my gut was telling me that the guy on the phone wouldn't be into vandalism.

"What guy?" Steve asked.

"Don't know. Some whacko. Tech, did you figure out anything from the phone number?"

"Nada. It was a burner, and I couldn't trace it. The only thing I know is that it pinged off a tower in Pittsburgh."

I shrugged. I didn't know anyone in Pittsburgh. It was pointless trying to put the pieces together when there was so much work to get done. "How long before we can start cleaning up?"

"Give us a half an hour to take some pictures and check around. No point in trying to collect evidence with as many people coming and going as there are around here."

"Okay, coffee break for me. I will call the troops and let them know they can come in at 7:00 and to wear comfort shoes and bring some paint."

In the back room, I retrieved my travel cup of coffee and breakfast sandwich, which were now cold.

# Chapter Six

By 9:30, the store looked presentable enough to open. Katie had managed to find a glass installer to cut and replace the window. It wasn't tinted yet like the rest of the windows, but it kept the cold wind out. Lisa and Alex painted the graffiti over the walls with a white primer which would have to be sufficient until we closed down for the holidays. Goat got the floor buffing machine going and was able to clear enough of the paint so no one would recognize the swear words. We realized the overhead to the stock room had been painted a big 'fuck you' but we decided to just leave the door up for the day and deal with it some other time. And, everyone, including the Devil's Players, pitched in rolling out tubs and racks of clothes for restocking, while hauling the damaged clothes to the dumpster.

Noting that all was well, once again, I went to refill my coffee and find something else to wear.

"Kelsey," Lisa called as I entered the breakroom. "I found some clothes for you to wear today. This will be perfect for you."

The clothes in question consisted of a mint green polyester pantsuit and a white ruffled blouse. It would make my super white skin look ghoulish, and the style was at least three decades off.

"Uh. Thanks, but I can find myself something. I was thinking it was more of a jeans and boots kind of day," I responded while filling my coffee cup.

"Don't be silly. This is a power suit, and it will look great on you," Lisa insisted and set the suit over a chair, placing matching shoes on the table before leaving. I looked back at the suit and sighed. What the hell… If it will make her happy … I've worn worse.

Customers were lined up outside in the cold when I opened the doors at 10:00, but within minutes, they were all happy campers. I turned toward my office when I heard someone calling me. "Kelsey, Darling!"

I smiled knowing who it was before turning around. "Dallas, I thought we were meeting after work?"

"Yes, dear, but I need your assistance," Dallas said pushing Tammy, Dave's wife, in front of her.

It was obvious that Tammy had been crying.

"Fix her. I do not deal with tears. I stopped at her house this morning to steal some fresh baked muffins, and this is what I found." She gestured at Tammy like she was an enigma. "I thought you or one of the other girls could handle it," Dallas said wringing her hands looking at her daughter-in-law.

"Tammy, what's wrong?" I asked.

The answer I received was big crocodile tears, and her lower lip started to tremble. I escorted her, shoving a little here and there, to the office. Katie was inside, but one look at Tammy and she rushed out saying she had to take care of something. Katie didn't do tears either.

I sat Tammy down and handed her a box of tissues.

"Okay, I can't do anything to help unless you stop crying and tell me what is wrong," I sternly reprimanded. I wasn't trying to be mean, or insensitive, but in my experience, coddling a crying woman could turn into an all-day event. And, I had maybe 10 minutes before I would be called to take care of the next crisis.

"I am just emotional. Dave and I have been trying to get pregnant for over a year now. And the doctor has me on these pills. They make me cry all the time. Dave got upset this morning and threw the pills away. He said he didn't want to get me pregnant anymore!" she bawled.

The whole confession came out a whiny, hysterical ramble. *What the hell was Dallas thinking, bringing her to me?*

"Blow your nose, wipe your tears, and stop crying," I ordered.

This seemed to do the trick, and she straightened up and complied.

"Now let me get this straight, you were all stressed out because you couldn't get knocked up, so your doctor put you on hormonal stuff, now you're a mess, and Dave wants his sane wife back. Is that about right?"

She was able to nod assent without more waterworks so we were making progress.

"Do you want to stay on the pills and drive yourself and Dave nuts?"

"No, but I want to have a baby. And, I don't know what else to do. We already tried all the positions, the temperature monitoring, the special diets, the strange schedules, and everything else that I read about."

"And this has been going on for over a year?" Oh my goodness, no wonder Dave lost it.

She nodded again, and I was cringing because it appeared the waterworks might restart.

"So, when was the last time you guys had sex for the fun of it?"

She turned bright red and looked at the floor but didn't answer, which in itself was an answer.

"Okay, this is what you are going to do. No more baby making until June. No temperature taking, no testing, no pills, no pro-pregnancy positions, no pregnancy books, nothing, for six months. You need to get your marriage back together before you do anything else."

I opened the file cabinet, pulling out a half dozen black thongs and bras, and then went to the bookcase and selected three erotic books. I dumped it all in a tote bag.

"Here, take this home. Go call your doctor and tell him you're on hiatus for six months. Take a long soak in the tub, give yourself a manicure, style your hair, paint some makeup on your face, and then put on these undergarments. Once you're all relaxed and feeling gorgeous, then it's time to curl up and read one of these books. For the next six months, you are not to wear any granny-panties. And, all underwear must match, and be dark colors – no whites, no pastels."

She stood and robotically walked out of the office peering into the bag. I could see her face getting bright red as she sped up, heading for the exit. I had little faith that she wouldn't faint when she starts to read the books.

I was on my way to the registers when I saw Bridget skipping in through the entrance. She was beaming. When she saw me, she ran up and hugged me. "You won't regret this! I promise. I will be the best worker ever!" she sang as she abruptly released me and skipped to the back room.

I turned and saw Whiskey approaching. He was carrying a bouquet of daisies and laughed as he watched Bridget skipping to the backroom.

"You have no clue what she was talking about, do you?"

"None, what-so-ever."

"Goat called her and asked if she wanted to work laundry services during the week and floor stocking on Saturdays. She started screeching and jumping around so loudly that the whole club came running."

"Does this cause any problems with the club?"

"Nah. She'll work the earlier shift during the week, and the Players are already here on Saturdays anyway – so it will give her something to do. She's been bored," he grinned.

"Excuse me," a woman interrupted, "Sorry to interrupt, but could you point us in the direction of human resources?" She was middle aged and accompanied by another woman and a young man.

Before I had a chance to answer, Katie approached and directed them to follow her to the office. If my theory was correct, Goat was making good progress on his 10-employee hiring quota.

I was still watching Katie, when she stopped, pivoted around and look at me again. She then gestured for her group to wait for her, and came back. I expected she had a question or needed something, but when she reached me, she removed my name tag.

"You cannot wear a nametag that identifies you as the owner while wearing such a hideous suit!" she hissed. She clicked her heels back toward her awaiting party and continued to the office with them in tow.

I pouted as I looked down at myself in the gross mint suit. Whiskey laughed and agreed it was ugly. I thought about sneaking to the back room and changing until I heard a ruckus up at the registers. Moment over, I decided to see what chaos was brewing.

Dallas was behind the register and arguing with a customer over the total being correct or incorrect by a dollar. She had a 'hello my name is' tag stuck to her blouse and Carol, one of the cashiers, was trying to interrupt and handle the situation but Dallas wasn't giving her a chance. I leaned over the register, grabbed a dollar and a coupon out of the drawer and passed them off to the customer. Then I dragged Dallas away from the register by her elbow and proceeded to the back room with her.

"I don't know why you caved. I am sure I added the order up correctly, and she was being utterly rude," Dallas barked. "And, you gave her a coupon to boot! You should have thrown that hussy out the door and told her where she could stick that attitude."

"I am sure that's what you think I should have done."

I spotted Goat and waved him over.

"Goat, nice try, but not happening. Dallas can't work at the registers."

I turned and left Dallas with him. He created the problem, he could figure it out.

From the center of the sales floor, I heard Anne yelling and looked up to see her toss the daisies at Whiskey and tell him to leave her alone as she stomped back to menswear. Sara and Haley were entering the store's front door as Whiskey stormed past them. He gave Sara the flowers on his way out. Poor guy. Maybe it was time to have a chat with Anne and see what was going on with her.

"Hey, little-bug!" I said, giving Sara a half toss in the air that made her giggle, before putting her down. "Why are you two so late getting back?"

Sara was about to answer when Haley interrupted. "Traffic was crazy, and the library was busy. Sorry, we are late. I will make up the missed time."

Haley used to be a club girl, until she drew a line in the sand last summer and declared her independence and started working for me. She worked the front registers on most days, but also helped out in the back stockroom when needed. She also took Sara regularly to the local libraries and bookstores when time allowed.

"It's fine, Haley," I grinned. "Sara, why don't you take your laptop to the breakroom today. Tech is still behind on his project, and we have people coming and going from the office for interviews."

"Can you come with me and help me set-up, Aunt Kelsey?" Sara asked.

"Sure," I answered because I wasn't sure what else to say. Sara didn't need help setting up her laptop. In fact, she seldom let me touch it, with my infamous record of messing up electronics. But no matter how busy we were, we all made time for Sara when she needed it, so I went to the breakroom with her.

When we entered, Tech was getting a soda out of the fridge. Sara closed the door after us. Tech raised an eyebrow in question, but I just shrugged and had a seat.

"So, if someone asks you to keep a secret, but you think it will help if you don't keep the secret, is that good or bad then to tell?" Sara asked.

"Well, that's tricky to answer without knowing the secret. If it's gossip or something said to you in confidence, you should keep it. If you think someone is in danger or needs help in some way, then you should tell."

She pondered that for a moment before admitting, "Haley might get mad, but I think I should tell."

She nodded her head as if confirming with herself that she was doing the right thing.

"Do you want to tell your mom, instead of me? I can go get her," I offered.

Sara and I were close, but I didn't want her to feel like she had to confide in me because her mom was working.

"No," she answered after a moment of thinking on it.

I looked at Tech, but he just shrugged.

"Okay then, spit it out," I grinned.

"Haley's getting her bachelor's degree, and she is out of money for the books for her last semester. She was going to use the ones at the library, but the librarian wouldn't let her check them out. The librarian said that those books were available for people that needed them. And, she took my books away from me too."

"That bitch!" Tech said shaking his head. "That's not the first-time Haley has had issues at the library. They look down their noses at her all the time."

I was still trying to process the fact that Haley was finishing her bachelor's degree and somehow I never even knew she was going to college. "Sara, do you have a list of the books that she needs?"

"Uh-huh." She shuffled around in her computer bag and pulled out a piece of paper. "I told her I would try to find some cheap copies online for her."

I pulled my cell out and called Hattie.

"Well, Hello, Sunshine. I am just coming in the back door, what do you need?"

"We are in the break-room. I was wondering if you had time to take Sara to the college bookstore?"

"Sure, sure... Sounds like fun. Be there in a moment."

When Hattie arrived, we explained to her what we needed, and I asked her to add on whatever books Sara wanted and a gift card for Haley too. By the time they left, they seemed giddy about their secret mission.

I was still sitting there pondering things when Tech pulled me back to the real world.

"What are you thinking so hard on?"

"How did I not know Haley was going to college, let alone one semester away from getting a degree?"

"She didn't want anyone to know in case she couldn't finish. She has been scraping by to pay one semester at a time. I knew because I helped when she had computer problems and sometimes she had me quiz her before a big test."

"What's her degree in?"

"Pre-med. I've seen her grades. She's aced all her chemistry and biology classes, most of her core classes too. She will make one hell of a doctor some day. She has to wait a couple years to save up before she can apply to medical school, though."

"Damn. I knew she was smart, but that's smarty-pants smart."

I always had the impression that Haley had a rough life before she met the club, and because of that, she remained close to them even after splitting off to follow her own path. They protected her. The fact that she had been working at a college degree for years on her own, was impressive.

I was already planning on talking to Katie to see what we could do to help Haley get into med-school earlier, rather than later. But that would have to wait as the PA was calling for assistance to the registers already.

"On a different topic, can you copy the last 72 hours of surveillance on to my computer? This morning's break-in is still bothering me, and I want to just give it a run through."

"Sure. I will set it up to play on the flat screen in your office. But even on fast forward, it will take several hours to review that much footage."

"I know. I will have to watch it in bits and pieces."

The PA called again for assistance, and I started to leave.

"Hey," Tech stopped me before I got too far. "Was there anything about that phone call last night that would help identify the caller?"

"No. But, somehow I just know it wasn't related to the break-in. The man seemed educated, calculating, cold. Not the type to spray paint swear words on a wall."

"Could it be related to our search for Nicholas? Could someone have found out we are looking for him?" Tech whispered.

"That doesn't fit either. The guy on the phone was warning me to stay away from his son. During the adoption process, I had to track down Nicholas's biological father and get his sign off. He was all for it. He didn't want to worry about paying child support to Nola."

"It would probably be easier if there were a few less bad guys to scratch off the list," Tech said.

I had to agree with him.

# Chapter Seven

Several hours later, the store had calmed down enough for me to grab a sandwich and start watching some of the surveillance videos. To make the process faster, Tech had set the TV to run six cameras on one screen. I didn't think there would be anything surprising on the indoor footage, so in fast forward motion, I tried to concentrate on the outdoor parking and driveway footage. I was about an hour in when someone knocked on the office door.

"Come in," I answered as I hit pause on the screen.

Right as I hit pause, though, I noted a familiar looking van driving by the store. The van was a plain white contractor van with no logos to identify it.

"Got a minute?" Goat interrupted my thoughts a few minutes later. He must have been standing there watching me stare at the paused screen.

"Yeah, sorry," forcing myself away from the TV again. "I seem to be easily distracted today. What can I do for you?"

"Well, I am not real clear on whether I need to talk to you or Katie. I don't understand which one of you is in charge of what, around here. It's about the contractors and their billings."

"The rule is that any employee can talk to either one of us, at any time. Then Katie and I act as we think is appropriate and update each other when the dust settles. We are both on the run all the time, so it makes it easier on everyone else just to ask whichever one of us is available or passing by, no matter what it's about."

"Strange. Can't see that working well for a lot of companies, but with you and Katie it makes sense because you think a lot alike," he nodded. "So, I went over everything last night, and then checked out the buildings this morning. Some of the equipment installed is not matching up with what you are being billed. To keep it simple, you're being scammed. I think that good ole Billy knows you guys are so busy right now, that you don't have time to pay that close attention, and he is using it against you."

"How much money are we talking?"

"Ten grand minimum, from what I have found so far, but I get the feeling that the labor charges might be off too for the sub-contractors. It could be as high as twenty or thirty by the time I finish digging into everything."

"Corner the sub-contractors and confirm your theory, especially the electrical contractor. He has worked for me on some other projects. Then get vocal with Billy. I would love to fire him outright, but it will cause delays in the construction. If he admits everything and gets in line, he can stay on the job. If he doesn't, get his ass and crew off my property. But I want it settled in the next day or two. That will give us a week to hire a new crew before we close for the holiday break."

A loud, very loud, crash came from the back loading docks, and I started around my desk to head that way, but Goat but his hand out to stop me. "I got it. I will let you know if it's anything serious," he said over his shoulder as he jogged that direction.

"I kind of like having him around," Katie commented from just outside the doorway.

"Yeah, and just a heads up - I gave him the green light to get in Billy's face. They are cheating us out of a lot of money."

"I'm sorry, Kelsey. I should have been on top of it."

"In your spare time?" I laughed. "Look, we both knew that there was a problem and neither one of us seemed to be able to schedule it in."

I was distracted again by the paused screen of the white van.

"Did you see something?" Katie asked looking at the flat-screen.

"I don't know. Something about that van is nagging me. I can't seem to shake it. Maybe it's just one of the contractor's vans, and that's why it seems familiar." I rubbed my temples. I was starting to get a headache. "Or maybe I have just been staring at the screen for too long. Ugh!"

"Well, we are getting busy again, so you can take a break from being a detective and join us on the floor," she grinned.

# Chapter Eight

It was a long day and throwing the sign to Closed was the best thing that had happened. I congratulated all the new hires on a great job and sent them and the other hourly employees on their way, all except for Bridget and Haley, whom I asked to stay behind for a few minutes.

Sara was waiting as patiently as a seven-year-old could, but couldn't wait any longer.

"Now?" she asked.

"Yes, now. Have Tech help you bring the bags up front," I smiled.

Sara grabbed Tech's hand and was dragging him until he caved and started jogging to the office with her. When they came back, they had two large bags and took them to Haley.

"What's this?" she asked looking inside. "OMG! No way. But I can't afford these. I'm broke."

"It's called a gift, Haley. All we ask is that you let us know when graduation is because we want to be in the audience hooting and hollering when you get that bachelor's degree," I said.

"Deal!" Haley grinned with teary eyes.

* * *

"For everyone else that was in the dark with me, Haley is finishing her bachelor's and then will be going on to med school."

Everyone whooped, hollered, and whistled as expected.

"What she doesn't know is that she won't be waiting for a couple years to go. We have made arrangements for tuition and books to be covered and Doc has offered to help you with anything you need as well."

"My medical school tuition?" Haley shook her head. "I can't accept. It's too much," she insisted.

"Haley, I have a lot of money and no real need for any of it right now. And you would make one hell of a doctor. I can't think of a better way to spend it."

Haley looked stunned but launched herself at me in a hug. "I will pay you back. I promise. It will take a long time, but I will figure it out."

"No Haley. I don't want to be paid back. But someday, you can pay it forward by helping others. You will be one of very few doctors that can make that connection with people in need."

"Promise," she said through teary eyes. "I will pay it forward."

"Alright, enough of this sappy crap," Alex interrupted, but he put an arm around Haley's shoulder and gave her a kiss on the cheek. "We need to talk for five minutes about inventory before we pack it up. I got confirmation today that the business I mentioned last night is going to be seized by the IRS in the next couple days. The owner wants to liquidate anything and everything by Saturday, but we can have first dibs tomorrow if we can get there. It's a two-hour drive, and the building has 40,000 square feet of merchandise and equipment. Are we in or out? I need to call him back."

"We'll make the trip. Katie, we'll need funds available. I will call Chops about a semi. Goat, reach out to the Players and see if anybody is interested in being hired for manual labor. We might end up taking racks and such, and if so, we will need to disassemble some stuff. Tech let me know if you can free your schedule. I will want you to check out any electronic equipment. Everyone that's going, meet here at 7:00 a.m. sharp. We will need one person to stay back and oversee the restock and laundry staff tomorrow while we are gone."

"I can do that," Hattie assured me.

"I'll stay too, in case there are issues with the contractors. And, I have a few more new hires starting tomorrow too," Goat grinned. "I am already up to 6, and I have two more days left," he bragged, rocking back and forth on his feet.

"Don't count your chickens just yet," I laughed. "Anything else?"

No one commented so everyone dispersed to make their calls and I started shutting down lights and closing blinds.

"Now darling, we must talk!" Dallas insisted coming over and laying claim to my elbow to steer me away.

I hadn't even realized she was still in the store. She handed me a pair of jeans and a blouse, which was Dallas speak that I needed to change clothes before she would be seen in a bar with me. Eyeing the wrap around emerald blouse, I wasn't about to argue.

"Dallas, I forgot you were here. How did it go today?" I smirked.

"Well dear, that's what we need to talk about. This just isn't going to work for me. But the real issue is, if Dave finds out I quit another job after only one day, I will never hear the end of it. So, you have to fix this for me."

"You're fired," I smiled.

"Splendid! I knew you would understand." Dallas clapped her hands together in delight.

"Go tell Goat he's down to five employees, and then we will get those drinks I promised."

She grinned and flounced her way toward the back to find Goat while I went to change and ditch the mint green suit. I planned on throwing it in the closest trash bin on my way out.


Dallas drove us in my SUV to the body shop first so I could ask about the semi. Chops said it wasn't a problem, and he would get with James and set up someone from the Players to drive it. I noticed a silver crotch rocket sitting off to the side with a sale sign on it and asked about that, but he refused to give me any information. His girlfriend Candi was behind him making 'call me' gestures, though, so all in due time. I wasn't sure if I would even be able to drive one, but it looked like fun.

Dallas and I each drank three cocktails and two shots within the first hour of arriving at the saloon, and I was feeling a lot less stressed. Hanging with Dallas was like riding a fast roller coaster, and I knew I would have to slow down or end up hurling all over the floor. I didn't listen to my own advice, though, and by the completion of the second hour, we were beyond trashed. We were dancing in the middle of the bar by ourselves to the jukebox when Dave and Steve came in, uniforms on, grinning at us. The bartender must have called them to give us a ride. They helped us fill out our credit slips and calculate the tip, which seemed as mathematically challenging as my college calculus class, before guiding us out the door.

"Until next time Bitches!" Dallas yelled as the door was closing behind us.

The remaining patrons responded favorably back to her.

The fresh air felt great but didn't last long as we were shoved in the back seat of the squad car.

"What about my truck? I need it tomorrow morning," I questioned.

Steve sighed, dug my keys out of my shoulder bag and went to drive it for me. I grinned at how spoiled I was.

We were barely out of the parking lot when Dallas started snoring loudly. Dave just shook his head.

"So, why are you still working? You've been on since dawn," I asked as I tried to fiddle with the window but it wouldn't move.

"I picked up some overtime. I'm planning on taking some time off to spend with Tammy this weekend." He looked at me in the rearview mirror. "She said she talked to you today. What was that about?"

"The meds that were making her coo-coo for cocoa puffs. Don't worry, though, I got your back," I snorted.

"Now I'm scared. What does that mean, Kel?" Dave looked at me with his serious, 'I'm-a-cop' stare in the rearview mirror, which just made me snort again. And, of course, my snorting just made me laugh. By the time I got control of myself, we were pulling into my driveway. Dave let me out of the backseat and helped navigate me to the door.

Lisa opened the door for us, and I was escorted to the dining room and shoved into a chair. This was a good thing since the floor seemed to be moving when I walked. I crossed my arms on the table and used them as a pillow to lay my head on. That's the last thing I remember.

# Chapter Nine

I woke up to the smell of coffee, but I wasn't ready to open my eyes yet. Then something thumped the hard surface my head was laying on, forcing the issue.

"Time to wake up, Sunshine!" Hattie bellowed.

I opened my eyes to see a cup of coffee on the dining room table; the same table that I was surprised to find I was laying on top of.

*What the hell?*

"Why am I sleeping on top of the table?"

"Well, when we all went to bed, just your head was on the table. Every time someone tried to coax you to your room, you told them to go to hell. So, we left you."

She pulled out a chair, and I maneuvered off the table and into it. She slid a bottle of aspirin to me that I eagerly accepted.

"I must also confess that when I saw you stretched out on the table this morning, I took a picture on my phone and sent it to everyone."

"Oh, you're going to pay for that Hattie!" I laughed. It was something that I would do so I couldn't be mad at her for it.

"Serves you right. What were you thinking, getting that drunk?"

"I wasn't thinking – and that was the intention. I am so damn tired of thinking."

"You have to survive one more week, and then we close the store for three long weeks for the holidays. Just hang in there until then. And your butt better get in the shower, because you are meeting everyone in forty-five minutes at the store and you smell like the bar. So, get a movin'…"

I stood slowly, cringing when my head seized.

"Thank you, Hattie," I said as I kissed her on the cheek before wobbling on unsteady legs down the hall to my bedroom.


I felt better after showering and went to my closet to find something to wear. I noticed another horrid dress was hanging on the hook next to the closet door. *Where the hell does Lisa find such ugly clothes? And, why does she keep insisting that I wear them?*

I ignored the dress and pulled on my favorite pair of hip-hugger jeans and a snug v-neck ribbed sweater. I applied ample make-up and clipped my wet hair up in a messy bun. I finished the look with my knee length black heeled boots with the hidden switchblades inset into the linings. The knives always made me feel better when I wasn't wearing my gun. Ready to start my day, and feeling like my old self again, I went to refill my coffee.

"Didn't you see the dress I put up for you?" Lisa questioned when I walked into the kitchen.

"Yes, I did. I chose to wear this instead." I filled my cup, grabbed my shoulder bag and coat, and left.

I might be feeling better, but I wasn't up to dealing with whatever drama Lisa was having over my wardrobe. That conversation would have to wait until later.

"Hey, wait up and let us ride with you," Anne hollered following me out the door with Sara in tow.

"Hey, little-bug! You going to make the trip with us today?" I asked Sara.

"Yup. Mom says I can be the navigator!" she grinned.

"Super cool. Maybe I can take a nap on the way there then."

"Ha," Anne laughed. She handed me a folder. "Tech and Alex put together this bio of info for you on the seller and his store. You need to study up before we get there."

The file was at least an inch thick and was going to take most of the trip to go through. I jammed it between the console and my seat as I started up my SUV and Anne and Sara buckled in. As I was pulling out the driveway, I noticed a white van, turning left off our road. Our three houses were the only buildings on the road. I thought of the van that I saw on the video and decided to follow it.

"Why are we going left?" Anne asked.

"The van up ahead- it was pulling off our road, and I want to see where it goes."

"He could have been trespassing back in the woods. It's not the first time someone has been down by our houses."

The van turned right off the highway, down a residential road, and I made the same turn but hung back at the intersection. I watched it turn left into a suburb.

*Okay, you're losing it, Kelsey.* It's just someone that lives in the neighborhood. Shaking my head at myself, I swung a U-turn.

"You okay Kel?" Anne asked quietly.

"Yeah, sorry. Just still out of sorts about the break-in I guess -or maybe some lingering alcohol from last night is still messing with me." I smiled to reassure her that all was well.

# Chapter Ten

"Where did you guys go? You left before us," Lisa asked when we got there. She was waiting by Katie's SUV, and it appeared everyone else was ready to roll-out as well.

"We were just checking something out down the road, nothing important," Anne answered.

"Has everyone figured out who they are riding with and such?" I asked.

"Yes-um, boss…" Alex drawled, walking up to us. "Everyone's ready to go. We were just a wait'n for the Queen B to join us. And, by the way, how comfortable was the dining room table last night?"

Everyone that heard his comment chuckled looking down at the asphalt.

"I recommend you drop the commentary until my hangover is gone," I smart mouthed back at him. "You look stunning though this morning, Mr. Alex."

Alex was dressed in a black and white striped suit with a red bow tie. His shoes were almost as shiny as the fake diamond he was wearing in his ear and the bright white smile on his face.

"And, you look bitchen, Luv," he winked and kissed me on the cheek. "Let's hit the road!"

Tech ended up jumping in with us to ride in the back with Sara, and Anne took the keys to drive while I studied the file on both the business and its owner. We were about halfway there when I noticed a white van pass us on the highway. I tried to get a better look, but it was going too fast.

"It's not the same one. That one is a newer model than the one we were following this morning," Anne answered my unspoken question.

"What are you guys talking about?" Tech asked.

He and Sara were playing some computer game in the backseat, and I was surprised he even heard Anne over their own banter.

"It's stupid," I sighed. "I saw this white van on the security footage yesterday, and I can't get it out of my head. Then I saw another white van this morning turning off our road. I followed it, but it turned into a residential area. It must be someone that lives in the area. And, for some dumb reason, the whole thing just keeps nagging at me."

"How far into the footage were you when you saw the van?" Tech asked.

"That's the thing. I think I saw it several times passing the store before I paid any attention to it. But I was an hour in on fast forward when I hit pause on the screen. It could be the guy I followed this morning or one of the contractors. It's such a common make that it could be multiple ones that look alike."

"I'll pull up the video and check it out."

"Too slow!" Anne giggled. "I already have the video up, and I am looking for the van."

"Don't be trying to steal my job now!" he teased and elbowed her. Sara giggled again.

"Found it," she announced.

"It is a common make and model. It could be anyone. We'll do some digging though and let you know if we come up with anything," Tech said.

I felt better that the dynamic duo was checking into it. And, if it turned out to be nothing, then at least they would be entertained by something other than computer games for the rest of the trip. I focused back on the pile of papers in my lap.

We arrived at our destination without incident. The Devil's Players hung back in the parking lot while the rest of us did a quick walk through of the store equipment and merchandise. The owner provided his own inventory list and purchase prices, but I started crossing off his prices and adding my own while I directed others to take a closer look at things like the jewelry case, the registers, and the security equipment.

I saw a freight truck was itemized on the list, and Whiskey and James went to inspect it for me. I went to the owner's office and commandeered his desk and calculator and started adding numbers up as the others reported back to me counts and values.

"Okay, for all the merchandise except the jewelry, I will offer $45,000. The wall racks, shelving units, all the display cases, registers, security cameras, dollies, and ceiling lights, would be an additional $19,000. I have no interest in the round clothes racks. The freight truck is old, but I will offer $17,000 for that. So, we are currently at $81,000. Why don't you think it over while I go take a look at the jewelry? I will need an answer by the time I come back, though. We have significant payroll going just to make the trip here." I handed him the revised log sheet and left the office.

The jewelry case was located in the center of the store, and the owner's wife was there to open the case so I could take a closer look. It was the typical items you would find at a 70% off fine jewelry sale. There weren't enough lower end items to make sense for The Changing Room, and the higher end items would have to be sold online. I was about to vote against the jewelry when a diamond ring caught my attention. I pulled it out of the case and tried it on. Containing my excitement behind my poker face, I admired the ring that I always promised myself I would buy some day: a large emerald-cut diamond, flanked by pear-shaped diamonds, all deeply set into a white gold band. It was perfect.

I handed the ring back and returned to the office. "I'll pay $18,000 for the jewelry and the jewelry case together, which brings the total up to $99,000. Are you in or out?"

"I would like to get $20,000 on the freight truck and $25,000 on all the shelves and equipment," the owner said.

"I'll go up to $22,000 on the shelves and equipment, but not a dime higher on the truck. And, that's my final offer."

He sat looking at the sheet again. I knew he owed $76,000 to the IRS, which seemed like cheating. He needed to clear that debt before the IRS swooped in and sold everything for pennies, including the building itself.

"Deal," he said, standing to shake my hand.

After returning his handshake, I opened the office door and waved for Katie to enter. She would arrange a wire transfer of the funds and handle the sales contract. I walked to the front, gaining everyone attention.

"Alright everybody, everything is ours except the round racks. I also want the ceiling lights and security cameras, so those have to be disassembled. Fill merchandise in all the SUV's and freight trucks first, and equipment and such in the semi. The freight truck out back is also ours, so be sure to fill it up. Hope you all had plenty of coffee, you're going to need it," I smiled and grabbed some of the boxes to start filling.

I asked Lisa to load all the jewelry in a hard tote, but to pull the emerald-cut diamond from the stock for me. She looked puzzled but returned a few minutes later holding the diamond. "It's gorgeous. I didn't notice it the first time I looked. It's worth at least $10,000 alone," she said still admiring the ring.

I took the ring from her and put it on my right hand. "Yup, and, tonight remind me to write a check to the store from my personal account," I smiled.

Within three hours we had everything loaded to capacity, and the store was empty except the built-in counters and the round clothing racks. We were just cleaning the place up a bit when Alex walked up.

"Well, we have Saturday stock now. How did the numbers come out?" he asked.

"We did good," I smiled. "We'll recoup our money tomorrow on the merchandise, including the cost of the truck and all the equipment for the new buildings."

"You sure you don't want any of the round racks? They might work well in the bridal building."

"Ugh – Never!" The racks in my store had always been straight and long, and that's how I planned on keeping it. I liked the nice neat rows. And they were easier to restock.

Grabbing a stack of unused packing boxes, I carried them out to the freight truck and passed them up to awaiting hands. It had turned out to be a clear and sunny December day. And, the colder temperature felt good after working up a sweat. Walking to my SUV, I reached into the glove box and pulled a cigarette out, lighting up. I seldom indulged, but always enjoyed the calming effect.

I was thinking of where to store all the equipment when I noticed another white van. This one was parked just down the road, on the opposite side of the busy street, facing our location. Tech and James were walking my way, and I turned so my back was to the van.

"Tech, tell me that's not the same van across the road, to the Southwest?" I was becoming paranoid, which wasn't like me.

"Damn. It's the right year, has the half tint on the windows. Do you have your truck keys?"

I pulled my keys out of my back pocket and handed them to him before I jumped in the passenger seat. By the time we pulled left onto the road, the van had pulled out into traffic. We had lost it before we made it a block.

"I'm imagining this, right? Whoever that was just happened to be leaving at that particular time, right?"

"Sorry. That's sending up red flags for me too. And, I haven't told you about the video yet. We counted 37 times that van has passed the store since last weekend. It has a dent above the rear driver side fender, so we know it's the same van. Once, it pulled up to the back of the store, but stopped and reversed out when they spotted the security camera. I was guessing they were casing out the store. But following us all the way over here? That doesn't make sense."

"Did you get a plate or a picture of the driver?" I was biting my lower lip. I hadn't wanted to be right about the white van. I had wanted them to tell me it was one of the contractors or someone that lived around the corner.

"Not even close. We think the driver has a brown beard. And, we have nothing on the plate. Sara is still working on it, but our cameras are positioned to monitor the building entrances. And, as you know, we don't have any cameras on the new buildings yet."

"Get a hold of Goat and tell him I will pay whatever extra it costs, but I want new security cameras and exterior lights in the new parking areas as soon as possible."

"Got it." Tech parked us back where we started, and we looked up to see James, right where we left him, with his hands on his hips, scowling at us.

"I will call Goat, and you can handle the Prez," Tech chuckled, getting out of the SUV and walking the other direction.

"Don't get your knickers in a twist," I said to James when I got out.

"I came over to ask you something and you two did your secrecy spy talk shit and just took off. What the hell is going on?" James barked.

I reached under the passenger seat and unlocked my gun case. I strapped my holster on, followed by snapping my gun in place. "There's been a white van watching the store, and it followed us here today. Not sure what they are up to, but put a warning out to your crew. I will get a warning out to mine."

James nodded and took off. I signaled to Lisa, Anne, and Katie to join me.

"Katie, did you bring your gun?"

"Yeah. It's in my truck."

Whiskey walked up carrying Sara in one arm and her laptop bag in the other. I filled everyone in about the van and rearranged who was riding with who, to best protect everyone.

"If you see the van, hit the gas and go. Drive as fast as you can. If you get pinned down, shoot first. Got it?"

"Who's riding with you?" Anne asked.

"I am," James answered walking back up, joining us. "One of the other guys will drive the semi back. I am assuming always-in-charge Kelsey will want to take the tail of the convoy, and there won't be any convincing her otherwise. Bones will kill me if anything happens to her so I will be with her."

I had to grin. I was planning on everyone arguing with me about trailing behind them, but they must have figured James would keep me out of trouble because they all packed up into their assigned vehicles and started pulling out.

"Do you have another gun?" James asked.

"Yup, under the driver's seat, in the lockbox," I answered, handing him the car keys which had the lockbox key as well.

James reversed the SUV and waited for the semi to pull out ahead of us, followed by the two freight trucks.

"What are your Spidey senses telling you about all this van stuff?" he asked.

"Someone's watching one of us. They are trying to catch a pattern or an opportunity. They could be targeting someone in the club, but I expect it's me or someone working at the store."

"Why would anyone come after one of you?"

"Some of the girls weren't born with the same name they go by now. They've led hard lives and left dark pasts behind."

"Well, your family is club family too, so the Players have your back. I hope you know that."

I didn't say anything else on the long drive. I just kept watching out the windows and mirrors for the van and anyone else that looked suspicious. There wasn't anything else to say. It could be several possible enemies. The list of possible suspects was too long without knowing who they were targeting.

# Chapter Eleven

We were all exhausted by the time we unloaded all the clothes and set the store up to open for the next day. I called Chops, and he agreed to rent the semi to me for the week to store all the shelves and equipment. The new freight truck also still needed to be unloaded.

"Damn girl," Alex said as he grabbed my right hand and inspected my new ring. "It's the one! It's the one you always promised to buy yourself some day. It was part of the jewelry you bought?"

"Yup. I was about to walk away from the jewelry when I saw it." I grinned. I loved the ring. "And, I noticed some diamond earrings as well, one of which might do nicely to replace the fake one that you wear. It might be time to upgrade for the sake of the store image and all."

"I need to check it out. Which direction did the jewelry go?"

"Lisa is in the office pulling the most expensive pieces to put in the safe. I'm sure she still has it all out, so go shop. Tell Lisa I said to bill your new earring to me personally, and I will add it to the check I write later."

"You're not going to hear me arguing."

I saw Tech was up in his loft office with his sidekick Sara. As I climbed the stairs, I heard footsteps behind me and looked to see James and Whiskey following me.

"We've got nothing," Tech stated before I even asked. "We just keep coming up with the same images of the van, with no way to identify it."

"I think we spooked whoever it was today. If they have a brain at all, they are going to either lay low or switch vehicles," I said.

"Then what's the plan?" Whiskey asked.

"Can we rig the security system to run a live feed on the other flat-screens in the building? Maybe set up a couple more TV's in the back and a large one up by the registers? If we are all keeping an eye on the feed, then we have a better chance of noticing something out of place."

"Oh! I know!" Sara chimed in, getting excited and standing on her chair. "We can re-write the facial recognition program to search repeat identities. So, if the same person passes a camera more than five times, then it will alert us. As it identifies each of us, we can tell it to skip that identification, and continue searching."

"Damn little genius, that's golden!" Tech praised and they high fived.

"Sure, what she said," I laughed, shaking my head and leaving.

* * *

James left to purchase more flat-screens while Tech and Goat started running cable to connect them and Sara did her computer programming thing. I was walking the sales floor to do a last check when Anne came over.

"Is it them?" she asked nervously.

"Right now, I can't say. But they are only one of many possibilities. We just don't have enough information. This could be just some crazy from the store that started stalking one of us."

"Isn't it sad that I am hoping one of us picked up some nut-job stalker?" she asked, wringing her hands together.

"I know. But for right now, we stay together and wait it out." I gave her a hug because I knew she needed it. "It's going to be okay."

# Chapter Twelve

Leaving my bedroom and atrium curtains open all the time served two purposes. One, the space appeared larger. Two, when the sun came up in the morning, it glared at me in bed telling me I was late, *very late*. Diving off the bed, I ran through the shower and threw on some clothes in record time. I picked tight jeans that would look good in my favorite boots and an oversized knit shirt that would hide my shoulder holster and gun.

Rushing into the kitchen, I greeted Hattie and grabbed a cup of coffee.

"Why didn't anyone wake me? It's already 8:00."

"Katie said everything at the store was set and to let you sleep. And, then I was ordered to ride with you to the store."

"Yeah. Sorry, Hattie. But until this thing is settled with the mysterious van, no one is to be left alone. We'll try to figure something out so you don't have to be there so much, though."

"It's fine. I want to clean the break room, and I can use the small stove to make something up for lunch today for everyone. Maybe a pot of chili so everyone can grab a bowl when time allows. And, I already have muffins and croissants ready to go with us too."

"You are the best." I snitched a croissant out of the basket and grabbed my coat. "And, chili for lunch sounds perfect. I can have Bridget and Goat run to the store to pick up everything you need."

"Bridget can go with me. I have my gun if we need it. We will be fine."

Hattie had mentioned before that she carried illegally in her purse, but I had never seen her gun or seen her shoot. "Hattie, when was the last time you shot your gun?"

"Oh, must be about twenty years now. Not since my husband Simon and I lived out on the farm."

"And, it's been in your purse this whole time?"

She nodded and smiled.

"When was the last time you cleaned it?"

She frowned.

"Hattie, let me see your gun." I held my hand out, and she dug to the bottom of her purse and passed it to me.

"I guess it is a little dirty," she admitted.

The gun was tarnished and had lint and other unknown substances stuck all over it. I released the barrel, and it grudgingly popped to the side, but when I tipped it back, the bullets didn't want to come out. I set the gun down and went to my bedroom to retrieve a spare glock. I held it in front of her and showed her the safety and clip release. Securing it in a holster, I put it in her purse.

"I will see what can be done to salvage yours, but it's a bit neglected. And, next week you are to practice shoot with us," I insisted as locked her gun in the credenza and gathered our stuff to leave.

I pulled into the store's parking lot, as Henry, one of our best sellers, was pulling out, smiling and waving at us, driving one of our freight trucks.

"Huh…," I said to myself.

I continued driving around to the dock entrance and parked out of the way. After getting Hattie and all of her stuff settled in the break-room, I went looking for Alex and found him in Katie's office.

"Why is Henry driving one of the store freight trucks?" I asked.

"Because, Goat is a genius!" Alex replied, and Katie grinned. "Goat talked to Henry yesterday and found out that he wanted to make more buys, but couldn't make it worth his while with gas prices and his vehicle not being big enough. Katie got a liability insurance rider for him and worked out a deal with the gas/mileage against the price we pay him for the purchases. So now, he will be able to bring in a freight load every few days instead of just his pickup load.

"Damn. That's great. Henry has a good eye for clothes, and we seldom have any that go in the charity bin from his stock. This was Goat's idea?"

"Yeah," Katie said. "He cornered me yesterday afternoon while we were unloading. We were able to get everything set up easy enough. I just hadn't caught up with you to let you know yet."

"Did Hattie bring any food in?" Alex asked abruptly changing the subject.

"Muffins and croissants are in the break room," I laughed. "And, she's going to make chili for lunch."

"Yum. I'm starving!" Alex took off with Katie close on his heels. And, I do mean heels. Today Alex was sporting tall red leather heeled boots.

"Hey, Alex –,"

"Yeah?"

"Nice earring!" I smiled, and he winked back at me.


I was about to leave the office when I noticed Donovan barreling my way.

"Hey, stranger. You're back early," I greeted him.

"I was working a bodyguard thing in Chicago, and my partner called and said the store placed a large order for some security equipment and wanted it by this morning. The distributor was in the Chicago area, so I was able to pick it up."

He had his serious face going, which was his normal face when Lisa wasn't around. When she was around, he was all gooey-eyed in love.

"What I want to know, is why the rush? What's going on?"

"We are on yellow alert around here. Everyone's safe and being careful. Tech should be up in his office. He can get you up to speed on the security plans. I went over them last night, and they looked good to me. But let us know if improvements can be made."

"Who's idea for the extra TVs?" Donovan asked.

"Mine. You like?"

"Surprised, but yeah – smart. The more of you watching, the less chance someone will get by you."

"Looks like it will be a non-issue since Sara built her new computer program. But, I'll let her show you that."

I needed to check the registers, so I turned toward the front of the store as Donovan turned toward the stairs that went to Tech's loft office.

"If you see Lisa, tell her I will track her down before the store opens," he grinned.

"Will do."

I got the registers settled in record time, and I was enjoying the fact that we had eight cashiers standing ready to go. To my knowledge, Goat was up to nine new hires and needed one more by the end of the day to make his goal. With only five registers, the extra cashiers would bag until the lines got crazed; then we would start rows of cash only check-outs. The cars in the lot were already overflowing into the field, and the Devil's Players were working the crowd to keep everyone on their best behavior.

Moving to the back room, I found Alex and his share of the staff had all the spare racks ready, and another team was working laundry for what appeared to be recent buys from this morning. From there, I went to Bridal only to find Lisa and Donovan lip-locked, catching up.

"Fifteen minutes," I hollered out. "You better make it a quickie."

Lisa blushed, but Donovan started to push her in the direction of the dressing room causing her to giggle as I made a fast exit.

Menswear appeared to be stocked, and Anne had two employees with her. She asked me to check on Sara and I went back up the stairs to Tech's office. I instructed both Sara and Tech that Sara was to stay in Tech's office unless she had an escort. I received head nod acknowledgments from both of them, but they never looked up from their computer screens.

Back downstairs, I locked up the office and checked the clock. Two minutes. Several of the Players came in through the back door and spread-out throughout the store for security. I closed my eyes and took a deep breath.

Saturdays were the most fun and most physically and mentally challenging day of the week. By late afternoon, thoughts of the potluck party and consuming large quantities of alcohol would serve as the only motivation to keep us going. Today, I would rather skip the rush and head right to the food and booze.

Moment over, I picked up the PA and announced the store would be opening in sixty seconds. This wasn't part of the normal routine, and several staffers gave me a strange look, but I wanted to give Donovan and Lisa a warning in case they were still in the middle of 'other things'.

Standing ready at the door, I waited for James to give his Saturday sermon to the crowd on minding their manners or being forcibly dragged out. When he turned and gave me the official nod, I threw the lock and opened the door.

Within a half an hour, customers started checking out and by 11:00 we started up all four cash-only lines. The others working on cash sales with me were seasoned cashiers, and some of the Players helped us bag. We had a steady stream of customers exiting as new customers were being let in at the same pace. Most of our customers knew that if you weren't in line when the birds started to stir, there was a chance you wouldn't make it inside at all. We just didn't have the capacity for everyone.

By noon, I called Katie to bring the portable safe to the front. The fanny-packs were ready to burst and needed to be unloaded. Donovan and Bones built the safe with a drop slot in the top to slide the money easily inside, and the base of the safe had casters to roll it to and from the office to be locked down. It also had a sensor installed so that if it was tampered with or taken out of the building, an ear-piercing alarm went off. Two of the Players escorted Katie and helped us transfer the money inside the safe, before escorting her back to the office, where someone would stand guard nearby.

I was just getting started on another sale, when Haley interrupted, taking my spot and telling me that Tech needed me up in his office.

"What's up?" I said breathing heavy from running up the steps. I needed to get back on the treadmill.

"We need you to look at a couple video shots and tell us who is familiar and who is not. You know the construction workers the best."

I looked through the videos and cleared most of the people from the construction crew. That left one man inside the store and two contractors unaccounted for.

"How did this guy get five hits already?" I asked, pointing on the surveillance monitor to the man inside the store.

"He's wandered around a lot. Been toward the backroom but didn't enter. Been in Menswear, grabbed some jeans and then wandered back out to the main sales floor. Might just be a bored husband."

"Can you go to the first video of when he arrived? See if he came in with anyone?"

Sara pulled it up and hit play, but it appeared he came in alone. If any of the women standing around him were his wife, they weren't on speaking terms.

"Ok. I'll check out John Doe, and send the two contractor photos to Goat to ID."

While walking back down the stairs, I watched Alex skate into the room, literally. He had swapped out the red heeled boots for his roller skates. He replaced one of the long empty racks, with a full one and several women cheered him on while he skated off again. I wasn't sure if the cheering was because he delivered fresh stock or for his skating style, but I was glad to see both Alex and our customers were having so much fun.

I spotted the mystery man coming out of the men's bathroom, picking up his pair of jeans from the attendant. By the time he turned around, I was blocking his path.

"Hi, I'm Kelsey, the owner. I need you to follow me," I grabbed his elbow and steered him toward the back.

He looked like he was going to bolt, but after looking behind me, he changed his mind. My guess was that a couple of the Players had moved in. I was under constant surveillance on Saturdays.

I led him through the backroom doors and down to a small storage room that I knew would be empty. I unlocked the door, and he followed me into the room, along with Whiskey, James, and Tyler.

I kicked his legs out from under him, startling him. I pulled my gun and held it to his forehead. "You have ten seconds to tell me who you are, and what you are doing here before I turn my friends loose on your ass."

"Shit. They told me this was no big deal. They gave me a hundred bucks. Said, they would throw in an extra hundred if I could scope out the back rooms."

"Who?"

"I don't know who they are. We didn't exchange names. One is medium height, a little heavy, brown beard. The other is tall, bald, psycho-mean looking. I was at the motel where they are staying and didn't have enough money to stay another night. They offered me money to tell them what the layout inside this place was like."

He was sweating, and his hands shook with fear as he held them out in front of his face for protection.

"Said I had to get here by 8:00 or I might not make it through the doors. I didn't believe them, but I got here at 8:00 and the parking lot was already full. I had to wait until eleven before it was my turn. This place is crazy."

"What's your name?"

"Umm…"

Whiskey leaned over and flipped the guy over on his belly and pulled his wallet. "Joshua Smelzer, local address."

"What motel?"

"Umm..,"

"She asked you a fucking question!" James yelled in his face while dragging him up from the floor by his neck and pinning him to the wall.

"The Motor Lodge on Cranson Street! I checked in on Tuesday. Those other guys were already there. They have the two rooms after mine," he choked out.

His eyes were watering from the pressure against his neck, and I gave James a tap on the shoulder to have him back off a bit.

"Kelsey, go ahead and head back to the sales floor. We'll see about getting the details and relay them to Tech and update you later."

"Just remember that we don't bury the bodies here onsite," I winked as I holstered my gun.

I unlocked the door and handed my key off to Whiskey, before sneaking out alone.

Alex was in the backroom loading another rack. He looked at me and then glanced back at the door. "Everything kosher?"

"Peachy-keen. If you hear any loud noises, just ignore them."

"I was ready for some music anyway," he shrugged and went over and cranked the stereo to some classic rock. "Hey, take a full rack of jeans out with you. It's wild out there."

I dragged a full rack of jeans out, but it was half empty by the time I pulled the old rack out of the way. I repeated the process several times, working shoes and jeans with Bridget while Alex directed another team on shirts and dresses. Alex would occasionally skate off to startle an unsuspecting woman and do his personal shopper routine, which was the equivalent of giving a woman and head to toe review, feeling sorry for her fashion sense, and personally selecting an armful of clothes that would not only fit, but would complement her to perfection. I had been his voluntary victim on many occasions and happily cheered along as he rewarded customers with his expert skills.

Working the racks for long periods of time was physical challenging, but it was taking my mind off everything else going on, and I turned up the music on the sales floor. Alex winked at me as he skated passed, singing off key. I laughed and lost myself in the work.

I was so into the frenzy of it all, that when Godsmack's Voodoo came on, I started singing along in earnest and grabbed a hanger as my pretend microphone.

By the time the song ended, Anne and Katie had joined me for the rock performance, and I realized we had gathered quite a crowd.

"Only you white chicks would favor a song about heroin addiction," Alex laughed.

"Compared to that rap crap that's all about killing people?" Katie countered.

"And, shall I start a list about country music?" Anne asked.

"Touché," Alex grinned.

"Alright, everybody needs to grab some empty racks and let's cycle them again," I laughed.

"Shit, I forgot that's why I came out this way!" Anne laughed. "Menswear needs to be restocked."

I helped Anne pull four new racks down the back hall while Katie helped Alex reload another round for the women's section. By the time I returned to the backroom again, Henry was pulling the freight truck up. "Back so soon?"

"Hit the mother-load!" He rubbed his hands together as I opened the back. "I know typically you don't accept deliveries on Saturdays after 10:00, but thought I would swing in and see if someone had time to check me in."

"Damn Henry!" The truck was packed to capacity with bin after bin of clothes. I started rolling the bins out as Alex grabbed the clipboard and started writing out an intake receipt. After he had marked a bin clear, then another set of hands hauled it off to laundry.

"I'm not done yet either. I still have two more sales to check out. So, I might be back yet today. If I'm not here by five, though, I will swing by tomorrow to unload."

"Well, have at it! Just don't push yourself too hard. Do you need someone to help you do the loading and stuff?"

"Nah. Most the time the sellers jump in and help. Sometimes even strangers help, seeing an old man like me hauling the bins," he grinned.

Henry was retirement age, but there was nothing 'old' about him. He had more energy than a second-grade schoolboy. But he was also smart. I was sure he intentionally played the old-man card to gain free labor.

"Hey Henry, will you keep your eyes and ears out for some old pulley systems for me?"

"Any particular size or kind?"

"Cheap and in good shape," I smiled. "I want to play around with mounting the pulleys to the walls and hanging some racks from them. Then layering them so when one is empty, we lower the racks to the next round. That way we aren't fighting the crowds to restock the outside walls."

"Might work. Maybe something more like garage door openers instead, though, motorized, but can handle the weight. What do you think?"

"That would be easier for some of the employees to run and go over better with our insurance company too. But they will have to be commercial grade to take the weight. Good idea."

"Was your idea, I just tweaked it," he winked. He closed the back of the truck and hollered over his shoulder, "I'll see what I can do, but got to get going. Places to be, shit to buy." He waved and was off.

I turned around to close the overhead, and Alex was staring at me still holding the clipboard.

"What?"

"Where do you come up with these ideas? The layered racks - that would be amazing!"

"I don't know. It's been in my head awhile now, but then someone always pulls me another direction. Goat was right about getting the staff situation fixed so we'd have time to focus on other things. It feels good to work the sales floor again."

"I know. It's been months since you've been able to spend this long on the floor. And, I haven't had to go help with the laundry today either, which makes me happy."

We both pushed the bins over to the laundry area and then turned back to the restock racks.

"What happened with our guest in the storage room?" I asked.

"I think he's still in there. The others walked out about an hour later, but either he's dead, or they chained him up. Either way, the less I know, the better. And you should follow that same logic."

I was hoping that he was still alive. It didn't seem like he deserved to be killed just for taking a casing job. Hopefully the club thought the same. The problem was they were too protective of us.

By 4:00 I called a halt to all restocking. We had already sold our original stock and all the morning drop-offs that had been laundered and racked. I didn't want to hit the afternoon stock that Henry brought in, or we might not have inventory for Wednesday. About half the sales floor was empty, and we had another hour to go before we closed. I decided to let the customers fight it out for the scraps.

Menswear was about the same at half stocked, and Anne looked a little more frazzled than usual. I jumped in to help her for the rest of our shift, and by 5:00, the department was down to about a quarter of its' inventory. I heard the PA system announcing it was closing time and ushering customers to the front of the store to check out. Anne and I joined the cash-only checkout while the Players herded the remaining customers to the front.

Two players stood guard at the rollout safe. Money was being tucked into it at such a steady pace, that it wasn't worth wasting the time hauling the safe back and forth to the office.

James was pushing the last of the customers up to the checkout lanes when I looked past him at the sales floor. Alex was picking up empty hangers from the floor and putting them on the barren racks. Other than a few pairs of shoes, it appeared we had sold out of everything on the floor. That would make record volume considering the stock we went through. I would have to schedule time in the morning to help Katie balance the sales receipts and prepare the bank deposit. I looked back at the safe, and to the two Players guarding it. They both smiled. I was pretty sure there was enough money in there to buy an upscale house. I smiled back. It was a good day.

The last of the customers exited and the doors were locked behind them. The Players scattered to recheck all the rooms and make sure no one was hiding anywhere. (Women sometimes lose all their senses when it comes to clothes shopping.) I helped Katie push the safe back toward the office.

"Umm. We have a problem," Katie said.

"What?"

"We don't have anywhere to lock up the register drawers tonight. I already had to empty the roll safe, into the wall safe today, and now the roll safe is full again. I'm not sure where else to lock the money down. And, with the recent break-in, I don't trust leaving cash in the filing cabinet."

"Let's see if we can fit the cash from the register drawers in the roll safe. Then it's only the credit card receipts that are in the filing cabinet. We just won't bother reconciling the register drawers.

We stuffed the roll safe to capacity, and what was left over was crammed into my shoulder bag. We both stood there staring at the roll safe. It was about 2 feet wide, 2 feet deep, and 3 feet tall. Even if it were filled with one dollar bills, which it wasn't, that would be a lot of cash. We were both nervous about leaving it in the office, alarm rigged or not.

"So what now?" Katie asked.

"You two about done?" Donovan asked from the doorway.

"No. The wall safe is full, so we filled the roll safe. But it's jam packed."

"It's full?" he asked while looking through the top drop chute and seeing you could pull the money back out without any effort. "Holy shit."

"It was an awesome day," Katie said while we both grinned. There were worse problems than trying to figure out where to hide all the money.

"Okay, well the backroom is the most secure with no windows, and every door rigged with sensors. We can lock it in the storage room back there."

"Ummm," I hesitated. "Can you ask Whiskey if the storage room is available yet?"

Donovan raised an eyebrow but left to go find Whiskey while Katie and I finished loading the credit card receipts into the filing cabinet. Donovan returned as I was locking the cabinet.

"I was told it wasn't available yet, but that it would be cleared in ten minutes and ordered to head back to the office." Donovan had his super serious face on now.

Katie stopped working and looked at me too.

"Unless you are okay with becoming an accessory after the fact, I wouldn't ask any questions or think on it anymore. I know I don't want to know anything else, and I'm the one that started it." I was still curious whether the guy was alive, but I didn't want to know if he was dead, so I refused to go check.

Donovan had his hands on his hips and was looking at the floor either contemplating life or thinking about punching something. Either way, I let him ponder on it alone and returned to the front of the store to help close the remaining blinds and start shutting and locking the overheads.

James and Whiskey caught up with me after I locked down Bridal & Gowns.

"We helped Donovan move the safe. Be sure to have Katie schedule security for the bank run on Monday. I want at least four guys with her," James instructed, handing me my set of keys back.

I nodded agreeing that the extra men were necessary.

"Half of the Players are going to escort everyone to the house, and the other half will be with me on an errand. Spread the word that no one's allowed to leave tonight without the Players with them."

Again, I nodded, and we parted ways after shutting and securing all the backroom overheads and doors. I checked the drop off clipboard before locking the back door. Henry hadn't made it back before closing so I would have to make sure someone was here early enough to unload for him in the morning.

# Chapter Thirteen

Hattie had convinced some of the Players to escort her, Sara, and the chili that no one had a chance to eat, back to the house before everyone else arrived. By the time the last of us walked in, she had everything running smooth and the kids corralled in the family room playing. Lined up on the counter were our individual preferred drinks, mine conveniently in a large water glass, instead of a cocktail glass.

"Thank you, Hattie," I said as I passed by and kissed her on the cheek.

"You're most welcome, Sunshine."

In the dining room, Alex was explaining to Goat the stacked wall racks with the garage door openers. I went to pull my sketchpad out of my shoulder bag to show them the design, but forgot about the money and dumped a bunch of it on the floor. They laughed and helped me pick it all up. I kept the sketchpad and Katie took the shoulder bag to put in the house safe. Flipping it open, I found the sketches of the wall rack design and left Goat and Alex to study it. I had no problem with them taking the idea and running with it. I had other things I could do with my time.

The living room was packed, and one of the French doors to the back deck was open, moving some cool air through. I could smell a hint of cigarette smoke, and I followed the aroma outside to bum one from somebody.

"Hi Tyler," I greeted one of the prospects.

"Hey Kelsey" he grinned while pulling out his pack of cigarettes and offering me one.

"You're my hero," I laughed.

"It was a long day. You must have walked 100 miles in that store today."

"That's what my sore feet are telling me at least," I inhaled the cigarette and held it for a moment before exhaling. "Ah, better."

"Those things will kill you, you know," said a familiar deep voice from behind me. Strong, muscular arms wrapped around me and hugged my back against a firm body.

"Thought you wouldn't be back for a week or so?" I questioned without turning around to look at him but leaned further into his body. Tyler excused himself, leaving Bones and me alone at the far end of the deck.

"I got a call yesterday that trouble was brewing. I came back earlier than planned, and came straight here. Where's James and Whiskey?" he asked as he nuzzled my neck.

"They are out on an errand. Not sure how much trouble they are getting themselves into. You might want to drop a call to them and see if they need you."

He kissed my cheek and took the side stairs off the back deck and into the backyard to make the call. Hattie walked out to join me. "That boy's nuts about you, you know."

"Maybe. Or maybe it's just about sex."

"Naw. It's more than that. But," she hesitated while looking at Bones in the backyard.

"But what?"

"I just get the feeling sometimes that he's troubled about something. And, that it has to do with why he's always taking off out of town."

"I know what you mean," I sighed.

I had so many secrets of my own, that I didn't think I could handle Bones' too, even if he was willing to share them. And, my gut told me that whatever he was hiding, I wouldn't like it one bit.

"I'm stuck," I admitted to Hattie.

"I know, Sunshine. I know." She patted me on the shoulder before turning and walking back into the house. I could see Bones was still talking on the phone, so I decided to get a bowl of chili before it was all gone.

I went to my bedroom to eat my dinner and enjoy a bit of quiet. The chili was excellent as expected and I realized too late that I ate too fast and too much. I was settled in my favorite chair in the atrium and set my empty bowl aside and leaned back, relaxing for the first time all day. I had left the atrium inside lights off, but the outside lights glowed enough to see. Darkness had settled, but the skies were clear, and I could see the slight glimmer of stars even with the outside lights on.

A light knock on the bedroom door, pulled me back into the here and now.

I called out, to enter.

Lisa came into the atrium carrying yet another putrid suit.

"Everything alright?" she asked looking concerned.

"It was until I saw that outfit. What the hell is going on Lisa? Why are you insisting that I wear such horrid clothes?" I was annoyed and had had enough.

"It's not horrid!" she insisted, holding the suit up and looking at it again.

"Bullshit. I know you, Chicky! You have impeccable fashion sense. But for some reason you want me walking around looking like a jackass. Why?"

She threw the suit down on the loveseat and placed her tiny curled fists on her hips. "Because YOU treat me differently! You never yell at me. You never tell me no. You never get mad at me. And, I'm sick of it!" she yelled.

"What the hell are you talking about? Have you lost your mind?"

"You keep telling me I'm part of the family, but you don't treat me the same! You fight with everyone else, but not with me, like I am too fragile or something. Or maybe you don't even notice I'm around."

I just sat there staring at her, dumbfounded. Laughter broke out near the bedroom door, and I turned to see Katie, Alex, and Anne.

"Don't just stand there. Get in here and explain this shit to me! Because I don't understand a word she is saying!"

"You wouldn't," Alex laughed.

"But we do," Katie added.

"Explain," I ordered. I was really not in the mood to have my ass chewed for things that I couldn't even comprehend.

"She's been trying to piss you off, but you just kept wearing the ugly clothes and not saying anything," Anne said.

"Why do you want to piss me off?"

Katie snorted, and Alex elbowed her in the ribs.

"I told you already! If I were part of this family, you would get pissed off with me too!" Lisa stomped her foot like a child, which made me snort.

"Sit."

"No."

"NOW!"

She sat on the love seat and pouted, but I could see her eyes starting to water and realized she was serious about all this nonsense.

"The rest of you can leave now."

Alex, Katie, and Anne left, closing the door behind them.

"Lisa, have you ever picked a fight with a customer at the store?"

"No, of course not," she answered annoyed.

"Have you ever intentionally broke something, intentionally hurt one of the other's feelings or lied to me about something important?"

"I don't think so."

"So other than the recent ugly clothes issue, what did you do in the past that you feel I neglected to yell at you about?"

"I don't know, but you yell at the others all the time and never me."

"That's not true. I yell at Alex and Katie all the time because they intentionally push my buttons right up to the danger line. I only yell at Anne when she's being a drama queen and needs to chill. I never yell at Hattie or Sara."

I let this sink in a bit before I continued.

"So let me assure you, that from now on if you ever ask me to wear some butt-ugly outfit again, I will not only yell at you, but I might knock you on your ass too, because you, my dear, are family. But I prefer you better being the sensible and mature one of the group."

"You think I'm sensible and mature?"

"Before this conversation, I did."

She laughed at that and wiped her eyes.

"Lisa, how could you think you weren't part of us?"

"I don't know," she sighed. "I guess I had the *daddy's little princess can do no wrong* song, stuck in my head. I've been all over the place. I don't know what my problem is. Maybe it's Donovan going back to work. Maybe it's because I live next door and not in the main house with you and Anne. I just go from happy to sad to mad to happy again. And, I haven't been feeling good," she pouted.

"Holy shit," I laughed. "Are you serious?"

I laughed so hard that I started to cry.

And, Lisa was right. Her emotions were all over the place, and she was up off the love seat and getting mad all over again. She started pacing back and forth which just made me laugh harder and fall out my chair.

"QUIT LAUGHING AT ME!" she yelled.

But I couldn't stop.

Donovan came rushing in along with Bones, Anne, Hattie, Alex, Katie, and Whiskey.

Donovan went to Lisa and got her to stop pacing, but she was still yelling. "Make her STOP!" she yelled again.

"Okay, okay! I will stop laughing if you quit yelling!"

Anne offered me a hand to help me up off the floor and raised an eyebrow in question. I winked at her and turned back to Lisa.

"I'm sorry, Lisa. I know you are not in an emotional state right now to handle my picking, but I promise you that eventually you will look back at this and laugh."

"And, why is that?" she snidely asked.

"Because my friend, I think you're pregnant," I laughed.

Everyone turned to look at Lisa, who was still glaring at me, when what I said sank in. Then I could see her fingers twitching, counting out the weeks.

"Holy Shit!" she said and sat down abruptly on the loveseat.

"Quick! Someone get a pregnancy test!" Katie hollered.

We all looked at each other excitedly until we realized that none of us other than Lisa had a sex life, so we had no reason to have a pregnancy test handy.

"Okay fine. I will run to the store and buy one!" Katie started to leave when Whiskey stopped her.

"No one leaves without an escort, remember?"

"Damn it," Katie pouted.

"I know where to get one that can be delivered," I said, pulling out my phone.

"You have a dealer for pregnancy tests?" Alex asked with a raised eyebrow.

"I have all kinds of connections, but let's not get sidetracked," I winked.

I called Dave and asked him if they were still coming over and if so, if he could sneak one of Tammy's pregnancy tests out the door without her seeing it. He assured me he could.

"Why does he have to sneak it out?" Bones asked.

"Tammy's been trying to get pregnant for over a year now, and super emotional about the issue. It would be best if we all keep that in mind later if the test is positive." I looked back at Lisa, who was still looking at Donovan.

"So this is a possibility?" Donovan asked her.

"It might be. I think it's been about two months since my last period." She blushed realizing she said that out loud in front of everyone. "I have been sick to my stomach a lot too. I just didn't put it together." She looked at me and started laughing. "Ha! I get it. I'm an emotional basket case!"

"Told you it was funny," I smirked.

"Ya, know what's even funnier?" Whiskey chuckled. "How's Donavan going to explain to her father, the reigning mob boss of New Jersey, that he knocked up the little-unwed princess?"

"Oh, fuck me," Donovan sighed but chuckled.

"It's okay, Donovan. We'll just have Kelsey tell him. He goes along with whatever she says." Lisa giggled.

"No……No….No…. You two are getting hitched. End of story," I insisted.

"That's not a problem," Donovan said as he pulled a ring box from his pocket, slid off the couch to one knee and proposed on the spot to Lisa.

"Don't you want to wait to see if I am pregnant?" Lisa asked.

"Babe, I already had the ring. Whether you are, or not, I want to marry you. So, yes or no?"

"YES!"

We all cheered, and it wasn't long before more people gathered, and I had to boot everyone out of my private space. Everyone but Bones left to other areas of the house. Bones came up behind me and wrapped his arms around me.

He had become so familiar to me. He made me feel strong and protected all at the same time. But, it wasn't real. As much as I didn't want to, I stepped away from him and put distance between us. When I turned around, he was watching me.

"If I asked for the truth, would you give it to me?"

"I don't know."

"Then for both our sakes, walk away now."

"I don't know if I can." He stepped toward me, but I stepped away from him again.

"If I knew what you were doing when you left town, would there be any chance of a relationship between us?"

He didn't say anything which was all the answer I needed. I walked passed him and sat back in my chair.

"Please leave."

I never heard him walk across the room, but a minute later, I heard the door open and close. I curled into the arm of my chair and cried.

"Kelsey?" I heard a voice that woke me. I must have dozed off in the chair.

"In here…"

"Hey. You okay?" Dave asked. He kneeled down in front of me.

"Yeah. Sorry. I was having a little pity party and then must have fallen asleep. I'm all better now."

"And, what was the pity party about?"

"Ah. It's nothing. Did you get the pregnancy test?"

"As soon as we entered, Katie dragged Tammy into the kitchen under some girly pretense, and Lisa pounced on me for the test. I'm guessing it was for her since she and Donovan ran upstairs with it." He chuckled and sat in the other chair.

"I don't need to see the results to know she's pregnant."

"Is that why you were crying?" he pushed again.

"No. I'm happy for her. Speaking of which, is Tammy better?" I asked, changing the subject.

"She is much happier. And, she seems to be intent on making me a very happy and physically satisfied husband right now. What the hell did you do to her? And where did all the sexy underwear come from?"

"That depends. What color is her underwear?"

"At first just black, but today she had hot pink with black trim. And, she told me on the drive over, she switched to purple, but I would have to wait to see it," he grinned.

"Good for her," I nodded. "I gave her the black, but the colors were a suggestion. And, I have banned pastels. I also have to warn you that she is reading a few of my books. Some of the stuff in them will freak the shit out of her."

"I haven't read any of them. Thought it would be weird with us being friends. But that makes sense. She was jumpy when I came home yesterday. She ran into the bedroom and then back out, but wouldn't tell me why."

I crossed the room and retrieved one of the books from the shelf. I flipped through to one of the first sex scenes and handed it to him to read, before reclaiming my favorite chair. He quietly read until he abruptly slammed the book closed. He seemed upset.

"Are you mad at me for giving them to her? I just thought maybe it would help distract her a bit from all the baby stuff."

"No. No. I'm not mad at you," he sighed and leaned forward to pat my knee reassuringly. "I'm grateful to have such a good friend that would help my wife. And, it has helped her. She's laughing again. She's baking again. She's going for walks and volunteering."

"Then what's wrong?"

"I think she tried to play out this scene the other night, and I ruined it for her."

Ahhh. So he was upset with himself.

"You have to remember that this stuff," pointing to the book, "is out of Tammy's comfort zone. You are going to have to help her become more comfortable communicating with you about sex and what she wants. Use the books to help you through it, though. Go home tonight. Find the book and then read that section out loud to her. Make it a couple's thing. Then it will be easier for her to express to you what turns her crank and what turns her off. It will help build her self-confidence as a woman too."

He thought for a moment and nodded his head.

"How the hell did you start writing this smut anyway?" he laughed. "You don't even date."

"I needed money and as a teenager, employment options were minimal, but there wasn't an age requirement to write," I shrugged. "I started writing action books, then romance, and eventually ventured into erotica. It paid the bills. And, it's a great way to relieve sexual frustrations."

"Please tell me that you were at least of legal age before you started writing this book," he said looking uneasily down at the book.

I laughed and nodded. "I was already a cop when I switched to writing what Katie calls my porn movement."

"So are you still sexually frustrated? What's up with you and Bones?" he asked.

"Nothing," I tried to just shrug it off, but Dave saw right through me.

"Ahh, that bastard." Dave knelt down again and gave me a much-needed hug. "It will be okay, Kelsey. You're strong, funny, creative, and one of the most loyal people I know. You'll find the right person for you."

"I'm fine. It's not like I was all gung-ho to get involved with someone anyway. I have a lot going on in my life, and I don't know when or if that will ever change."

I got up and walked over to the window. The stars were brighter now, not a single cloud in the sky.

"Are you sure you guys won't work it out?"

"It doesn't matter. I have plenty of other people in my life that make me happy and until I deal with things from my past, I can't commit to anyone."

Dave saw my resolution and nodded. I knew he would always be on my side.

"Well then, there is only one thing left to do."

He came over and pulled my hand toward the door. "Tammy hid some oatmeal raisin cookies for you."

This made me smile. Nothing worked better to cheer me up than oatmeal raisin cookies.

## Chapter Fourteen

I didn't stay up much later than it took to down four cookies. I was tired from the long day and even longer week. I went to bed and woke before dawn. Reluctantly, I rolled out of bed and dragged myself straight into the shower. I knew that Katie would want to hit the books, and I didn't want her to have to work all day. We tried to work only a few hours on Sunday mornings, if at all.

By the time I arrived in the kitchen, Hattie was already up and around. "I heard you stirring, so I started the coffee. It's not quite done yet, though."

"That's fine. I'm going to make some toast. Do you want some?"

"Sure, sure. That sounds lovely dear."

I loaded the toaster oven and retrieved the butter and jam. We still had some frozen strawberry jam that Hattie made last summer, which made me smile. "Hattie, are you happy?"

"Happier than I ever thought was possible after my Simon died, my dear." Hattie always lit up when she talked about him. "Why do you ask?"

"No real reason. Sometimes we just get so caught up in the day to day, I forget to stop and see what everyone is up to."

"Or maybe you forget to stop and see where your own life is at and whether you are happy?"

"Maybe that too."

"And, are you?"

"I have some unfinished business in my life, and until it's resolved, I don't know if I can be happy," I admitted.

I thought of Nicholas. His eighth birthday passed last month, and it was the hardest one yet. I couldn't handle the thought of another year of his life passing by without him.

I shook off the thought and turned to see Hattie quietly watching me. I offered a brief smile.

"I think I have a good life, though. I have great friends like you, a good business, a nice home. Does that make sense?"

"Of course, it does. And, whatever it is that weighs you down, you will figure it out. You always do. But until then you need to balance it all out a bit better. You keep yourself so busy that you barely sleep. You need to do something crazy and just for you." She patted my hand going over and filling our coffee cups.

I pulled the toast out and spread the fixings on. "I think I'm going to buy a motorcycle today. But, don't tell anyone. They will all yell at me."

She laughed at that. "You're right. They will yell at you, but because they worry about you as much as you worry about them. But do it. The thought of you speeding down the highway with your hair flying sounds perfect to me. And, if you don't like it, then you sell the motorcycle. No big deal."

We both enjoyed our toast and sipped our coffees before speaking again. "So, who are you going to ask to teach you to ride?"

"Candi. Chops has a bike for sale that he won't sell to me. But Candi let me know to call her about it. So, I'm going to be all sneaky and catch up with her later. Chops spends his time at the clubhouse on Sundays so he won't be around."

"Hah. I like Candi. She's all bubbly and happy. And she and Chops make a good couple."

I nodded in complete agreement. They were both good people. "Well, I need to get going. I want to get the deposits ready so Katie doesn't get stuck spending most of her day at the store."

"You need to have an escort, remember?"

"Shit. I forgot to check in with the club last night. I'm not even sure if they have any new information."

"Something about the guy in the storage room was returned in one piece to his car and encouraged to leave town and some hotel rooms were already cleared out that were booked under fake names."

"The guy is alive? I am very excited to hear that since I'm the one who dragged his ass to the storage room and then held a gun to his head!" I snorted.

Hattie's eyes got big, and then she looked over at me, and we both broke out laughing. My conscience was clear.

There was a light knock at the side door. I approached, moving one hand to my back to be ready to pull my gun if needed. On the other side of the locked storm door, Tyler nodded at me.

"What brings you over at the crack of dawn?" I asked while opening the door so he could enter.

"I drew the short straw last night. I have the early morning duty," he said. "We all knew you would be up with the birds and not wait for someone to escort you to the store. I was here at 5:00 a.m., waiting for the lights to come on."

"But I've been up for about an hour. Why did you wait so long to knock?"

"You're kind of scary before your coffee, and I thought it best to give you time to adjust your caffeine level before telling you that I was assigned to babysit," Tyler admitted.

"Smart thinking, Mr. Tyler," Hattie cackled from the kitchen table.

I just shook my head. I retrieved my shoulder bag out of the safe, kissed Hattie goodbye and left. At least Tyler's truck was already warm. The temperature with the wind chill factor was hovering around the negative 15 mark, and my hair was still damp.

Two hours later, Tyler and I had the money from the rolling safe counted out and bundled. He found a large suitcase in the back room that we moved the cash into.

"What are we going to do with it until tomorrow when the bank opens?"

"I have a walk-in safe in the basement at the house. We can lock it in there."

I wrote out the deposit slip for the total and sealed the suitcase up. We rolled it back into the empty storage room and relocked the door.

Next, we went to the office and opened the wall safe. We both groaned when cash tumbled out.

"Never thought it would be a bad thing to have to count so much cash," he chuckled.

"It can be a dirty chore. The credit card receipts can be a pain too, but they just need to balance to what the computer says. The money is already in the account."

"Why do you encourage people to make cash sales then?"

"The card readers are too slow, and the customers that use them almost always want receipts. I can clear more customers than three cashiers running the card machines, by doing cash deals."

We both settled in counting and bundling the cash with rubber bands. When we were done, we looked around to find something to put it in, but could only find the paper tote bags that we used for clothes. We split the bundles of money into two bags.

Then we both just stood there, staring at the tote bags. Anyone could glance in and know they were filled with cash. It wasn't smart to leave them this way.

I had an idea that I thought would work and opened up one of the cabinets. I took out some fancy tissue paper and poofed it out of each bag. Then I pulled out some ribbon and tied the tote handles together and added ribbon streamers down the side of the bags.

"Perfect," Tyler laughed. "I would never guess those were loaded up with green." He carried the bags as I got the doors and we locked them in the storage room with the suitcase.

"What now?"

"Now, you go make some fresh coffee while I start on the credit card receipts."

Neither of us made it very far before the back buzzer went off by the loading dock. I checked the screen and saw that it was Henry with the freight truck and opened up the overhead.

"Henry, you're extra early this morning," I yelled while locking the overhead into place.

When I turned back around I saw a portly man with a dirty gray beard holding a gun to the back of Henry's head.

I froze.

Tyler went for his gun, but the fat man yelled at him not to move, or he would blow Henry's head off. He nudged Henry into the building with the end of the barrel. Following behind him, with a gun of his own, was my ex-boyfriend Brett.

"Well, isn't this turning out to be a crappy day," I sighed. "Hi, Brett. How the hell are you?"

Brett and I had a history, a bad one. There was a time, shortly after I moved back to Michigan, that I was so deeply shadowed by guilt that it drove me to some bad dating choices. I allowed Brett to inflict his physical and verbal abuse on me for a few months before I was smart enough to walk away. We had crossed paths a few times since then, resulting in a quick trip to a jail cell for him followed by a restraining order. After the break-in, I had checked in with his sister Barb, and she assured me he was settled with a woman in Battle Creek, a city a few towns over and in the next county. He had even sold his house. I should have known better.

"You look like shit, Brett. Been overdoing the whole drug addict thing?"

"Shut the fuck up, before I shut you up for good," he yelled.

He raised his gun and pointed it at Tyler. "You. Slowly reach for your gun and drop it on the floor. Then your cell phone."

Tyler glanced at me, and I nodded. He set both on the ground and kicked them both toward Brett without being asked.

Brett looked around and saw the storage room door. "Unlock that door, Kelsey."

I wasn't sure how he knew the money was in there, but I was more worried about Henry and Tyler than the money, so I did what I was told.

"Now both of you get in the room," Brett ordered Tyler and Henry.

*Ha!* He doesn't know the money is in there after all.

Tyler and Henry both seemed unsure but since they didn't have a choice they entered the room, and Brett pointed with his gun for me to relock it. The door couldn't be opened without a key, so I knew they were trapped for now.

"So who's your new friend? Fellow cokehead?" I asked.

Pissing Brett off wasn't the smartest thing I had ever done, especially when I had two guns pointed at me. I earned myself a backhanded slap across the cheekbone.

Ok. One point for Brett. Hot pain throbbed across my cheek up to the tip of my ear.

"Come on, man. Let's go get the money and go. No telling how soon the others will start arriving," his fat partner in crime whined.

"He's right. Move. Head to the office." Brett shoved me toward the front rooms as he walked behind me. He still held a tight grip on the gun, but lowered it, perceiving no immediate threat. The cocky bastard would never guess in a million years that I was capable of fighting him, let alone armed.

"I saw how busy it was yesterday. I know the safe is full," Brett said.

We entered my office, and I turned to the safe and started running the dial.

"Terry, keep an eye out so no one sneaks up on us," Brett ordered.

"I'm not leaving you alone with all the money," the fat-man, aka Terry, said.

So much for honor among thieves, I thought.

"I didn't say for you to leave. Just stand in front of the office window or door and holler if someone is coming into the building."

I finished opening the safe and swung the door wide.

"Where the hell is the money?"

"At the bank," I answered, sitting down behind my desk.

"Impossible. You closed the store after the bank closed."

"They have night drop chutes. We wait until late at night and make deposits through the chute that goes down into the vault in the bank's basement," I said.

This was sort of true. Our bank did have this option, but we weren't stupid enough to travel with that much money at night to a bank drop off. When I had the smaller store, it was fine. But with the bigger store, there was way too much money involved to take the risk.

Terry must have been listening and came into the office and looked into the safe. "Shit man. You said this was a sure thing. There's nothing in here but a couple of files and these little boxes." He pulled out one of the small velvet boxes and held it up.

"Hey, wait a minute." Brett set his gun on the desk and took the box from Terry, opening it up. "It's jewelry. How many boxes are in there?"

Terry pulled all the jewelry boxes out, and they opened them up. While they were occupied, I leaned forward and stretched my foot out under the desk to hit the silent alarm. The old alarm would have just triggered some strobe lights. The new alarm sent a text message to my entire crew and several club members. Brett reached down and grabbed the trash can, emptying it on the floor, and they loaded it up with the jewelry. Terry tucked his gun in the back of his pants. I was about to move when Brett picked his gun back up.

"Come on, let's go," he said to me.

"Why? You have what you want. Just leave."

"You're coming with us," he insisted, reaching to grab for me. His gun was pointed at the floor, so I jumped out of his reach and pulled my gun from the holster. I was aimed at his chest.

He took a step back.

I could see all the bad ideas filtering through that tiny brain of his.

"Don't do it, Brett. Set the gun down or I *will* shoot you."

"Doubt it," he answered before raising his gun.

I fired twice. The first bullet entered his shoulder, knocking him back and the gun to the floor. The second was somewhere in the same vicinity but was an accidental second tap to the trigger so I wasn't watching for it.

I re-aimed at Terry. "Are you going to be smart or stupid Terry? It's your choice. Set your gun on the desk nice and easy, or you will be leaving in a body bag."

He looked at Brett bleeding out on the floor and started to remove his gun from his waistband. He leaned forward as if to set it down but jerked back at the last second to aim it at me. I fired a single round in his shoulder, which caused him to drop the gun to the floor.

I was still holding my gun on them when the police arrived. It took me a moment to realize they were talking to me, and I lowered my gun, placing it on the desk and stepped out of the office.

I went to the storage room, warning Henry and Tyler that it was just me, as I unlocked the door.

"Holy shit," Tyler yelled when the door opened, and he swallowed me in a hug. "Are you okay? We heard the gunfire. You scared the shit out of me." He was checking me from head to toe and rubbed his fingers against my cheekbone, which made me wince. "Sorry."

"I'm fine. How are you guys? Henry, I am so sorry you got dragged into this mess!"

"I'm just sorry they used me to get to you, honey. I was so worried about you." He hugged me tight. We both were tearing up. It had been a stressful morning.

"So who the hell is Brett and who was his buddy? And, do the cops have them?"

"Brett's my very pleasant and charming ex-boyfriend and the other guy was someone named Terry. They have a few bullet holes in them now, but I was nice when I doled them out. They should survive the injuries just fine."

I was still a little shaky from the adrenaline rush and leaned over to put my hands on my knees to calm myself.

"And, I can't believe the stupid fucker didn't even realize he locked you both in a room with all the money!" I laughed. This made Henry and Tyler laugh too, and we all hugged each other again.

"Let Tech into the building and you can have your damn video!" I yelled at Detective Atwood.

It had been an hour of giving our statements, being tested for gunshot residue and re-questioned again and again. Atwood had patrolmen keeping all of the employees and club members out of the building.

I saw Dave badge his way in and approach me. "She's right. Tech and Sara are the only ones that can access the feed. Kelsey doesn't even have access to Tech's office. And, you wouldn't want her to. The last time she messed with the security system, she wiped everything out."

"Fine. Go get him," Detective Atwood grumbled. "But no one else comes inside until I have cleared the scene and watched the video. And, I have to witness the video being copied or it won't hold up in court."

Detective Atwood had transferred in from Detroit about two months ago and was used to doing things a bit more by the book than what a smaller city required. I had met him a few times, but my association with the club seemed to be a big negative in his opinion. This was the first time we had had any real interaction, but based on his attitude, I doubted it would be the last.

Dave went out to collect Tech, who came flying in the back door seconds later, grabbing me and swinging me in a big circle.

"Damn it, Kelsey. You scared the shit out of all of us," Tech said. He looked at the bruise on my face. "Get some ice on that."

He nodded for Atwood to follow him, as he led the way to his office.

I went to the break room, and Tyler followed me. He pulled a towel and some ice and handed them over. Henry was already sitting at the table looking bored.

"How much longer are they going to take? I got places to go, shit to do," he grumbled.

At least I knew there was no permanent emotional damage for Henry. He was the same ole Henry as always.

"Oh! I forgot why I came so damn early this morning! I was all excited because I was driving home last night when I passed a big industrial building that was being emptied. I swung in and guess what I made a deal on buying?" he grinned.

"Garage door openers," I beamed back.

"Yup. Bought six commercial units for a hundred a piece. The crew on-site even showed me they were in good working order before I supervised them taking them down. I can go back tomorrow and pick them up. I didn't have enough room in the truck for them yesterday."

"You filled the truck again?"

"Sure did," he continued to grin.

It was another half an hour before we got the all clear and the others were let into the building. They converged like a wild mob and descended on us with tears and hugs. All three of us were feeling a bit crowded and overly emotional.

Dave came back and told us the surveillance video showed there was no question of me acting in self-defense. The district attorney would still need to watch the video before making it official, but he didn't see any reason to worry.

I noticed Bones watching me from the loading dock. I started to walk that way when he lowered his gaze, gripped the sides of his head in frustration, and spun around to walk out of the building. James came over and placed a hand on my shoulder.

"It's complicated. He just wants to do the right thing by you."

"Go make sure he's okay, James. Please."

He nodded and followed Bones' path out of the building.

Tech walked back into the back room with a big smile. "That stupid fucker locked Henry and Tyler in the room with all the money! What a dumbass!" he laughed.

"I know, right!" I grinned.

"What are you talking about?" Katie asked.

"We came in early to count all the cash. We moved it into the storage room. Then Brett locked Tyler and Henry up in the storage room."

Katie walked over to the storage room and looked in.

"It's a suitcase and two tote bags that look like presents. He didn't think that was weird? That they were just locked up in an empty room like that?"

Everybody looked in the room.

"How much is that anyway?" Dave asked.

"About three and a quarter," I answered.

"You have Three-Hundred and Twenty-five THOUSAND dollars sitting in a damn *storage room*!?" he yelled.

He was mumbling something about 'women' when he stomped away.

Not ready to go back into the office just yet, Tech and Whiskey locked the store down, and Tyler and Goat escorted Katie to the main house to secure the cash in the basement walk-in safe. Everyone else followed in that direction.

I decided I needed some space and opted to take a drive. The drive was short, ending at Chops' garage. Chops and Candi lived in the house next door to the service garage, so a few seconds later Candi came running out and barreled into me with a hug so tight I couldn't breathe.

"I'm okay, promise."

She saw the bruise on my face and mumbled *that bastard*, under her breath.

"I stopped in to see what the deal is on the bike." We walked over to it.

"Sign says eight thousand, but we picked it up at six," she said.

"How about seven and a half?"

"We can go lower than that."

"And, I can afford to pay twice that, so, seven and a half?" I smiled.

"Done," she grinned. "Let's go inside. I will do the paperwork up before Chops comes home. Do you know how to ride?"

"Nope. Are you going to teach me? Or do I have to figure it out for myself?"

She grinned even wider. "This is going to be fun. The boys are going to shit bricks over this one."

# Chapter Fifteen

I pulled the comforter up over my head and burrowed further into the bed, while exposing one arm in search for the elusive snooze button, to stop the annoying alarm from disturbing my dream. It was a good dream, and I wasn't ready for it to end. It involved strong arms, a wicked tongue, and devilish deep dark brown eyes. Hmmmm….

Knocking the alarm clock off the stand, it seemed to blare even louder. Huffing angrily, I threw back the comforter and forced myself up and out of bed. I turned the alarm off and stared at the time. 6:00 a.m. Shit. Now I'm up.

I complained and grumbled to myself all the way into the shower.

I chose to wear loose jeans and a warm knitted turtleneck sweater, both for comfort and to decrease any rubbing against the patches of missing skin and bruises I acquired during my first motorcycle lesson. I was glad I bought a used bike since it had a few more scratches on it than it did before I owned it. Candi was a good teacher, though, and after a couple hours, I was able to take it on the road.

With a slight limp, I meandered into the dining room. Hattie smirked and gestured for me to have a seat while she retrieved my morning caffeine dosage. Anne, Katie, and Sara were already at the table, eating eggs and toast. Sara was showing them a printout of her class schedule for the next semester. Anne and I had looked it over last night, and it was impressive, and intimidating.

Hattie set my coffee down and a plate of breakfast.

"Thank you, Hattie," I smirked.

"You're most welcome, Sunshine" she smirked back. "So, did you notice it snowed last night?"

"What? No way. That sucks!" I knew it was a bad time of year to buy a motorcycle, but I was hoping to practice a few more times before the weather turned too hazardous to ride.

"Yup. Looks to be about three inches, and the forecast is calling for more this afternoon."

It was a good thing that Candi and I had sealed the bike up in her oversized shed in her backyard. Looks like I wouldn't see the bike again until spring. Dang, I had a lot of fun on it yesterday, I pouted to myself.

"Kelsey, are you going to the store at 7:00?" Anne asked.

"Yup. You need something?"

"I have some errands to run and Sara doesn't want to go with me. Can she go with you?"

"Of course. I am sure that little-bug and I can find some trouble to get into without you."

Sara giggled and looked excited. We didn't get as much time together as we used to, with all the construction projects going on.

"I need to stock up on some new clothes. How about we spend a bit of our time this morning having our own fashion show?" I asked Sara.

"Yes!!" she yelled. Playing dress up was her all-time favorite activity.

"I am so jealous. I am behind on all the books and need to lock myself down today, or I will never get them caught up. If you guys find something super hot in my size, be sure to set it aside for me," Katie pouted.

"Can I tag along?" Hattie asked. "I've been thinking of sprucing up my own wardrobe. I'm kind of tired of the same old clothes I always wear."

We all turned to look at Hattie.

"Sure. This could get interesting," I wagged my eyebrows.

Hattie had always worn simple khaki or navy pants with plain oversized shirts. She was never into the flair of clothes and always straddled the line between nice and comfortable. I don't think I have even seen her wear a pair of jeans.

"This is going to be fun," Sara giggled.

"I wish I didn't have errands to run now," Anne laughed.

"Stop it, all of you. This is no big deal," Hattie insisted.

We all grinned at each other. It was a big deal. Something was up with Hattie, and I intended to find out what.

# Chapter Sixteen

Goat was already at the store when we arrived and was on the phone in the back room. He looked to be deep in serious conversation. I didn't see any of the contractors on-site yet, so I figured he was neck deep in their drama. Sara went to the break-room to drop off her laptop bag, and Hattie trailed her to check the coffee pot.

Goat disconnected the call with a *"Come pick up your shit then."*

"Was that the contractors or your wife?" I laughed.

He snorted. "The contractors. Billy and I went over the books on Friday. It didn't go well. He was trying to play off that it was some accounting error. Best I figure, you don't owe him the next payment, but he still owes you about a grand, which I am sure you will never see."

"Well, it is what it is. Don't stress about it. Let's just move forward." I patted him on the shoulder and Hattie delivered us both a cup of coffee. "We need to install new locks on the buildings, pull their tools and get our supplies locked down. Then we can focus on finding better contractors."

"I know a guy. He's good and has loyal subs. I called him over the weekend, but he's tied up all this week and wouldn't be able to start until next week. That will put the project behind."

"So, let's close for four weeks for winter break instead of three. I know I am not the only one that wouldn't mind having a little more time off."

"Awesome," Katie said coming in the side door and overhearing. "I'll update the website and send out a mass email right now."

"Well, okay then," Goat grinned. "I'll give him a call after I get the buildings locked down. Mind if I borrow some of the staff to help?"

"Go for it. Do whatever needs to be done. Hey, did you make your quota by Saturday for the ten employees? I forgot to ask."

"Sure did. The last hire was for laundry services, and was approved by Katie just before the deadline."

"Great job. It's not easy finding new hires, but you seem to have a talent for it."

"Thanks, but I think I'll be a little more careful before I stick my foot in my mouth next time," he chuckled.

"I'll let you get back to your work. Can you keep an eye out for Henry? He's bringing the garage door openers in today, and they'll need to go over in one of the new buildings for now."

"He found them already? Dang, he's like a hound dog. Maybe I'll have him do a walk-through of the buildings for the rest of the supplies we'll need. If that's okay?"

"Sure. Just remember he's paid accordingly."

Sara reappeared and dragged me by my arm toward the new inventory racks.

"Looks like my time is up," I laughed and allowed her to have her way.

Alex arrived and helped us pull the full racks of stock onto the sales floor so we would be closer to the dressing rooms. We no longer carried a kids' clothes line, but we always kept a rack for Sara and the other kids. I think Alex was just as excited as us about having a dress-up party. Every time the back door buzzer went off he would groan and roll his eyes before heading that way.

I noticed Hattie picking through the same types of shirts and pants that she always wore, so I grabbed a couple pairs of jeans and some more flashy tops and handed them to her.

"You said you wanted to spruce things up? So, let's do it right," I smiled.

She looked embarrassed for a moment but then pulled back her shoulders, raised her head and nodded to me, heading off to the dressing room. Sara giggled, following her with a few dresses.

Alex took the jeans I was holding away from me. "You also need to have more of a variety in your wardrobe," he said shaking his head. He handed me some dresses. "I've been saving these for you. And, I want to see every outfit before you turn it down!" He was sporting a very devilish grin. *Oh boy.*

"Holy Shit, Alex!" I hollered after putting on the first dress. "There's not much material going on here!"

"Don't be shy. Come out and let me see the goods, Luv," Alex yelled back.

Alex had moved a shoe rack over, and tossed me a pair of sling back shoes to shimmy into. I walked over to the three-pane mirror and laughed. "I can't wear this! I look like a high-class hooker."

"You look hot," Katie said, walking our way.

"Damn girl," Alex laughed. "I knew it would fit well, but it's like a second skin. You are so keeping that. Your breasts alone look amazing, but then your ass seals the deal."

The dress was beautiful. It was floor length in a shimmering midnight blue, off the shoulder sleeves and a plunging bodice. And, it did fit like a second skin, wrapping tight around my body until it flared out from mid-thigh down.

"Where would I wear it?" I laughed.

"Actually," Lisa said joining us. "It would be fun to have some theme days at the store, and all the employees can dress accordingly. This could be like a 'Nite out on the town' theme or 'Oscars at The Changing Room' theme. If we were all dressed up, you wouldn't stand out as much. And, we can dress the manikins up too."

"I wouldn't bet on Kelsey not standing out in that dress, but I am all for the idea," Goat laughed standing by the backroom door with Henry.

Hattie walked out in a pair of snug jeans and a low-cut sweater top that showed off her ample cleavage. She was grinning as she walked toward the mirror. Alex stopped her with a pair of short black boots that worked well with the outfit that she quickly put on. When she looked in the mirror, her face turned a little pink. When Goat, Katie, and Henry started cat-calling her, it turned dark red.

"I don't know, is it too much for someone my age?"

"Not even a little. You look smart and sassy – just like you are. You got the goods girl – show them off a little!" Alex insisted.

Hattie smiled bright, before turning back to try on another outfit. Sara paraded a dark green velvet dress, and after she was abundantly complemented, we both returned to the dressing room to try on our next items.

The next dress in the pile would work well with the sling backs, so I picked that. I had a little trouble getting it put together, as it was more form fitting than the first. It was a wraparound slinky number in a shimmering champagne color with several sections that opened to the bare skin. There was no way to wear underwear with it either, so I went commando.

"And, what would the theme of this one be?" I asked whoever as I walked out. No one replied so I looked up and saw them all staring at the dress.

"Umm… I think that one is a theme all on its own," Lisa smirked. "Maybe, 'Kelsey needs to get laid' theme."

I laughed my agreement while viewing my image in the large mirror.

"Fuck me," I heard from the doorway and looked over to see Bones, Whiskey and James standing there. Bones rubbed his eyes, turned and walked out.

I didn't know what else to do, so I went back to the dressing room. I sat on the small bench and tried to pull my emotions back in before the dam of tears broke. Alex pulled the curtain and stepped in.

"I like Bones, but he is pissing me off. He's strung my best friend along for almost a year now and still doesn't have his shit sorted. So, screw him. It's time for you to strut your stuff girlfriend. So, quit moping, and try on some more dresses. And, come Saturday, when the store opens, you are wearing *that dress* to work. I'll make sure the other girls are geared up too. It's time to let your hair down a bit." He turned to leave but then stopped.

"Or," he grinned, "maybe with that dress, sweep the front hair in an up-do and let it curl down your back."

I smirked, stood, and hugged him.

"And what the hell is the deal with the bruise on your hip and skin missing on the side of your leg?" he asked while looking at my leg again.

"I had a bit of an accident yesterday afternoon. If I tell you about it, you have to promise to keep it a secret," I grinned.

He agreed, and I explained the riding lessons and the bike that I bought.

"Well, I am glad it snowed so you have time to heal that shit up before Saturday's fashion show," he laughed.

He kissed me on the forehead and stepped back out.

We spent a good two hours trying on outfits, and my stomach was sore from laughing so hard. But we claimed almost everything we tried on. Alex did allow me to pick two more pairs of jeans, but only because he deemed they looked bitchin on me. Hattie had indulged in a much more daring line of clothes that complemented her body and her personality. Sara had a party dress for Saturday, and the rest was more sensible everyday wear, in all her favorite pastels.

Katie had been escorted to the bank and had returned. And now, she was in lock down in our office to work the books. On the way to the office to see if I could lend a hand, I ran into Carol, one of the cashiers. She was crying.

"Carol, what's wrong?"

"Nothing. I'm fine Kelsey," she insisted while trying to slide by me.

"You are not fine. What's wrong?"

"I just… I just needed to talk to Katie about Saturday. And, she insisted I couldn't have any time off without listening to why I needed it." She wiped her eyes and took a deep breath. "It's fine, though. I understand how crazy Saturdays are. I totally get it and shouldn't have asked."

Carol was a great cashier, and she was right, Saturdays were sacred at the store. My issue was the part where Katie didn't even take the time to hear her out. "Follow me, Carol."

Carol followed me into the office, and I directed her to sit in the guest chair at Katie's desk. Katie looked up at me and then at Carol.

"I'm in the middle of these numbers, can this wait?" she asked.

"Let's see. An employee had a problem, came in to talk to you about it, and you blew her off without giving her a chance to explain. What do you think?"

"Damn," Katie rubbed her forehead and set her pen down. "I'm sorry, Carol. I was a bitch. You have never asked for time off, and I am so focused on my own shit, I didn't think," she admitted.

I stepped back out of the office and closed the door. Katie would make sure things were settled and rebuild her respect level with Carol on her own.

"Is Katie talking to Carol?" Haley asked as I walked up front.

"Yeah. Do you know what's up?" I asked.

"Her only sister is getting married on Saturday, and they got into a huge fight when Carol told her Saturdays were mandatory to work. Her sister has helped Carol and her kids get through a lot of rough patches, especially with money problems. I hope Katie agrees to give her the day off."

"It's not always that easy. We need someone to cover for her."

"What if Carol could help Katie get all the books caught up this week? Then Katie would be able to help more on Saturday. Carol used to do accounting work. And, I could train Bridget to work the register too. That would help."

"Since you already know Carol's situation, why don't you interrupt them and pitch the idea. I think Katie might go for it. But the final decision is up to her, and you have to respect whatever that decision is."

She nodded and walked off toward the office.

Since I was back in jeans and comfortable shoes, I decided to clean the bathrooms and wash all the handprints off the front windows. Satisfied everything was nice and shiny, I returned to the office.

Carol was at my desk using my computer when I entered. She started to get up, and I gestured for her to sit back down. She was working on the bookkeeping, and I didn't want to interrupt her rhythm. I took a seat in one of the guest chairs at Katie's desk and she handed me two red folders and three blue folders. I leaned back and started reading each folder and signing off on purchasing orders and payroll approvals.

Hattie entered around noon and delivered a pizza to us, giving us all a much-needed mental break.

"May I make a suggestion?" Carol asked.

"Sure," Katie replied gulping her pop.

"What about instead of me working laundry on Mondays, I help keep up the books? It seems Goat has some good new hires handling laundry right now, and Katie could use the help."

"Sold," Katie grinned.

"Better you than me," I grinned in favor of the plan.

Carol grinned and took a big bite of her pizza.

After lunch, I worked the loading docks for new deliveries and was surprised by a smiling Katie at around 2:00.

"Wow. A smile on accounting day?" I laughed.

"Carol is amazing with the books. She has all the expenses and sales entered through Saturday and is working on entering all the construction information into a database, something I have been trying to get to for two months now," she grinned. "I understand why you didn't want an outside accountant working our books, but with her knowledge and skills, I think I should pay a higher wage for the accounting work."

"I'm cool with that. Just make sure she understands that we don't have a full-time slot open yet for a bookkeeper. Maybe down the road when we get the other buildings open, though, we can increase her hours for it. Plus, I want her to sign a confidentiality agreement. Not that I think she is a gossip, but it's a nice reminder that it's our private business."

"I already knew you would say all that, so it's already taken care of. And, I gave her the green light for Saturday, and Haley is going to train Bridget this week on the register. Bridget said it was fine as long as it didn't turn into an everyday thing. She likes to be able to be more 'active' she said."

"I can see that. She's not the sit-still type."

"Well, it's my turn now," Katie said as she started to walk away.

"For what?"

"My new wardrobe," she grinned. "Alex said he was pulling me some new outfits too. He better have something just as hot for me to wear on Saturday as that get-up you squeezed into earlier." She sashayed away like she owned the world.

Tech walked in but was sidetracked by Katie swinging her backside toward the sales floor. He had a grin that could have a thousand meanings, but if any of them involved thinking of one of my best friends naked, I didn't want to know. Sometimes it was hard to remember that Tech was a grown man because of his preference for root beer floats and video games.

"She's in a good mood today," he said.

"She discovered that Carol is a wizard with bookkeeping. She magically has some free time on her hands."

The loading dock buzzer went off, and I opened the door while Tech grabbed the clipboard to fill out an intake receipt. On the other side of the door was one of our less liked sellers, Sleazy Tony. *Ick*.

"Must be my lucky day. Get the sexiest chick in town to *service* me," Tony grinned his rotted tooth smile as he leaned into my space.

*Ewe*! I took a step back.

"You'll mind your manners or get the hell out of here Tony Stamwell!" Hattie said as she bulldozed herself in front of me.

I turned to Tech, and we both smirked. Go Hattie.

"You will not disrespect Kelsey or any of the other employees, or you will answer to me. Understand?"

Tony looked at Hattie, then at me, then at something behind me, and nodded agreement. He started unloading his truck as Alex came up to inspect the delivery and I turned around to see Henry, Whiskey and James standing behind me grinning. *Macho nut-jobs*.

"What can I do for you, gentlemen?" I grabbed Hattie's elbow and meandered to the break room with her in tow.

"Henry found another deal of the century. He needs extra labor though to pull it off. We went to ask Katie, but she's in dress-up land, and we didn't want to interrupt her play-time," James smirked.

"What's the find?" I asked Henry.

"A resale store in Jackson is going out of business. We can have 1200 square feet of stock for $2500. Haven't looked at it yet, but know a gal in the area. I called, and she went and scoped it out for me. She says it's top of the line, designer labels, and stuff." Henry explained all this in his no-nonsense way as he leaned against the wall, but his eyes kept drifting over to Hattie. "They would also be interested in selling wall racks, mirrors, display cases and such, which is where the extra labor and truck space comes in."

"I'll go pull some cash," Hattie offered and swished out of the break room.

*What was up with all the butt swinging around here today?*

Whiskey must have noticed it too because he chuckled, but Henry was too focused on Hattie's retreat to notice anyone else.

"The semi is still full, and the other freight truck has stock for Bridal and Menswear. We would have to make multiple trips."

"Nah. I got a buddy that works at the truck rental place up the road. Said if you opened a business account, he would discount you 30% off on your rentals."

Henry was a wizard of a deal maker. I grinned my approval.

"Figured you would like that," he grinned back. "Had him fax an application to you already. You just fill it out and fax it back, and we can head out first thing in the morning."

"Saw application," Katie said entering the room. "Filled out, signed and faxed back said application. Now, how about this dress for Saturday?"

She pivoted around in a slow circle. She was wearing a slinky red sequin dress with a very high slit up the side, a diving neckline almost to her navel, and platform heels that had crisscross straps up her ankles.

We all had huge eyes and open mouths and just stared at her. She looked "HOT," I said. "Sizzling," Whiskey added. "Damn" was all James could come up with.

From behind us, we heard another opinion, "Hell No."

We turned to see Tech standing there pissed off with hands on his hips. "You are not wearing that on Saturday. What would people think?"

"That she's beautiful? Sexy? Single?" I answered on her behalf.

Katie looked back at me and winked before strutting back to the dressing area. Tech was right on her platform heels.

"Well that should get interesting," I mumbled.

"I had no idea he was still interested," Whiskey said.

"That's because you have been too busy watching another skirt that's around here," James teased. "Which, you should see what Anne is wearing on Saturday. I think there is even less material than Katie's dress."

"I need a cigarette," Whiskey grumbled.

We all laughed as he departed.

Hattie re-entered with a grin on her face. "Tech is not a happy camper right now," she giggled. She handed the cash envelope out to Henry, but he didn't take it.

"I think you should hang on to the money and ride out to Jackson with us in the morning," Henry explained. "We might need a woman's perspective on the display cases and such to make sure they will look right with what was already purchased."

"Well, sure. I suppose I can do that," Hattie agreed with a blush.

Hot damn, Hattie had a date. Well- sort of.

"Sounds like a great idea. You all run with it. I need to go finish up some things in the office," I said. I just needed to get out of there before I started giggling, but any excuse would work.

"Shit," James laughed following me. "Was that for real? Is our Hattie crushing on good ole Henry?"

"I'm not getting involved. She can figure it out for herself." But I was happy for her. She deserved to have someone in her life like Henry.

"You need anything else before we take off?"

"No. It's been a quiet Monday with the contractors all gone. I think most of them have picked up their tools, and some of the subs left their business cards hoping they will be re-hired under the new contractor next week. Everything seems calm at the moment."

"Okay. See you tomorrow."

Looking around the store, everything seemed to be set already for Wednesday, and since the bookkeeping was also caught up, I had an idea. I grabbed the PA phone and called Alex, Lisa, Anne and Katie to the sales floor.

"Somehow the tides have turned in our favor, and we are already ahead of schedule for the week," I said. "So, I am going to take advantage of some of the down time and go home and work on some other projects. And tomorrow, Goat and I will cover the store while you four take a much-needed day off."

They all seemed surprised and looked at each other.

"But what will we do?" Katie asked.

"Whatever the hell you want!" Goat answered as he walked up. "I know not coming in here for a day is the most bizarre thought in the world to you guys, but you have the rest of today to figure out what you want to do with your day off. Go have a spa day. Go to the movies. Go to the casino. The point is, do not under any circumstances come into this store tomorrow. The Queen B and I will handle it."

"It's settled then. Goat, I will see you tomorrow. The rest of you... don't be too serious today. We don't get the opportunity very often to kick back and relax."

"Who wants to have a spa day with me tomorrow?" Alex asked already forgetting me before I was even out of the building.

"Me!" Lisa answered.

"I think I will take Sara somewhere fun," Anne said.

"I want to go to an all you can eat Chinese buffet," Katie said.

I grabbed my shoulder bag and stepped out the back door. It was early enough, that I could run up to the state licensing office and get my motorcycle license. I grinned at the thought.

As I walked to my SUV, I noticed Sleazy Tony's truck was still in the lot. Or maybe he had returned. It was off to the side, though, near where Bridget sometimes takes a smoke break so I was concerned. I pulled my gun from my shoulder bag and tucked it into the back of my jeans. I left my shoulder bag sitting in the middle of the lot. I hurried around the corner. Tony had Bridget pinned to the wall and was groping her breast while she stood frozen in fear.

"Tony – Get the hell away from her!" I yelled and charged him.

He took a step back, and I punched him in the face. Then I planted a sidekick that had enough force in it to bounce him off his truck and back forward again. I utilized his forward momentum by delivering a powerful knee to the groin. He was in the fetal position on the ground holding his nose with one hand and his nuts with the other before I turned around to Bridget.

She was still frozen in place, white as a ghost and not hearing a word I was saying. She was in shock. I started guiding her back to the building when the others ran out to see what the ruckus was about. Haley saw Bridget and took over getting her inside.

She looked back and added, "She'll be okay. I've seen this before," she assured me. Haley didn't seem too worried, and she knew Bridget the best, so that made me feel better.

Goat dragged Tony up off the ground, only to have Tech step up and punch him, knocking him back to asphalt.

"Okay, Okay. That's enough," Goat chuckled.

Bones walked into the mix, from where, I wasn't sure, looked at me to make sure I was alright and then hauled Tony back up off the ground. Goat opened Tony's truck door, and Bones launched him into the cab.

"*If I ever see you here again, I will kill you,*" Bones declared with cold certainty and walked away.

Damn.

"You should have shot him," Alex said tapping the gun at my lower back.

"Thought three bodies in one week might be too much for our local PD to handle."

"It would look a bit suspicious," Goat agreed watching Tony drive away. "Though I think Tony feels like it would have been less painful if you would have shot him. Damn girl. Did you invert his nut sack?"

I grinned and walked back to my SUV to head home.

I noticed I had a voicemail message on my phone and called in to listen to it as I was backing out of my spot. I was paying more attention to the phone than my driving and backed into the dumpster. I got out and confirmed that I smashed out the rear light again before pressing 1 to play the message. Alex was at the loading dock with the door open shaking his head at me. *Whatever.*

"I can't believe it fucking snowed!" a woman's voice on the message said.

That was it, the whole message. I laughed as I disconnected and put the truck in drive. Candi had just as much fun yesterday with the bike lessons as I did.

# Chapter Seventeen

Tuesday started off much the same as Monday, with a battle between me and the alarm clock. Once again the alarm clock won. I was a lot less sore, but a lot more tired. I had stayed up until 3:00 a.m. working in my War Room in the basement trying to come up with new leads to find Nicholas. I re-read all the witness reports from the murder investigation of the burned bodies, and around 2:00 a.m., I found something I had missed before.

The witness was listed as Carl, no last name. And the notes the officer took didn't make much sense until I thoroughly read the words instead of scanning them quickly.

Officer: *Did you see anyone the night of the fire?*

Carl: *I didn't see Nicholas.*

Officer: *Did you see anything at all?*

Carl: *All the newspapers got it wrong. I read them all, it was all wrong. Why do I bother to read them if they are going to be so inaccurate? They are deceiving all their customers.*

Officer: *Did you see anything the night of the fire?*

Carl: *I saw the truth. Now I want a chili dog. I have to go wait for a chili dog.*

The police officer taking the statement must have thought that Carl was insane. And knowing this particular Carl, the officer wasn't alone. Most of the neighborhood referred to him as Crazy Carl. But while I had worked undercover, I had the opportunity to get to know him. He was actually so intelligent that he couldn't function with normal tasks. He could write chemical formulas up that I didn't even want to know what they were for, but was too absentminded to remember to charge his cell phone. When I met him, he had been living on the streets only because he couldn't remember where he lived and had left his wallet with his id at home.

It was too early to call the group home where he lived. And, most likely Carl would refuse to talk to me over the phone anyway. I would need to sneak into Miami and talk to him in person. His statement on the newspapers told me that he did see something that night. Carl religiously read every newspaper he could find from front to back. If he said all the papers got the story wrong, then he knew what really happened. He also said he didn't see Nicholas. So, he knew that Nicholas was alive. And the chili dog comment was a message for me. I was supposed to meet him outside our favorite chili dog restaurant. But that was almost three years ago. I had no idea if Carl was even living at the group home anymore.

Overthinking it right now, wasn't helping. I would just have to wait a couple hours and call.

I showered and dressed in comfortable hip-hugger jeans and a knit turtleneck. I would be working the loading docks all day, and it would be too cold for anything more fashionable. I finished the look with my lazy-ass slip on tennis shoes and went in search of coffee.

"Hey, Donovan," I smiled, seeing he was sitting at the table in the dining room. "What brings you over this morning?"

"Lisa threatened our sex life if I woke her before 9:00 this morning," he grinned and held up his coffee cup.

"Ha. Like she could hold out for long anyway."

"I wasn't going to take any chances. I even waited until I was outside to put on my shoes. Pregnant Lisa is a whole different Lisa."

Hattie came in and handed me my cup of Joe.

"Thank you, Hattie," I greeted giving her a kiss on the cheek.

"You're welcome," she said absentmindedly.

Donovan and I both looked up at her. She went to the fruit bowl and was sorting the fruit to make sure it was all fresh. Donovan looked back at me, and I just shrugged.

"So, Hattie, are you ready for your road trip with Henry today?"

"I think so. Not much to plan. I made some cookies last night to take along. And the money is in my purse. I'm not sure about my outfit, though. We'll be in a truck all day, and maybe I overdressed."

She seemed nervous.

"You look perfect. I like that blouse. It has a nice flare to it."

"Ha. You're biased."

"But she's not a liar. You look great. And, the weather will be clear today. So, you picked a good day to go," Donovan added.

She seemed to accept this and headed back into the kitchen.

"So I heard you were in a fight yesterday." He looked over his cup in a fake glare at me.

"He deserved it."

"I'm just sorry I missed it." He grinned and clinked our coffee cups together. "But remember to keep a low profile for the next couple weeks while the dust settles from the shooting. It wouldn't be good for you to get a reputation for being violent before the DA officially clears you."

"Is it weird that I have no feelings at all about shooting Brett and Terry? I mean, I didn't even think about it when I was in the office yesterday. I didn't even glance at the floor to see if all the blood was cleaned up."

"Bones had some of the guys help him clean the office, so there's nothing to see. And, no, it's not weird that you don't have feelings about it. You have been pushing Brett's threats out of your head for a long time, so you didn't get bogged down by them. Inside your head, it's the same old Brett shit as normal."

"Maybe." I wasn't convinced that his reasoning was a good enough excuse to being indifferent about shooting two people. "I'm glad I decided to shoot them in the shoulder, though. It was a little bit of a question in my head at the time," I admitted.

"Understandable. I heard a few gripes from some of the Players that you were too nice about it."

"I'm sure you did." I rolled my eyes.

"Kelsey, dear. Are you ready? We are going to be late," Hattie complained from the kitchen.

I looked at my watch. It was a quarter to seven. It takes less than a minute to drive around the corner. I smirked at Donovan, and it was his turn to roll his eyes. "On my way, Hattie."

"Where is everybody?" I asked Henry when we pulled into the back lot.

"I came down here to pick up Hattie and then we will meet the guys at the truck rental. I didn't want them to all start gabbing with you over coffee. We got places to be and shit to buy, you know."

I nodded and told them to have fun and find good sales, as Henry assisted Hattie into the truck along with her basket of goodies.

I punched in the security code and unlocked the back door. Stepping in I hit the first light switch and all was quiet and secure. I kept my shoulder bag with me and continued through the store opening up the rest of the rooms and turning on all the lights.

"Hey," Goat called out when he entered. "I meant to get here before you this morning, but Amanda wasn't cooperating."

I was about to argue that I didn't need him to protect me when I realized my right hand was inside my shoulder bag gripping my gun.

"I guess I'm a little on guard still." I set my shoulder bag on the counter by the loading docks.

"It's expected and understandable. You went through not one, but two scary incidents within a week in a place that you have always felt safe. Just give it some time, and until then, don't get shitty with any of us that try and make you feel safe."

He grinned and went to turn up the thermostat to warm the place up a bit. I made a pot of coffee while the other employees for laundry services arrived.

After handling a few drop-offs deliveries, I went back to the break room and retrieved coffees for both Goat and I. I found him by the dock doors and nodded to the stools to take a break.

"How do you like it here so far?"

"I'm hooked. I see why you guys get so addicted to this place. There's so much to do, but every day is so different from the next. It's the most un-boring job I have ever had."

"So, are you planning on sticking around?"

"I dare you to try and kick me out. I won't go easily," he grinned.

"Good. Katie and I want you to run future projects and developments. We still may need your help with staffing, especially helping to keep an eye on laundry services since Hattie stepped away, but the construction projects and the new ideas that we come up with would be your priority. We need you to take the lead and just run with them. You up for the challenge?"

"Bring it on. I can handle it."

"Okay then. I want the loading docks moved out another twenty feet. And I want three instead of two overheads bay entrances." I took another drink of my coffee and watched him turn to look at the loading docks and the big overhead doors.

"Okay. I can draw something up. Can you tell me why?" He was scratching his chin trying to figure it out when I giggled and slid my sketchpad out of my bag.

I showed him that by moving the docks back, we could have a corridor area that wouldn't have to be heated in the winter or cooled in the summer, and we could have roll doors with plastic sheeting to move everything further into the building. With the addition, we could add on another dock, and push the asphalt out for parking another twenty feet into the field.

"Damn. Okay, I'll get started on it. What else is in here you want me to work on?"

We went through my ideas to utilize the heat from all the dryers and pump them into the warehouse during the winter and better venting outside in the summer. Then I showed him the set-up I wanted for a farmers' market on the vacant corner property. Each sketch seemed to draw him further and further into the bubble, and he was asking all the right questions and coming up with additional ideas as we went along.

An hour later, he went to check on laundry services and then he was going to start on more formal plans for the docks so city permits could be pulled. The buzzer went off for another delivery, and I started the intake process again. Tuesday was a big day for drop offs, and Haley had to jump in and help me cover all the deliveries.

By 10:00, I still hadn't had a chance to call the group home where Carl lived so I asked Haley to cover for me as I slipped into the employee-only hallway that led to Menswear.

One of the house tenants was confused on phone etiquette and kept answering the phone, introducing himself and then hanging up. I laughed and kept calling back until Scott, the group home director, finally rescued the phone.

"Hey, Scott. It's Kelsey Harrison. Do you remember me?"

"Yes. Of course, I do. I tried for six months to get a hold of you, but all the contact numbers I had were disconnected. I went to the station, but they said you moved out of state. Is this about Carl?"

"Yes, I need to talk to him. How's he doing?"

"I don't know. That's why I was trying to reach you. He still has a room here, and the bank makes the payment electronically every month, but he took off a couple of years ago, and I don't know where he is."

"Did he say anything before he left?"

"The day before he kept ranting about how the papers got it all wrong. I filed a missing person's report, but I don't have any idea how to find him."

"I do. But I can't get there right now. Will you go get him?"

"Gladly. Where do I go?"

I gave Scott the directions to the chili dog restaurant. "He won't want to leave. You will need to go inside, buy him two chili dogs with cheese and mustard then sit down on the cement no closer than four feet to him and wait for him to eat his chili dogs. When he is done, tell him that I got his message, but he will have to wait at home for me. It will be another week or so before I can get there, but tell him I have to meet him at the house."

"How do you know he will be at the restaurant? It's been years."

"He's there because he sent me a message that he would be waiting for me. I just didn't get the message until last night. In Carl's mind, he has to keep going back to the restaurant every day until I meet him. It would be like a mantra repeating in his head over and over."

"You're right. When he gets his mind stuck on something, he can't let it go. I'll head out now and wait to see if he shows up."

I returned to the loading docks, just as Haley was closing the overhead door again.

"Wow. I am out of shape. I should have taken you up on the offer to use the house gym," she said wiping the sweat from her brow.

"You haven't been around the house much the last couple of months. Everything going okay?" I asked.

Haley had moved in with us briefly, but the last few months she was back to staying at the clubhouse.

"Yeah. Sorry. I should move the rest of my stuff out. Bridget was having a hard time with some of the other girls, so I've been staying in my old room. We've talked about getting our own place together, but neither of us has done anything about it."

"With all the shit that happened last summer, I was never able to go back to my old house. It's been on the market all this time. Seems not a lot of people are interested in a house where I blew a guy's brains out. But if that isn't a freak-factor for you guys – and you are interested in living there, you're more than welcome. You would just have to pay utilities and keep up with the mowing and such."

"Bridget and I have both lived in worse, trust me. I'll go talk to her and see what she thinks. It's a great house. I remember it from the old Saturday night parties."

While she went to laundry to talk to Bridget, I went to the break room to grab a bottle of water.

Bridget and Haley were both waiting at the loading dock when I came back out.

"So?" I asked.

"We've decided that paying the utilities isn't enough. You have to charge us rent."

"No. To sell now, I would have to sell cheap and take a loss. I don't like to lose money. And, five years or so from now, if I sell it, then it will be more marketable because time has passed. But I will agree to let you both pay the annual taxes in addition to the utilities. That way I have no expenses on the house while you two live there. How's that sound?"

"How much are the annual taxes?" Bridget asked.

"Twelve hundred a year."

"So, you're saying, a hundred bucks a month and the utilities?"

"Yup."

"Yes! Yes! Can we go look at the house tonight after work?" Bridget was about to burst she was so giddy. Haley was grinning too.

"Sure. I can even meet you there. I think it's time I visit again. I have a lot of good memories there, more good ones than bad ones."

The girls dragged full bins into laundry with them, and I heard several boos at their arrival. I turned around to see Goat leaning against the bay door.

"You sure you're ready to go back to the old house?" he asked.

"No, but it's time."

"You want me to go with you?"

I shook my head. "You have your daughter, and she is more important. I'll be fine."

"That wasn't a very convincing answer," he stated as he re-opened the overhead when the buzzer went off.

The overhead doors were open more often than closed as more and more deliveries rolled in and by 2:00 the Devil's Players returned with the rental truck.

I grabbed the clipboard and looked for the freight truck. "Where's Henry and Hattie?"

"They took a side trip to another sale. Henry said that his truck was half empty, and he didn't want to waste the fuel on such a long drive for a half empty truck." James winked at me.

In other words, Henry wasn't done impressing Hattie yet.

"So there wasn't that much available at the sale?"

"Oh no. You made out like a bandit," James said as he opened up the rental. Every square inch was packed. "Henry made sure that as much as possible was squeezed in this truck before we were allowed to put anything in his."

"That old dog. How the hell are we going to empty it without an avalanche?"

I heard bikes roll up and in trooped about a dozen club members. I moved out of the way and found a stool to sit on and marked on the clipboard as much as I could of the items unloaded. I saw four more light fixtures come in that would be perfect for the new Accessories & Such department I had planned. And, at least another half dozen rolling racks and several wall racks were unloaded. I directed the lights and wall racks next door, but the rolling racks could stay in the backroom. I also counted twelve overflowing rolling bins of clothes that looked to be top quality. The last two items to come out were wrapped in towels.

"What's that?" I asked, ready to write it down.

"This was Henry and Hattie's only disagreement today. Henry insisted no. And, Hattie insisted yes. Hattie won. I was told to deliver them to you." James pulled the towels away so I could see them.

They were landscape paintings of sunsets on the beach. The colors in the sky rolled and blended in blues, oranges, pinks and peaches. They were beautiful.

"They're perfect," Bones voiced my thoughts.

"Yes, they are," I whispered. I couldn't help but think of Nicholas as I stared at the paintings. His love for the ocean is what had always made it so special for me. I rapidly blinked my eyes and pushed the memories away. Now was not the time.

"Perfect for what?" James asked.

"For her atrium. She has two walls that she has refused to ever hang anything on because they had to fit the room 'just so'," Bones grinned

"So this is a girl thing," James laughed.

"No, James. This is a Hattie loves me and takes care of me thing." I couldn't stop looking at the paintings.

"Tyler – help me take these up to the main house and get them hung," Bones ordered, and Tyler jumped to do his bidding.

Bones laid his hand on my shoulder before turning and following Tyler out the door. I went to my office to take a moment to collect myself. *Stupid paintings - making me cry like a silly girl.*

I spent the rest of the day organizing the restock racks, packing the full ones as tight as I could. With the new racks that were purchased, the back room was maxed out. By 3:30 I shut down laundry because there was no more room for clean clothes. Hattie and Henry arrived, and we unloaded their full truck into the new Bridal building before the rest of the Players took off. Henry had filled his truck to the brim as always. Every rolling tote was full.

"Damn, I've never seen you guys this stocked," Henry said looking around.

"Half of it is because of you!" I laughed. "You keep forgetting how much bigger deliveries you are making now."

"I've been having a lot of fun in the freight truck. And, Hattie makes a good co-pilot," Henry winked at her.

"Oh hush. Did you get the pictures dear?" Hattie asked.

"I did." I went over and gave her a big hug and kiss on the cheek. "Thank you, Hattie."

"You're forever welcome, Sunshine" she smiled back.

"Bones and Tyler took them up earlier to hang them if you want to run up and take a look."

"Yes. I must insist that Henry sees them too. The old fool would not believe me that those pictures were important." She elbowed Henry, and he laughed. It looked like they enjoyed spending the day together.

"Well go ahead. Goat and I are going to close down for the day. I have an errand to run, and then I will be home."

"Since we are closing early, I am going to run with Kelsey on her errand and then, Henry, if you can wait for me, I will meet you up at the house. I want to go over some new shopping list items." He was still holding the sketch pad and had made a lot of notes and marks in it.

"Sure. I will search for some more of those cookies," Henry grinned.

*Henry - not in a hurry to be somewhere? What is the world coming to?*


Goat insisted on driving my SUV over to the house. "Just so you know if we get a ticket for that taillight being out, you are paying for it."

Ugh. I forgot about the taillight. I pulled out my cell phone and called Chops, my all-time favorite mechanic. He answered on the first ring. "Hey Chops, it's Kelsey."

"Right or Left?"

"Left," I sighed.

He laughed and assured me he could swing by sometime tomorrow and replace it. He had parts already stocked.

"Hey, I was going to call you. Candi sold that crotch rocket but won't tell me who bought it. Was it you?"

"I think you're losing it Chops, getting paranoid," I said.

"Oh yeah? Then how come you won't answer the question?" Chops said.

"Oh, sorry. We have arrived at our destination. I need to go. Bye!" I giggled after I hung up.

"Do I want to know?" Goat asked.

"Yes," I answered him as I texted a warning to Candi.

"You going to tell me?" Goat asked.

"No," I grinned and got out of the truck.

Haley and Bridget were already at the old house checking out the back yard. Bridget was all bouncy again.

"This is so awesome!" she squealed.

"Well, let's check out the inside." I unlocked the back door and let them go first.

Walking into the kitchen was like stepping back into a simpler time. I could imagine Hattie doling out the coffee and Sara sitting on my lap drawing on the tablet while Lisa and Alex argued about make-up and Katie and Anne chatted about their new favorite paperbacks. The new house has more bells and whistles, but it doesn't have the same home feeling.

"This was the hub girls," Goat said. "If you were welcome in this house, this is where it all happened. All the big ideas, the building of friendships, laughter, and tears of the original staff, all started here. Saturday nights were about celebrating their success and enjoying their time together and Sunday mornings were about coming up with new ideas and sharing a box of donuts. This was their happy center."

"How much do you think Hattie would hate me if I knocked down some walls in her kitchen and recreated part of this?"

"I think if you told her why you want to remodel, she would admit that she misses it too." He put his arm around me and kissed my temple. "Why don't you girls go check out the upstairs for a few minutes, while Kelsey and I finish walking through down here."

I didn't care for how he ordered them to leave, but I think Haley picked up on how hard this was for me and hurried Bridget up the stairs.

"I was so worried about the bad memories, I didn't think the good memories would hit me so hard," I admitted walking into the dining room.

"Want to know the first thing I remembered when we drove up?"

"If you say Bones and me in the driveway, I will slap you!" I laughed.

"Ok. I won't say it then. Just know that it was a good memory for me too," he chuckled.

I slapped him playfully in the gut. Bones and I had shared a not so private moment in the driveway last summer, clothes on, but hot as hell. Goat witnessed the event in its full orgasmic glory.

With no furniture in the house, the living room didn't seem to bother me. I could still remember Katie tied up on the workout bench, but I could also remember when the room had been filled with furniture and we had sleepovers with the kids. I passed the guest bedroom and walked into the master bedroom.

I looked around. I thought I would be hit with all the bad memories, but I wasn't. It was in the past. It was a blip of time, and I was okay with it.

"I'm okay," I smiled and looked at Goat.

"I see that kiddo." He smiled back and hugged me.

We moved back toward the kitchen and I hollered up the stairs. "It's okay. You guys can come down now. I didn't fall apart."

Bridget came bouncing down the stairs and flying around the corner. Haley followed more cautiously behind her, but smiled when she saw that I was truly okay.

"In here is the dining room, living room, and around the corner, the old guest room and master bedroom," I directed Bridget.

They decided that the house was perfect for them, and I handed them a key. Goat said the Players were already gathering some furniture for the girls and would help move their stuff. I would see if Hattie had time to fill the cupboards and refrigerator to get them started with groceries. We said our goodbyes and left the girls to figure the rest out and celebrate.

"I wanted to ask you something," Goat said on the way home.

"Well then get on with it," I laughed.

"Be nice," he ordered with a wink. "Um, your friend Dallas, how would you be about me asking her out?"

"Indifferent."

"What the hell does that mean?"

"It means that as long as you two don't drag me into any drama, you're both adults, and I would expect you to do as you please. I can guarantee you that Dallas is a handful, but to me, she's worth the trouble. I wouldn't have her any other way."

"I can't believe you fired your friend."

"What? She asked me to!"

"Huh?"

"She didn't want to admit to Dave she quit another job after only one day."

"How many jobs has she quit after only one day?"

"A lot! She doesn't have to work. She made a lot of money on investments over the years and still has a couple rental houses. Every once in awhile, though, she gets a hair up her butt and decides that it would be nice to have a job, followed by getting one, and remembering she doesn't like people telling her what to do."

"I can see that," he chuckled.

We were having a good laugh when we pulled into my driveway. Henry's freight truck sat alongside the road in front of the house.

"I wasn't positive he would wait for me."

"I have a feeling he's staying for dinner. Go pick up Amanda and bring her back here."

"Sounds good. Just don't let him leave before I get back."

I didn't have to worry about Henry leaving. He was in the kitchen laughing with Hattie, helping her make dinner. I set down my shoulder bag on the credenza and went to check out my paintings. They were just as perfect as I imagined they would be.

I noticed a note on the coffee table and sat down to read it.

"I miss you" was written in Bones' handwriting.

Me too.

# Chapter Eighteen

Everyone had returned in time for dinner, and they were bursting with stories of their adventures during their day off. Lisa and Alex had gone to the spa and later met up with Donovan to catch a movie. Katie went with Anne and Sara to a Science museum then ate lunch at a Chinese buffet before they went to an indoor gym and played a trampoline version of dodgeball. Sara proudly announced that she beat them.

Henry stayed as expected. After dinner, he went over the new projects and shopping list with Goat while Sara and Amanda played upstairs. It was after 10:00 by the time everyone left and I had a chance to go to my room.

After shutting the door, I pulled out my cell phone and tried to call Scott, Carl's group home director. I left the third message for the day, repeating for him to call me back.

Frustrated, I stepped further into the bedroom and flipped the light on as I tossed my phone on top of my dresser. I was surprised to see Bones sitting on the couch in the atrium. He was staring at one of the landscape pictures.

"How long have you been here?" I asked.

"Not long. I didn't want anyone to know I was here, so I slid in through the atrium door."

"Did I leave it unlocked?" I tried to be careful about locking the windows and doors with Sara in the house. I was surprised that I would forget to lock it.

"No. I have a few skills with locks," he grinned.

I grinned back. It was easy to be with Bones. Too easy.

"I heard your phone call. Is everything okay?"

"Sure. It's nothing to worry about."

He held my gaze for a few minutes too long, and I knew, that he knew, I was lying.

He turned his head away and looked about the atrium. "I think this is my favorite room. The colors, the plants, the furniture, it's all so peaceful in here."

"I know."

I joined him on the couch and looked up at the paintings. Bones slid his hand over and entwined his fingers with mine. Feeling my diamond ring, he raised my hand to look at it.

"Should I be jealous?" he grinned over at me.

"A girl should never need a man in her life to justify wearing diamonds," I grinned back.

He smiled and raised our joined hands to kiss my wrist.

"I keep trying to walk away from you, but I can't," he whispered, looking back at the paintings. "I should.

It's better for you if I do. But I just can't stay away, even if it's wrong to be in your life."

I rose from the couch and stepped away. I rubbed my temples with my hands to try and focus.

"But what does that even mean?" I asked.

He got up and walked over to me. He slowly lifted my chin to face him.

"It means that I need you."

Moving his hand to the back of my neck he pulled me in for a deep kiss. But the kiss didn't end. Want flooded my body. I needed him too. I slid his cut off his shoulders and pulled his t-shirt up as we continued kissing and moving back into my bedroom.

My hands roamed his heated skin from his tight abs to his thick shoulders. His hands roamed up my back until we both parted to remove each other's shirts. In a blink, he held me tight to his body again. I barely noticed when he laid me back on the bed or when the rest of our clothes disappeared.

"Are you sure?" he asked suckling my neck, his manhood stroking against my clit.

"Yes,"

I moaned loudly, as he entered me swiftly, stretching me to fit all of him.

"*Oh, Yes!*"

# Chapter Nineteen

"Kelsey, you better get up! It's almost 7:00," Katie bellowed outside my bedroom door.

"I'm up!" I answered as I nuzzled back under the covers.

"Liar," Bones whispered as he rolled into me and wrapped his arms around me. "But I am all for you staying right here in bed with me today." He started kissing my shoulder, working down my back.

"Hmmm. That sounds so good." I rolled over to face him. "But, I need to get in the shower, and you need to slip out before anyone sees you." I kissed the end of his nose and crawled out of bed.

"Too late," Bones responded grabbing me and pulling me on top of him. "I left my bike on the walkway. Everyone already knows I'm here by now." He was pleased with himself.

"Oh, great. So now I get to be the topic of conversation today," I laughed.

"Babe, you're always the topic of conversation. At least, this time, I get bragging rights."

He chuckled as I lightly punched him.

"Caveman," I laughed and got out of bed again, this time hurrying away to get to the bathroom.

I had just finished shampooing my hair when Bones joined me in the shower. Bones grinned and pushed me against the wall while pinning both of my wrists behind my back with one of his hands.

"I need to inspect you to make sure you properly washed," he grinned, as he went down on both knees and pulled me into his mouth.

"Make sure you're thorough," I smiled, before his teeth grazed my clit and my shoulders involuntarily slammed backwards into the shower wall. *Sweet Sassafras.* I guess I'm going to be really late for work today.

"Good Morning, Hattie," I said forty-five minutes later when I entered the kitchen.

She handed me my coffee as I gave her a kiss on the cheek.

"Good Morning, Sunshine" she grinned. "Did you sleep well, my dear?"

"Not well at all," I laughed. "Everyone already head out?"

Hattie nodded as she filled another cup of coffee.

"Good Morning, Hattie," Bones said, wrapping one arm around my waist while grabbing the cup of coffee Hattie offered him with the other.

"Good Morning, Bones. How about you? Did you sleep well last night?"

Bones laughed. "I could use a few more hours."

"Enough," I laughed and transferred my coffee into a travel mug, grabbing my coat and shoulder bag. "I have to get to work."

"You want me to give you a ride on my bike?"

"Brrr. No. It will be warmer to walk the field."

He kissed me on the forehead, and I left out the back deck doorway.

After I cautiously navigated the snow-covered steps and reached the safety of the ground, I noticed footprints in the snow. They didn't lead to the store but seemed to meander around the house. I walked around and could see that they went up to most of the windows. I walked back up the deck stairs again. I could see the tracks that I just made, but also other tracks that came and went from the slider to the other set of stairs.

Strange. Maybe Bones was out walking around last night before he came in. It would be like him to check out the house and make sure everything was secure.

I was getting cold, though, so I descended the slippery stairs once again and set a brisk pace across the field.

By the time I reached the store, I was thinking about the footprints again. As soon as I was inside, I took off my coat and called Bones.

"Missed me, didn't you," he answered.

"Get over yourself, biker," I laughed. "Hey, are you still at the house?"

"Yah. Hattie and I are enjoying our morning coffee. Why, do you need something?"

"No. Yes. Ugh. Did you walk around the house last night?" I blurted.

"No. I went straight to the atrium. Why?" I could hear the tension in his voice.

"There are tracks in the snow all around the house. I was hoping it was you. Maybe it was Donovan working on something, though. It could be nothing."

"I'll check it out and get with Donovan. And, I'll give Hattie an escort to the store just to be safe."

"Thanks. Let me know."


"Hey, Queen B." Alex greeted walking up to me. "Saw a bike parked out front this morning on my way in. Anyone I know?" He was grinning from ear to ear. He grabbed my coat and went to hang it up without further commentary.

Realizing I was still chilled, I searched the back storage racks and found a wool blazer to wear. Goat was chuckling when he walked up and saw me snitching the blazer.

"I wasn't too sure about your idea of moving the loading docks out and creating a split space. But this morning, every time I had to open the loading dock doors, I was more and more convinced it was a brilliant plan." He tucked the tag for me on the back neck of the blazer.

"Yeah, well, come February, I don't think you will see me working the docks," I laughed.

I started toward the break room, and Goat followed.

"Anything special you want me to focus on today?"

"Nothing in particular, why?"

"I was planning on meeting with your architect and picking up the forms for the permits. I also wanted to check on some more equipment for the motorized wall racks and work out the rest of the details on that design."

"Sounds good. You won't have as much freedom once construction starts back up, so go for it."

Goat nodded and left.


I was topping off my coffee in the break room when Tech came in. "The internet is down."

"So call and find out what's up."

"I did. They said they would send out a repair guy."

"So, move to the house or the clubhouse for the day to work."

"That's not the problem. All the security footage is down. It's all linked together through the wireless internet."

"Well, if that's the worst that happens, it will be a great day. Quit stressing."

I went to the office to check my inbox. Sure enough, Katie had dropped two blue folders and a red folder in it. I sat down and started going through the items, hoping to get everything cleared before the store got busy.

I wasn't that lucky. Between the folders, I juggled some employee issues, helped Goat with some documents needed for the permits and the Fire Marshall showed up to inspect our safety equipment. Hours had passed, and I was still stuck in my office.

I took a break and made another attempt to reach Scott on his cell phone since I hadn't heard from him yet.

"Sorry, Kelsey. It was really late last night before I had a chance to call and I didn't want to wake you."

"That's fine, but don't hesitate to call next time. Did you find Carl?"

"Yes. He was sitting outside the restaurant. I followed your instructions and he agreed to come home. But when I got him home and started to get him cleaned up, I noticed he wasn't doing so well. He had some bruises and was having trouble breathing. I took him to the hospital. They had to sedate him, and they are treating him for pneumonia. He's in pretty rough shape, but the doctors said he's going to be okay."

"Scott, does he need anything? Is there anything I can do? I feel awful about this."

"No. I have it handled, and he has insurance to cover the expenses. We just have to keep him doped until he is well enough to go home so he doesn't wander off. He keeps trying to go back to the restaurant to meet you."

"Call me if anything changes. And, I'll keep checking in if that's okay with you?"

"Absolutely. Talk soon."


*Damn it. This is all my fault.* I should have been paying more attention when I first read those witness statements months ago. I should have read everything a hundred times until I knew every word in that file. Once again, someone was hurt because of me. And, damn it – if they would have only given me a copy of that file years ago - again, and again, I begged for a copy.

I was pacing in the office, my hands trembling and the threat of tears just behind my eyelids. I grabbed a crystal figurine off the bookshelf and pitched it across the room into the painting that hung on the wall, shattering them both.

"Arghhhh!" I yelled.

Completely frustrated, I collapsed back into my desk chair laying my forehead on the desk to calm down.

At least a dozen people checked up on me following my meltdown. Even though I told her to leave it, Anne cleaned up the broken glass. Alex brought me a bottle of water. Hattie brought me a bagel and some tea.

I forced myself to finish up my paperwork, pushing my emotions back down into place. What was done, was done. Scott would get Carl back to good health, and I would find a way to make up the last few years to Carl.

"What do you mean the wires were all ripped out? Did someone drive into them?" I asked the internet service technician.

"No. There is an access box on the outside of the building. Someone pried it open and ripped the wires out. I will have to get a new box installed, but I should have you up and running by this afternoon."

"Show me."

I followed him out of the building and around the corner. Sure enough, there was an old phone access box that had a broken lid and wires were pulled everywhere. He continued talking as I looked around the ground.

"You got lucky that the phones are still working. It was a fluke that they stayed connected. If it rains or snows before I get back, they might go out."

I was half listening to him as I followed a set of footprints out around the new bridal building. They led to the already plowed East parking lot. The internet guy's truck was parked in front of the main store.

"Did you walk this way at all?"

"No, Ma'am"

"Ok. Do whatever you need to do. Try and get something a little more tamper proof if you can, but I need our security cameras back up and recording as fast as possible."

He nodded and hurried off toward his service truck.

I stood there another moment or two before I decided there was nothing else to see that was worth getting frostbite over. The store was busy, and while I was happy to see the registers were keeping up, Alex was getting behind on re-stocking. I moved some clothes over to condense racks and pulled two empty racks into the back to exchange.

My phone rang just as I started to pull the full racks out and I paused to answer it. Unknown caller. I hit the answer key.

"Well, good morning mystery person."

"I warned you, bitch. I told you to stay away from my son. You'll regret not listening when you had the chance." It was the same man, stern, older voice, no accent. "He's married you know. Only a whore like you would chase after a married man."

"Wow, it's always so pleasant talking with you. Maybe if you told me, *what the hell you are talking about*, I would be better at listening!" I screamed into the phone.

He disconnected the call.

"What the hell was that all about?" Goat asked, standing next to me.

"I have no idea. Really, I don't." Frustrated, I tucked the phone back into my butt pocket. "You don't happen to be from Pennsylvania, do you Goat?"

"No, Michigan born and raised," he answered. "Why?"

"No reason," I shrugged as I pulled the full racks of clothes out to the sales floor.

It had taken a couple hours before re-stocking slowed down enough for Alex, Goat and me to take a break. We were going through double our normal inventory for a Wednesday. I had noticed that Katie, Carol, and Bridget were running cash-only lanes to try and free up the lines.

In the backroom, Haley and one of the other girls from laundry were running the loading dock drop-offs. Alex hurried over to give them a hand. I was too tired to help. Bones hadn't let me sleep enough last night.

I smiled. I didn't regret the missed sleep one bit.

Goat followed me into the break room, and I was surprised to see Bones, Donovan, and James. I was about to smile again but then remembered he was here about the footprints. I decided to postpone the conversation by searching out a cup of coffee. The pot was empty, and I groaned.

"Not enough sleep last night, Babe?" Bones chuckled wrapping his arms around me and ushering me over to one of the bar stools. Goat grabbed the pot and started to make a fresh brew.

I was just about to inquire about the footprints when a loud crash thundered and shook the backroom. We all jumped up and ran to the loading docks.

Haley was just getting off the floor and checking on the girl from laundry. Damn, I wish I could remember the new girl's name. I spotted Alex closer to the docks and ran over to him.

"Alex! Alex!" I yelled throwing myself to the floor. "Come on, Alex. Wake up!"

He wasn't moving. I could hear someone talking to 911 behind me.

"Alex, you have to wake up, Luv. We have to go restock again. You wouldn't want to get behind." I leaned over him gently cradling his face, careful not to move him. "Come on my friend. You're scaring me."

He slowly started to stir. His eyes fluttered open, but I could barely see his face through my own tears. "Alex. It's going to be okay. You're going to be okay." He lifted a hand to my face and wiped a fresh tear.

He groaned. He tried to get up, but Goat pushed him gently down.

"Chill dude. You took quite a bounce. We need to get you checked out," Goat told him.

"You scared the shit out of me!" I cried leaning my head gently on his chest. I was shaking.

"It's all good, Luv," Alex said to me. "I just need to lay here a bit and rest. You know it's not that easy to take me down." He stroked my head as I continued to cry all over him.

When the paramedics arrived, James pulled me away so they could load Alex on a gurney. I ran to my locker and grabbed my shoulder bag and followed them out to ride in the ambulance.

# Chapter Twenty

Alex had a fractured skull and was in and out of consciousness. I sat next to his bed and held his hand as others came and went. Haley arrived and walked over to the opposite side and sat and held his other hand.

"He saved Pepper and me," she whispered.

I looked away from Alex's still face for the first time in hours and looked at Haley. She had tears rolling down her cheeks as she gazed at him. Pepper – that's the name of the new girl.

"We were the closest to the loading docks. He must have seen something, because he reached out and grabbed us, throwing us out of the way."

Her tears continued to stream, and her voice shook.

"And, then it was like the whole building was shaking around us, and this horrible crashing noise."

"Do you know what happened?"

She nodded and grabbed a tissue to blow her nose. "Some asshole backed the semi up into the building. They don't know who was driving it. They had jacked the wires on the truck and intentionally drove it right into the building. One of the loading dock overhead doors crashed down, and there was some other structural damage."

She grabbed another tissue and finished wiping away the tears.

"Goat was able to get some contractors over once the police were done and they started securing the building."

Someone had *intentionally* tried to hurt us? Or was it to scare one of us? Who would do this? Brett had been released from the hospital but was denied bail and sitting in a cell. The white van – was it even the vehicle that they were using?

I stepped out of the room and pulled my phone, calling Steve.

"How's Alex?" he asked as soon as he answered.

"He's hanging in there. His head took a hard blow, so he needs to stay at the hospital awhile." I rubbed my forehead. "I need you to check into something for me. There was a white van that had been watching the store and followed us out of town last Friday. Can you find out if it was either Brett or his buddy Terry driving the van? I just assumed it was them. But now I'm not sure."

"I know that the day of the robbery, they had Terry's sedan. I will check into it and get back with you." He disconnected, and I called Donovan.

"Any change?" he asked anxiously when he answered the phone.

"Nothing yet. Donovan, I want security hired. And, not some mall cop types. I want real security, bodyguards, military trained."

"I'll make some calls and set it up."

I disconnected and looked up and down the hall. Tyler and Sam were just getting off the elevator. I looked up at the clock. It was just past 9:00. "Can you guys stay tonight? Guard Alex's room?"

"Sure. Is there something we should know about?" Tyler asked as he handed me my SUV keys.

"I don't know what's going on. I would just feel better if he had guards."

Tyler nodded. "How's he doing?"

"I was just heading back inside. He's been unconscious the majority of the day."

Opening the door, I was surprised to see Alex sitting up, drinking water.

"Well, this figures. I sit in that uncomfortable chair all day, waiting by your side, the ever so loyal and dutiful friend, and when I step out for ten minutes, you wake up for the leggy pre-med student," I smiled. I was so glad to see him finally awake. "You scared me," I admitted, walking over and kissing his cheek.

"Sorry, Luv. I promise not to get run over by a semi ever again." He sounded good, but he was almost as pale as me. It was going to take awhile for him to recover from this.

"I'm going to call the house, and let them know he's up and awake. They are on pins and needles over there," Tyler announced. "Good to see you still kicking dude." Tyler made the piece sign and stepped out.

"Haley, I need to talk to Kelsey a minute. Do you mind?" Alex asked.

"No problem. I'll go get a cup of coffee from the café." She kissed his other cheek and left with Sam.

"What's wrong?" I asked taking his hand and sitting on the side of the bed.

"I need to tell you something, but I don't know what it means. I didn't see who was driving the semi when it hit the building, but I swear a bit before that, I saw one of the Players getting into it. I heard it start up, and looked up to see someone in a leather jacket and riding boots closing the door to the truck. I didn't think anything of it. Then a few minutes later, it was heading straight at the building."

He grabbed his cup and took another small sip. His hand was shaking so I grabbed the cup back from him, placing it on the stand.

"I just can't image one of the guys doing this, though. It doesn't make sense."

"Did you see any markings on the leather? The Devil's Player's logo?"

"No, it was just a quick glimpse, leather long sleeve, biker boot, big size guy."

"I don't think it was the club. If it was, it had to have been one of the guys we don't know very well. I asked Sam and Tyler to watch your room tonight. Maybe you would feel better if I find someone else?"

"No. I trust them, especially Tyler. I do. In fact, I trust all the same guys you do. If it was the club, I agree it was one of their members that we don't know well." He seemed sure. "I would feel better with Sam and Tyler here tonight. I'm not feeling like myself."

"Do you want me to stay too?"

"No. Go home. Get some sleep. You need to run solo on re-stock tomorrow, so you're going to need it." He was smiling, but I could tell he was getting tired again. I kissed him on the forehead, and when he fell back asleep, I slipped out into the hallway.

Haley was back and passing out coffees, handing me one.

"Thanks. I am going to head home and check on everything there."

"I'm going to stay the night and sit with Alex. I will call if anything changes," Haley said as she re-entered the room.

I turned to Sam and Tyler, and they gave me the nod, as they positioned themselves on either side of Alex's room.

"I don't want anyone other than you three, my crew or medical staff in his room. If you have any problems, call me immediately. I don't care what time it is. No one else enters." I said.

"We'll take care of him, Kelsey. Go home," Tyler said.

"I also don't want any other Devil's Players going into his room until I give the green light."

Tyler and Sam both looked at me, but I didn't say anything else before I walked away.

# Chapter Twenty-One

"I've got guys coming in tomorrow and the day after to run the security you wanted. Until then the Players are sticking close. They set up shifts." Donovan was giving me the update before I even had my coat off. "And, Lisa and Katie were both moved into the main house."

"Good. But, I don't want the Players coming in and out of the house. A few that we know well can stay inside, and then we set the alarm."

James, Bones, Tech and Whiskey heard me say this as I entered the dining room. James raised his eyebrow.

"Something I need to know?" he asked.

"Alex saw someone getting into the semi minutes before it hit the building. He didn't think anything of it. Biker boots, big build, leather jacket, that's all he saw. We both agree that it wasn't you guys or Sam and Tyler who are watching over Alex right now, but we don't know all your members. I need to keep the girls safe. I can't take any chances right now regarding the members I don't know."

"I can vouch for all of my guys," James stood up defensively.

"Good for you. *But I can't!* And, it's my family and my staff that are the ones that could get hurt if you are wrong James."

I sat down. A cocktail was slid in front of me, but I pushed it away. James picked it up and downed it.

"I get it," he sighed.

He turned and gave Whiskey the approval nod. Whiskey pulled his phone and went to the living room.

"You're right. It's best to play it safe until we figure out what the hell is going on."

"The footprints around the house?" I asked Bones.

"Two different sets of prints, both men, but we don't know whose they are. We cleared your crew and ours."

Whiskey came back in and set the alarm on the security panel. I watched the lights turn, and the indicator light blink twice before going solid. If any of the doors or windows were opened with the alarm set, we would know. Whiskey sat down in the chair next to me and put an arm around me. I wanted to break down and cry but now was not the time.

My phone rang, and I saw it was Steve.

"Hey, Steve. Anything?" I asked.

"Neither Brett nor Terry had access to a white van that I could find. And both of them have alibis for last Friday. They couldn't have followed you."

"Damn."

"Any other leads I can follow up on?" he asked.

"No. I wish there were," I said.

"How's Alex?" he asked.

"Better. Haley is staying with him. I was able to talk to him for a bit."

"Did he see anything that could help?"

"No. He was pretty tired, though, and I encouraged him to go back to sleep."

"It's not every day you get run into by a semi and live to talk about it," Steve sighed. "If there is anything else you think of, let me know."

"I will."

We disconnected.


"Well, I am an idiot!" I announced, bouncing my forehead on the table.

Bones came over and picked me up and sat me back down on his lap.

"Talk to us," he encouraged as he wrapped his arms around me.

Anne, Katie, Hattie, and Lisa had joined us in the dining room.

"The white van didn't have anything to do with Brett. They alibi out for last Friday. Whoever was following us is most likely the one behind the semi truck, the internet wires, and the footprints around the house."

"The internet wires?" Tech asked.

"Yeah, the same type of boot prints went up to the phone and internet junction box, where all the wires were ripped out. The box had been demolished."

"Shit." James threw himself back into his chair and slammed the table with his palm.

"So, they were intentionally trying to shut down the security system. Smart," Tech nodded. "I am rewiring the system tomorrow, so we won't have the same issue in the future."

I nodded, but I was less worried about the future and more worried about the present.

"You need to get some sleep babe," Bones said.

"We all do," James said. "I'll take the couch in the family room."

Whiskey looked up at Anne, and she raised an evil eyebrow. "Guess I'll take the couch in the living room," he pouted.

Everyone looked at Tech. He looked up from his laptop when the silence registered, "I'll figure it out. Don't worry about me." And, he refocused again on whatever he was working on.

"Well, I don't recommend sleeping on top of the dining room table. Hattie takes pictures of you," I said.

Everyone grinned, and I got up and went to my room.

No one said a word when Bones followed me. I got out my favorite old MSU t-shirt and changed into it and a pair of sweat pants. With everything going on, it was best not to sleep naked in case something happened in the middle of the night. I laid my glock on the nightstand and crawled under the covers. Minutes later,

Bones curled up beside me and settled my head in the crook of his shoulder.

"It's okay. You can cry now," he whispered as he stroked my back.

And, the dam burst.

Seeing Alex hurt, and almost losing him, knowing that my family was still in danger, knowing someone was out there just toying with us, Carl in the hospital, my son missing after years of searching, I couldn't hold back the tears anymore. I cried myself to sleep as Bones comforted me.

# Chapter Twenty-Two

I woke up with a start and looked at the clock. What the hell? It was 5:00 a.m., and I was wide awake for no reason. *Ugh*. It must be all the stress. I crawled out of bed to go shower. Before I entered the bathroom, though, I thought I heard a vehicle drive by. I hurried out to the atrium, but I couldn't see anything.

I showered and was quietly getting dressed when I bumped something on top of the dresser, and it fell to the floor. I picked it up and realized it was Bones' wallet, and it was open to his driver's license. Declan Jerome Hartwood was the name printed on the driver's license. Huh, Bones was a 'DJ' in a past life. This made me smile.

While he didn't look anything like a DJ, Declan was a strong name that suited him well. I looked over at him, still in my bed. He had replaced holding me with one of my pillows, which he was crushing in his sleep. He looked so peaceful. I went to set the wallet back down, when I noticed the address, Pittsburgh, Pennsylvania.

*No.* The crazy guy on the phone couldn't be Bones' dad. That was insane. The man said his son was married. I would know if Bones was married. Wouldn't I?

I shook off the thought and set down the wallet. I'm sure it was just a coincidence. I grabbed my favorite boots and carried them to the kitchen to make a pot of coffee.

"You're up early," Hattie said, coming up behind me.

"I woke up out of a sound sleep at 5:00 a.m. Then I thought I heard a car drive-by, but no one was out there."

I poured us both a cup of Joe, and we settled at the little kitchen table.

"I went to the old house the other day. Would you believe it was the kitchen that made me start crying?"

"Why would the kitchen make you cry? We all loved hanging out in that kitchen."

"That's it exactly. The kitchen was what Goat called our 'hub.' We built our friendships and our business in that kitchen."

"I remember. It was nice that we all had a sunny room to hang out in together, eat and drink coffee. This kitchen is spectacular, but it's not homey at all. It's what Lisa calls elegant. Bah."

"I know. That's why I want to knock this wall out and open the kitchen into the dining room. We can build pantries on the end wall bordering the living room and then take out the upper cabinets on the outside wall and install windows all the way across."

"Yes," she answered immediately looking at the walls imaging the changes. "And, let's do big garden windows. I can grow herbs. And we can have a rollaway breakfast bar." She beamed with excitement looking around. "What about the dining room table?"

"Gone."

We both smiled. Neither of us liked the fancy overbearing mahogany set.

I retrieved my sketchpad, and we worked on the designs until 6:00. We had managed to go through half a pot of coffee in the process.


"Do you think some of the guys could stay here at the house with Sara and me today? I want to get some stuff done, and I think it would be good for her to spend some time away from the store. She doesn't have any more classes until mid-January, so it will help break up her day. Maybe she can put the new kitchen design on that fancy computer of hers and we can move stuff around and see how we like it."

"I'll talk to one of them when they wake up."

"I'm up," Whiskey said passing us, heading for the coffee pot. "You girls have been gabbing for almost an hour. The remodeling ideas sound good. Yes, we can split up to cover the house and the store today. And, yes, next time I get the *family room* couch so I can sleep in."

Hattie and I grinned. I don't think either one of us even remembered that Whiskey was sleeping in the living room. We turned when we heard Tech sneaking down the kitchen stairs, pausing when he realized three of us were staring at him with raised eyebrows. He just smirked and went into the dining room.

The doorbell rang, and Whiskey turned off the alarm to let Goat inside. Hattie made us all to go cups and Tech, Goat and I were off to the store.

After the store was searched, Tech went upstairs, Goat went to the loading docks, and I went to my office and started up my computer. I grabbed the remote for the TV and turned it on. The screen was still on the video feed of the white van from last week. I switched it to live feed, but it was still too dark outside to make out anything.

I looked back at my computer, contemplating what I was about to do.

On one hand, doing an online search of the guy you are sleeping with seemed a bit tacky.

On the other, if his father was the crazy old dude that kept calling, he was a threat, and I needed to find out more information. I had naively trusted the wrong people in the past, and people I cared about were hurt because of it.

Decision made, I typed the search information and hit enter.

I don't know what I expected to find, but it certainly wasn't a picture of Bones with his parents and sister, posing for an upscale fundraising gala. Bones wore an expensive tailored tuxedo and had his arm draped around a beautiful young woman.

The story headline read: *'Declan Hartwood's wife-Missing.'*

I didn't know how to process all the information that I found. There were several news articles regarding the disappearance of his wife and the business exploits of his father. His mother was also the chairman of several national fundraising boards, and his grandfather was the original owner of an international company that was now run by his sister and their father.

I looked up at the clock, registering that it was almost eight. Not knowing what else to do, I got up to refill my coffee when I spotted something on the TV screen.

"Hey Goat-," I yelled.

A moment later he appeared in the office doorway. "What's up?"

"What's that in the parking lot?" I pointed. It was still pretty dark out so I couldn't make out what was in the parking lot other than something was laying in the center of the lot.

He came up behind me and looked at the screen.

"I'm not sure. Stay inside and I'll check it out."

I watched on the cameras as he walked out the front door. Tech was coming down the stairway and followed him out. I moved to the front windows, but where they stood, they blocked my view. I saw Donovan pull up as well, so I figured I might as well get my coffee rather than staring at their backs.

I started a fresh pot, took my shoulder bag to my locker and double checked my glock in my shoulder holster for the third time that morning. Katie, Lisa, and Anne came in the back door followed by James and Bones.

"Where is everyone?" Katie asked.

"The boys are out in the parking lot out front. There was something out there."

I was glad that this peaked Bones' interest and he left the room in that direction. I wasn't ready to face him yet. I wasn't sure what to say, but it didn't feel right not telling him that I knew about his family, most importantly that he had a wife he never told me about.

Laundry and stock employees started to arrive, and I made sure everyone started their day before I went back up front.

Lisa, Katie, and Anne were all looking out the window.

"Are they still outside?" I looked out, and now a squad car and several motorcycles were also present. "I saw on the security screen something lying in the parking lot. Goat went out to check on it for me. It was too small to be a person, though."

Standing here thinking of the possibilities was just going to drive me nuts. "This is stupid. I am a grown ass woman, and this is my property. I'll be right back and let you guys know what's going on."

Bones saw me approaching and stepped in my path. I shook my head at him, and he resigned to step aside. He followed close behind me as I walked around Tech and saw what was lying in the parking lot. It was a dead dog, surrounded by a pool of blood.

I reached my hand out to the side, and Bones grabbed it and wrapped another arm around my waist. When I felt solid on my legs again, I stepped away and moved around the dog in a slow circle. Club members moved out of my way so that I could see the other side. It was a black pit-bull. Its throat had been slit, and its eyes had been cut out.

*"Oh My God. Oh My God. SARA! GET SARA!!! She's at the house with Hattie!!! Go! GO!!!"*

Almost everyone jumped in a vehicle or on a bike and started flying to the house. Through my tears, I saw Bones confiscate someone's bike and drive straight up through the snowy field to the back deck. Tech was trying to move me away, back to the store. Dave followed us trying to get me to explain what was going on.

It was all a blur, though. I couldn't process it all. I needed to see Sara. And, Hattie. I needed to know they were safe.

Someone held the door open, and Tech dragged me in. I heard the door locking and Dave and Steve ordering everyone to stay up front while they searched the back. Katie was trying to talk to me, but I couldn't hear what she was saying. Tech sat me in a chair and brought me a blanket from somewhere, wrapping it around me. I knew I was shaking, but the only thing I could do was stare at the backroom entrance and wait to see if they brought Sara through the door.

And, then it happened.

Whiskey carried Sara into the main room followed by Hattie. I launched out of the chair and ran across the salesroom floor. Sara jumped out of Whiskey's arms and ran to me. When we met up, I held her tight while we both cried.

"It's them, isn't it? They found us!" she cried.

"It's going to be okay. I promise, little-bug. I am going to keep you and your mom safe. I won't let them get to you." I held her tight, not knowing which one of us was shaking more.

*"No! No! No! It can't be!"* Anne was behind me, and just starting to grasp what was happening. *"You're wrong. They didn't find us!"*

I turned to her, and tears streamed down her face streaking her perfect make-up. She was shaking as hard as I was. She just kept shaking her head no, looking at me.

"It's a black pit-bull. Its neck was slit."

She fainted, and Whiskey barely caught her before she hit the floor. On shaky legs, I stood up, still holding Sara.

"Carry Anne to the couch in my office, please."

"Kelsey, you have to fill us in here. What's going on?" Dave asked again.

"Not yet. I need to talk to Anne first. Get rid of the dog. I don't want anyone else seeing it."

"We'll need to file a report. It's against the law," Steve said.

*"For fucks sake, get rid of the damn dog!"*

I took a deep breath to calm myself.

"Sorry," I sighed shaking my head. "If you need to file a report, say it appeared like it was hit by a car. Find some rags to soak up the worst of the blood, and get rid of the dog. *Please.*"

I followed Whiskey into the office, where he laid Anne down on the couch.

"I need to talk to her, alone, Whiskey. It's a family matter." He didn't want to leave, but out of respect, he did.


It was a few minutes before Anne came to enough to sit up. She was trembling but reached out to take Sara. Hattie came in with a hot tea and lemon for Anne and water for Sara. I asked her if she could get the blanket for Anne and within seconds she returned with it, patted my shoulder for support, and left, closing the door behind her.

"We need to decide what to do. We need to either stay and fight, or we run far and fast. But if we are going to run, we need to leave right now," I said slowly, watching Anne to see if she was absorbing the information.

"How sure are you? I mean I know that the dead dog is a bad sign, but has there been anything else?"

"The dog's eyes," I had to look away. "I'm sure."

She took several gulps of air as Sara clung tighter to her. "If we leave, we can't ever come back. What if they just keep tracking us down? We don't even know how they found us this time." Anne was upset, but she was holding it together pretty well.

"Anne, it's time to tell everyone who you are and who they are. If we stay to fight, we can't do it alone. They will have to decide if they want to help or not."

Anne nodded and kissed the top of Sara's head. "We trust you. Do whatever you think is best."

Anne and Sara stayed in the office curled up on the couch while I went out to talk to everyone. They were all waiting where I left them on the sales floor. I turned to Dave and Steve and told them it was a private matter, and it was best if they leave. Dave looked upset but nodded his understanding. Sometimes being a cop made things messier, and he knew that. Steve kissed me on the forehead and followed Dave out.

Before I had a chance to say anything to anyone else, Marcy, Goat's wife, walked in through the back and sauntered up to Goat. Goat was just as surprised as everyone else to find his wife hanging off his arm.

I looked at my watch. It was a little after eight-thirty. It was kind of early in the day for a crack-whore to be up and about.

"Everyone on the payroll, let's get back to work." Several of the employees took off. "Marcy, what brings you here so early?"

"I just thought I would check in with my husband. I ain't seen him around lately," she said.

"I bet that's hard for you." I faked sympathy. "Hey, I had some clothes set aside, that you might like. Why don't you come to the storage room with me and take a look?"

I walked off to the backroom and Marcy naively followed. I unlocked the storage door and walked in. She was already in the room by the time she noticed that it was empty, and I closed the door behind us.

She frantically looked between the door and me, realizing she was trapped.

"What's happening? There ain't no clothes in here."

"No, there's not. And, you didn't come here to see Goat or check-in on your daughter. Did you?"

"I don't know what you're talking about. I was just dropping in for a quick chat is all."

"Drop the act, Marcy. Tell me everything or I will *bleed* it out of you." Fury and fear backed the truth to my words, as I stepped toward her.

She was starting to shake, and I stalked toward her until her back was against the far wall. I was so terrified for Sara and Anne that I could easily kill her. And I knew she could see it in my eyes.

"I swear. I just stopped in for a visit. I don't know nothin' else."

All rational sense left me, and I punched her in the face, another fist landed hard to her gut and then I slapped her just for the hell of it. My hands were shaking from rage. My own ragged breathing and pounding heartbeat thundered in my ears.

She was bleeding from the nose and holding her stomach.

"Stop. Stop," she cried. "I'll tell you. It wasn't my idea. I've been dating this guy in Indiana. He's with a different club. They do drug runs cross-country. They had a couple guys from another chapter come in, just passing through."

She was crying hysterically, and I was having trouble making out the blubbering words.

"They were talking how they had a job this way and mentioned the store. I told them I knew this place and most of the employees. I didn't know, I swear. I didn't know what they wanted."

"Who? Who's here?"

"They'll kill me!" she shrieked.

"*I will fucking kill you, you skank!*" I punched her in the gut again, hard. I could hear a rib crack in response. She dropped to the floor and held one arm over her head and another around her legs that were pinned up tight to her body.

"The guy in charge, his name is Digger!" She gulped for air. "And two of his crew, Hyena and Barrel, I think."

"F-U-C-K!!" I screamed at the ceiling, my fists clenched to my sides.

I kicked her again just because I was filled with so much rage I couldn't stop myself.

I stepped back.

I took another step back.

I needed to calm myself down, or I wouldn't be able to think this out.

*Think. Think. Think-Kelsey.* Okay. I just beat the shit out of a woman. I am holding her against her will. That's what? Fifteen? Twenty years in prison?

I was glad I refused to allow security cameras in here.

"Where are they staying?"

"Some shitty motel downtown. I don't know which one. All three are together in a white van. Last night they made me loan them my car." She continued gulping for air. "They didn't want the van spotted."

I couldn't listen anymore. It was making me sick. I walked back to the door and used my key to unlock it. Several club members were by the loading docks, and the music had been turned up. Haley started moving my way with a big rollaway laundry bin. I looked inside, and she had a sheet of plastic laid on the bottom, and a couple of bed sheets draped across the side.

"I didn't kill her," I whispered, my voice shaking.

"I figured with that bitch, it was a fifty-fifty thing. I have a nice little sedative to keep her calm until we get her out of here."

Haley pulled a syringe partially from her pocket, and I gave her the nod and unlocked the door. James followed Haley in to assist, and I closed the door. I waited until there was a knock on the door and Haley rolled the bin out like she was just moving clothes as normal. She even hollered at the guys to go find something to do and get out of the way, as she rolled the cart into the back of one of our freight trucks and shut the door. It appeared that Sam was driving it when the truck pulled out. I didn't even care where they were taking her.

"Katie, can you find me some clothes?" I asked.

She nodded and rushed off. Hattie brought me some coffee and a plate of toast. I took the coffee but shook off the toast. I was too keyed up to eat.

Goat walked up to me. "Whatever that bitch did, I am so sorry, Kelsey. I will do anything to make it right."

"It's not your fault, Goat. I don't blame you. And neither will anyone else."

A tear rolled down my cheek, and I quickly wiped it away and shook my head. No time for tears. Too much shit to do.

"Can you get someone to sanitize the storage room? I would hate for her to file a report and have any evidence around."

"She'll never have the chance to file charges, but I will go clean it up anyway." He kissed me on the forehead, took the key and walked off. Katie brought me some clothes. I still hadn't moved more than a few feet away from the storage room. I wasn't ready to face the Players, and they were directly in front of me.

"Come on, Kelsey. Let's get you to the bathroom before anyone notices that's blood spattered on you."

"I didn't kill her, Katie."

"Then you are a better person than me. Come on." With her arm around my waist, she guided me into the restroom.

I quickly changed clothes while she washed the blood off my boots. When she was done, I slid them back on. Evidence or not, I wasn't willing to go without my switchblades that were hidden inside, and Katie must have sensed that I needed as much brave as I could get right now.

I exited the bathroom. Katie, Lisa, Donovan and the Players were all waiting for me. The girls looked scared and the Players looked pissed.

"I owe all of you an explanation. And, you'll get the full story, but this isn't the place for all the dirty details. What I can say right now, is that Anne and Sara have been on the run since before I met them." I took a deep breath and plunged forward. "Anne is married to Scar, Enforcer for the Hell Hounds motorcycle club. Sara is Scar's daughter."

It was silent.

Katie, Lisa, and Donovan looked around and realized they were the only ones that didn't understand. I turned to them to explain.

"The Hell Hounds are a very violent and powerful bike club. Their women aren't known to escape and live. Their children are raised to either be whores or members."

"This is bad," James said.

"I know. And, there are at least three members already in town. I need to decide whether to run with them or stand and fight."

"We fight," Bones answered stepping forward.

"Anne and Sara are not going anywhere. I will kill any mother-fucker that comes near them," Whiskey yelled.

James walked up to Whiskey and put a hand on his shoulder. "We have to put it to a vote, brother."

Whiskey wheeled on James and grabbed him by his throat. "Go have your fucking vote, Prez. But if it's voted down, know that I will be turning in my cut."

"Same here," Bones said.

"That goes for me too," Goat added.

"You can relax, brother. I will fight with you either way. We just need to vote to see if the rest of the Players will fight by our side," James assured Whiskey.

Whiskey released James and started pacing.

"Has the party started without us?" A male voice spoke from the salesroom doorway. I spun around pulling my glock instinctively, aiming it at the newcomer.

I froze, staring at the man I hoped I would never lay eyes on again. The man next to him stepped slowly in front of him blocking my shot, and I realize I was still holding my gun aimed their direction. I lowered my gun and re-holstered it, before turning away. I leaned over, placing my hands on my knees and slowly inhaled as my small world spun just a bit too fast.

"Wild Card, you have the worst timing of anyone I have ever met," Donovan said. "And, Reggie, how the hell are you, my friend? I didn't realize you were coming out for this job."

"Yeah. It was strange," Wild Card said. "I told Reggie where I was going and what the job was, and all of a sudden, he insisted he was coming along. I thought maybe he was worried about his big brother or something."

I could hear Wild Card approaching behind me, stopping just a few feet away. "But now I know he was worried about someone else. How the hell are you, Kelsey?"

Everyone was silent again, watching me.

I kept my back turned to him and looked at Donovan.

"He part of the security team?" I asked.

Donovan nodded looking between us.

"Fine," I said dragging a hand through my hair. "Assign him to Alex until he's cleared to come home. Reggie can stay with me."

Donovan nodded again, and I walked to the front of the store to check on Anne and Sara. Reggie followed.

"You should have warned me," I said over my shoulder to Reggie.

"You would have told him not to come. And, no matter how pissed you are at him, if a shit storm is brewing, you know he's someone you want on your side," he said as he stopped me with a gentle arm around my waist. He turned me to face him.

"I know it," I sighed. "But, I don't have to like it." I looked about, but no one was in the immediate area at the moment. "How do you know Donovan?"

"We met in the military. Know most of the Players. Bones comes down to Texas a lot."

"So, you're all friends?"

"Yeah. Good friends. Why?"

Reggie had been my personal confidant since the day I met him. He was the one person that knew all my secrets and unconditionally loved me for the person I really was. The person hiding from the rest of the world. I knew I could trust him.

"Because I've been sleeping with Bones, and now I suspect his father is one of the people that has been threatening me lately, and I don't know what the hell to do about it," I confessed pacing back and forth. I was beyond rattled. Reggie was family, sort of, and I knew he would understand. "And, now I'm finding out that my ex and my current, are friends from the service? This shit is so unbelievable! And, none of that comes close to the fact that a violent biker club is after us, and I have new clues to follow on Nicholas's disappearance, but can't get away right now. My son should be my priority, *not all this other shit!*"

Reggie gently grabbed my arm and pulled me closer to him. In a low whisper, he asked, "Where can we talk privately?"

"I have to check on Anne and Sara first," I sighed in frustration, wiping fresh tears away.

I continued to the office, took a deep breath to calm myself, and unlocked the door. Sara was asleep, curled up on Anne's lap. I sat next to Anne as Reggie shut the door, staying outside to give us some privacy.

"We stay and fight," I said.

"Are you sure? It might be safer for everyone if we left."

"And, then what? You and Sara spend the rest of your lives looking over your shoulder? No. We have the support to stand our ground, and everyone agrees. And, we have hired muscle too. We'll have the numbers. It's time to stop running."

Anne leaned forward and cried. I held her the best I could, with Sara bundled between us on her lap. Whiskey came in and took the seat on the other side of Anne and pulled her and Sara closer to him. She laid her head in the crook of his neck and continued to cry. He nodded to me, and I slipped out.

Reggie followed me into menswear, and when Katie spotted us, I signaled her to keep quiet. She nodded and went back to her tasks, as we slipped into the employee hallway.

"Only a few of us use this hallway, and we will notice anyone coming through either door. Also, it's one of the few places Tech hasn't installed security cameras." I rolled my eyes. There must be twenty cameras by now on this property alone. Tech and I were still arguing about him wanting to install indoor security cameras at the house.

"First of all, what the hell do you mean by Walter Hartwood might be threatening you? What does that SOB have to do with any of this?" Reggie growled.

I explained the calls and then everything else that had been going on, my relationship with Bones, the Hell Hounds coming after Sara and Anne, and finding the message from Carl. I admitted that I couldn't figure out how the hell it all fit together.

"Ok. I will try to find a video or phone message or something with Walter's voice. Then you'll at least know for sure if it's him." He dragged his hand through his hair. "If the Hell Hounds want a fight, well make sure we have the numbers to take them out. As far as Wild Card is concerned, he has no say about who you sleep with. He gave up his right to be part of your life. But, Kel, what were you thinking, sleeping with someone that was married? That's just not like you."

I started to cry. I couldn't help it. Now was not the time to feel sorry for myself over personal bullshit, but Reggie and I were close. I had spent many a night crying on his shoulder.

"I didn't know he was married until this morning when I found his real name and looked him up online."

*"That fucker-* I'm going to kill him."

Reggie stomped down the hallway toward the back room with me trying to stop him the entire way. Every time I tried to step in front of him, he pushed me back, until he went swinging out the hallway door and into the back room. Several club members were still standing around talking, including Bones.

Reggie charged.

*"You Fucking Asshole!"* he yelled as he threw a punch at Bones.

Bones was pushed back several feet, but Reggie charged again and hit him with a second blow to the ribs that would have crushed most men. That was as far as he got before Donovan and several club members physically restrained him.

*"You didn't think she had the right to know you were married?!? She's my fucking sister you dick!"*

Bones turned to me, and I knew he could see the devastation in my swollen eyes.

I walked away.

"Kelsey –," Bones called out.

I continued walking.

"*Your sister?*" Donovan asked.

"*What do you mean Bones is married?*" Tech demanded.

I walked faster. I didn't want to hear any more.

# Chapter Twenty-Three

The emotional coward that I am, I worked the registers for the rest of the day to avoid anyone being able to pull me aside and ask me questions, or worse, Bones trying to justify sleeping with me when he was legally still married to his missing wife.

He'd been searching for her for years. You have to love someone a lot, to be that diligent. I know that better than anyone. And, it explained all his trips out of town, which took him often to Texas, apparently.

Around 10:00, Katie asked if there was anything she could do to help. I gave her a mental list of things to get with the Players on and have set up at the house. Around 3:00, I still hadn't left the safety of the register. Hattie brought me a sandwich, and I ate as I worked. By 5:00 Katie dropped off a bottle of beer, carrying one for herself.

"Owning your own business has privileges," she said as she tipped her own bottle back.

"Then what's your excuse?"

"The owner was stupid enough to promote me to store manager," Katie grinned and walked away.

I drank the beer as I worked. Several customers smirked, but no one said anything. By 6:00, customers were being ushered out and the store was being closed down early around me. I was out of time.

I went to the office and Whiskey braced up Anne and carried Sara as they followed behind me. Everyone gravitated to the back room. Katie and Lisa shut down the lights, and several Players moved in a loose circle around us.

I found Donovan in the back room, talking to James.

"Alex?" I asked.

"He was released late this afternoon. He was moved to the guest room next to your room, and I have Sam, Tyler and Wild Card with him. Haley is playing nurse."

"Was he well enough to be released or was Wild Card pushing the issue?"

"Haley seemed concerned, so I had Doc swing in," Donovan admitted. "Alex needs to be in bed, and needs to be monitored, but seems to be out of the woods."

I nodded. I couldn't be mad at Wild Card for the decision. I was glad to hear Alex was home. I didn't like him being out of reach, and we could protect him better at the house.

"We ready to leave?"

Donovan nodded. "Your truck is outside the door, already running and an escort will follow you up. We'll do one more sweep of the buildings here, and lock it down."

I pulled my glock and turned the safety to off. Katie and several of the Players followed suit. Stepping out the back door, everything appeared to be ready, and Anne, Sara, and Whiskey followed me out as the Players continued to shield them. I opened the back door on the SUV, and they got in, and then I moved to the front passenger seat. I was not pleased to see Bones was driving, but he wasn't my main focus. With the open field, and the trees bordering it, we were sitting ducks.

"Let's go," I said.


The vehicles in the driveway had been cleared, and Bones pulled into the garage as someone was shutting the overhead behind us. It was the longest one-minute drive home ever.

"Where's Reggie?" I asked Bones as we all filed into the house.

"He should be here by now. He had to go pick someone up."

Walking into the dining room, I found the two best surprises I could imagine. The first was Alex, grinning at me, swigging a beer. He was still way too pale, but he seemed to be on the mend. The second was Pops, Reggie's dad.

"Alex, you are on pain killers and not allowed to have alcohol." I swiped his beer away and set it in front of my normal seat.

"And, Pops, damn, it is so good to see you."

He stood and gave me a giant bear hug.

"What the hell are you doing here?"

"Did you think I wouldn't show when I heard my baby girl was in trouble?"

"I didn't honestly think anyone would tell you," I admitted.

"Got on the first plane as soon as I found out where Reggie and Wild Card went. I brought Kevin and Harold along too. We couldn't bring any firearms with us on the plane, but I figure you will have some spares lying around that we can borrow."

"Yeah. I might be able to rustle up something," I grinned. "Everyone, this is Pops. He's my favorite daddy. Consider him family. He's also the one that made me practice shooting until I could hit a nickel off a tree limb from half way across the pasture."

"Well, I couldn't have you living in Texas and not knowing how to shoot properly. I just didn't expect you would get so damn good at it," Pops chuckled.

"I have to admit it's a little embarrassing," Donovan said leaning over to shake Pops hand. "She can out shoot all of us."

Pops laughed. "That's only because Wild Card was giving her lip that girls couldn't ride or shoot as well as men. It riled her up enough to prove him wrong on both accounts."

Pops turned back to me and winked. "Hey, brought you a present." He placed an oversized sweater box on the table. It had a roughly tied ribbon around it. I instinctively stepped back two paces as hands clasped my shoulders, ending my retreat. I was still staring at the box.

"Pops, I think you'll want to untie that yourself," Bones said from behind me. "Kelsey had a bad experience with a sweater box once," he chuckled.

At the time, it hadn't been very funny. Brett had sent me a large snake hidden inside a sweater box, with a similar ribbon tied around it. I freaked and ended up passing out, cracking my head open.

Pops removed the ribbon and the box lid. I stepped up to the table. It was a photo album. On the front was a picture of my horse, StarBright, and I standing in the middle of a large field. I grinned and wrapped my arms around Pops again.

"Thank you," I whispered.

"You're welcome, baby girl. I just wanted to be sure you remembered the good times you had in Texas too."

Kevin and Harold followed Reggie into the dining room, and more introductions were made. Hattie announced that dinner would be another half an hour. And, Katie was showing everyone to sleeping areas. On her to-do list today was to get some bunk beds delivered and set up in the family room and basement gym. She also had an oversized commercial refrigerator installed in the basement and filled with enough food for an army.

I was drinking Alex's beer when Katie came back and asked Pops how we were related.

"I'm her husband," Wild Card answered coming into the room and stealing my beer.

"Ex-husband," I snapped and glared briefly at Wild Card before turning back to Katie. "And, we were only married for four months. I had a whirlwind year, moving from Miami to Las Vegas, where I married this dumbass," pointing to Wild Card, "followed by moving to Texas with him for a few months. Then I divorced him and packed up and moved back to my home state of Michigan. But I never divorced Reggie and Pops. I stayed in touch with them." I explained.

"Damn. Did not expected that," Katie laughed.

"I cannot imagine you married," Lisa laughed. "Even if he is hot."

Donovan pulled her back and secured an arm around her as she giggled.

"You and your secrets," Donovan said to me, rolling his eyes.

Wild Card was hot, but that wasn't why I married him. He was sort of doing me a favor at the time.

"You were married to Wild Card, and you didn't tell me?" Bones gritted out between clenched teeth.

I turned to him. "You ARE married and didn't tell me?"

"Whoa! What the hell is going on?" Alex asked. "How long was I unconscious?"

Bones stormed off to the basement, and I could hear him ranting around. Reggie grinned. James shook his head.

"Hey, Sis, can I have a minute?" Reggie asked.

"Still keeping secrets, little brother?" Wild Card goaded.

"Cooper Wild Card Wesley, don't push my buttons," I glared. "You might be handy with a gun, but I still own this house and would love to have an excuse to throw you out on your ass!"

I followed Reggie to my bedroom and opened up my closet while he shut the bedroom door. "Help me get some guns out," I said.

I slid the clothes on the back wall over to the far side and slid a trim board up. The wall opened to a hidden gun safe.

Reggie whistled. "This is a lot more impressive than the gun collection you left behind in Texas."

"I have a lot more money these days, and can afford them," I grinned. "And, I left the guns in Texas on purpose. If I need them in the future, I know where to find them."

Everyone I was close with in Michigan knew I had a few glocks and a revolver, but I never showed any of them my gun collection. I had at least forty guns in different makes and models in the house and more stored in multiple locations around the country.

"AK's Kelsey? Really? You planning on World War III?"

"It's not that far out of the spectrum if the Hell Hounds show up. You'll be glad I was stocked."

We left the AK's, but pulled the handguns, rifles, and shotguns out, laying them on the bed. We also pulled ammo from the shoe boxes stacked on the shelf.

"Did you find a voice recording of Bones' dad?" I asked

"Yeah. I came back here and used your personal computer so no one would see what I was up to. I also got a bit distracted on your latest book. Had to take a cold shower," he grinned. "I have the video pulled up and the volume on. Check it out and see if it's him."

I hit play on the video and then stopped it a few minutes later. "It's him. I'm sure of it."

"We need intel, Kel. Maybe we should bring Donovan into the loop. He has some computer wizards that can dig into this further than what I am able too."

I smiled and pulled out my phone, sending a text. A few minutes later, Tech and Sara entered the bedroom and closed the door. Sara scrambled up into my lap at the desk. Tech paused when he saw all the guns on the bed, grinned, and sat in a guest chair.

"What's up?" Sara asked.

"I need a favor," I said.

"Anything. You know that," Tech said.

"This would require you doing some research behind the club's back, specifically behind Bones' back. And, he won't be happy about it when he finds out," I admitted.

"Seeing as I am super pissed at him about the married thing, no problem. What do you need?"

I explained the phone calls, the internet search on Bones and the confirmation of the voice. "I want you to dig in and see if you can find any connection between Bones' father and Bones' wife's disappearance. If this guy is so far off the rails that he is threatening me, he may have been behind her disappearance."

"I still can't believe he never confided with anyone other than James about this. I would have helped him look for her." Tech shook his head in disappointment.

Then he sighed and looked at Sara.

"To the *Bat Cave*, little genius. We have work to do!" he grinned.

Sara giggled, jumping off my lap and running to the door. Tech winked as he left. This would be a good project to distract Sara.

"Tech's good with computers?" Reggie asked.

"They both are. They are Donovan's secret weapons," I grinned.

We were all called to dinner, and I took plates up to Sara's room for her and Tech. They had crayoned a Do Not Disturb sign and taped it to the outside of the door, but that didn't stop me from entering. I set their plates down and told them both to pause to eat. They both nodded and picked up their forks without looking away from their monitors.

After dinner, I had the guys grab what guns they wanted from my bedroom and temporarily stacked the remaining ones in the atrium. I helped Alex to the guest room, and though it was early, I decided it was time to call it a night myself. Reggie was stretched out on my bed in his black sweats. The bed was plenty big enough for the both of us, and we had bunked up plenty of times before, so I changed into a t-shirt and a pair of sweatpants in the bathroom before joining him.

"Thanks for coming, Reggie."

"Anytime, Sis. Now get some sleep."

He pulled the covers up and tucked me in. I was so exhausted from the emotional stress of the day that it didn't take me long to fall asleep.

# Chapter Twenty-Four

I woke in the middle of the night but stayed frozen in place.

I laid there listening.

Then I heard something. It was a rustling noise outside the atrium door. I moved my hand slowly over Reggie's mouth, and his eyes opened and looked my way. He nodded, and I removed my hand.

I pointed in the direction of the noise and slid out of bed, donning my boots. Reggie did the same. I strapped my gun holster on and inserted my gun. Reggie kept his gun in his hand, and I shook my head at him. He reluctantly grabbed his holster and clipped it to his waistband. He went to use his phone, and I shook my head at him again.

I pulled a gun case from under the bed and opened it. Reggie grinned and nodded.

As quietly as possible we loaded the tranquilizer guns. I pulled out another box from under the bed and handed him a pair of night vision goggles. I opened the closet door closest to the outside wall and felt for the trim board, sliding it up, and the wall slid open. I bent over and went through the passage, but almost laughed out loud to see Reggie on his hands and knees to crawl through. We were on the backside of the second garage, between two oversized bushes. We both put on our goggles and looked around. The backyard appeared to be clear.

We made our way around the garage, kneeling to watch the men outside of the atrium. Two men wearing black leather jackets were trying to peer through the atrium windows. We watched them until they finally gave up and crossed the road into the edge of the woods. A third biker was waiting just inside the tree line.

"Did you see her?" he asked, his voice carrying back to us in the stillness of the cold night air.

"Naw. It's too dark. And, they installed those motion lights in the back so we can't check those windows."

"Fine. I'm freezing my ass off anyway. Let's go back to the trailer."

They started moving deeper into the woods, and I nodded to Reggie. We raised our guns and aimed. I landed my darts silently into both men on the left, but Reggie missed his shot for the third guy. The tranq-guns only held two rounds, so I grabbed his gun and shot the third guy with the last dart.

Reggie jumped up and was about to holler out in excitement when I covered his mouth. He looked around not seeing anything.

"I need these guys to talk before the Players know about them," I whispered.

He nodded and we moved across the street to retrieve our prey.

It took over an hour for us to drag their bodies down to Alex's house and secure them. We tied and gagged all three of them after we stripped them down to their underwear, and then locked them in a storage room in the basement. I threw all their belongings into a black garbage bag. It was time to go.

Reggie carried the bag as I led us into the mechanical room. Behind the furnace I pulled up the trim wood, to release another doorway.

"How many hidden doors and compartments do you have around here?" Reggie grinned.

"A lot," I answered. "I had a lot of money to spend, so I had fun getting creative. Only Donovan knows about this one. It goes through his basement and then to the main house, but we will have to be quiet getting through the gym and up the back stairs."

He nodded and followed me in. I hit the light switch, and the tunnel lit up. We secured the door, and I pulled a small chain that would slide the trim board back into place on the other side.

"Fancy," Reggie laughed.

The next two doorways worked the same to get through Donovan's basement and then the last door opened into the mechanical room in the main house. We unloaded the bag, goggles, and tranq-guns and hid everything behind the furnace. We slipped out into the hallway and crept silently across the open gym. Surrounded by bikers snoring, no one heard us as we finished crossing the room and went up the stairway. *We made it.*

As soon as Reggie closed the door, the kitchen light came on. Hattie was standing there with hands on hips, looking pissed. Haley was next to her grinning.

"Shit," I said looking down at the floor sighing.

"Busted," Haley giggled quietly.

"What do you know?" I whispered.

Hattie looked around, before answering just as quietly. "Haley saw you two out the window dragging bodies through the woods. She didn't know what to do, so she came and got me. Are they alive?"

"Yes. Make some coffee, while we go change our clothes. We can talk in my room where no one will hear."

An hour later the sun was starting to rise, but we had our plan formulated. Hattie and Haley stayed in my room, after gathering the supplies they needed to prepare, and Reggie and I started breakfast. We had cooked together for a few round-ups and social functions, so we slipped easily into our old roles and soon had piles of pancakes, french toast, sausage, bacon, and eggs going. We ate as we cooked, and as the aroma wafted throughout the house, a line of people started showing up to fill plates.

Reggie took plates to Hattie and Haley, and when he came back, his face was bright red. I was curious, so I took the coffee carafe back to fill their cups. Hattie was shaping ground sausage into a latex condom and shaping it into a penis. The way she stroked it, smoothing out the lumps, had me doubled over laughing. Haley was laughing too.

"You both better get that out of your system. If you laugh during this little charade you have planned then you'll have no choice but to turn them over to the Club," Hattie said.

"We're doomed then," Haley replied. "Kelsey sucks as an actress."

I stuck my tongue out at her. She was right, but that was beside the point.

"Where are we going to get the blood?" I asked.

"Marty's Meat Market," Hattie answered. "I'll complain that you cooked too much sausage up this morning and make the guys take me there to restock. I'll call Marty before we leave, so he will have everything ready and packaged for me."

"Hattie, you're a little too good at this scheming stuff," I said.

"I'm pretty good with this penis stuff too," she held up the fake penis. It limped over to the side. "Yup - looks pretty natural to me. We just need to adjust the color a bit and insert the tube. Hopefully, it stays floppy still with the tube inserted."

She passed the fake penis to Haley, to start inserting the clear tube. I decided it was safer in the kitchen with Reggie.

Donovan stopped me at the end of the hall.

"Phillip's, here. Did you call him?" he asked.

Phillip, Lisa's brother, is the right hand and only son of the Godfather of New Jersey.

"Yes, I did. He's here to help. If things turn ugly, I have a backup plan for him to get Lisa and the rest of them out of here through the tunnels and onto a private jet. He can keep them safe. But, he has promised to wait for you or me to make that call. Until then, he's offered himself and his entourage of henchmen to aid our cause."

"Nicely done," Donovan complimented. "So, does he know Lisa's pregnant?"

"I may have hinted at it, to soften the blow for you. But you need to get that girl hitched before her Papa finds out." I poked him in the chest with my finger.

Donovan smiled. "That's the plan. We just need to settle all this craziness first."

He looked at me funny before reaching up and pulling a small leaf out of my hair.

*Damn bushes.*

He raised his eyebrow at me, but I just shrugged. He tucked the leaf in his pocket before walking away.

Everyone was divided between the living room, dining room, and kitchen. There were at least forty people altogether. Most of them were already armed. I greeted Phillip and asked Katie to find him and his men a place for their belongings. Pops was grinning across the table at me and saluted me with his coffee. He had a pile of flapjacks half-gone on his plate.

"Damn, girl. I missed your cooking," he grinned.

The Players and my crew looked at me questioningly, and Bones laughed. Bones was the only one that secretly knew I could cook.

"Wait, what was that?" Katie asked coming back in the room. "Did you say that Kelsey cooked?"

"I know she did. I would recognize these homemade buttermilk pancakes anywhere," Pops answered.

They all turned to me again.

"What? You all just assumed I couldn't cook."

Most of the Players laughed, and Katie and Anne rolled their eyes.

"I've also got pot roasts slow cooking for lunch, but they won't be done until 2:00," I said.

Pops grinned. He loved my pot roast.

Since everyone was already up, I went to the basement to work out. I needed to burn off some excess energy and mentally prepare for the interrogation plan. Only Katie and some of the club members were going to the store today. They were going to help her get everything restocked for Saturday. Tyler, Kevin, and Harold agreed to escort Hattie to the meat market, and Reggie agreed to escort Haley to Alex's house under the guise of gathering some of Alex's things. Really, they were going to inject the hostages with another sedative, but no one needed to know that.

I ran five miles on the treadmill before switching to the punching bag. Bones came down and leaned against a wall, watching me.

"Don't start. I have you in a box, inside my head, and I have too much shit going on right now to open up that box," I said.

"Fine. But when this is over, you and I need to talk this out." He pushed off from the wall, ascending the stairs.

"You going to give him a chance to explain?" James asked, sitting up from one of the bunk beds.

"Haven't decided yet. As I told him, now's not the time to dwell on it."

"And, Wild Card?"

"That's none of your business, James. I suggest you stay out of it."

"Is it my business?" Wild Card asked coming down the stairs.

"Drop it, Cooper. We don't have anything to discuss."

I turned away from the bag and grabbed a clean towel off the shelf to wipe the sweat off.

"Finally. She calls me Cooper," he said to James. "She only calls me Wild Card when she's pissed, so we are making progress."

I marched toward the stairway, but he grabbed my arm to stop me. I spun and threw my elbow to his face, while turning to swipe the back of his knees, dropping him to the floor.

"Don't touch me," I stormed upstairs.

Pops watched me as I walked past the dining room to my bedroom. I wasn't surprised when he followed me.

"That's a lot of pent up anger there, baby girl. And, he doesn't even know why you are so angry and hurt. The least you can do is to tell him the rest of the story."

"No point in dredging up the past. Or making others feel as crappy as I do about it. Once this mess gets cleaned up, we both will go our separate ways again, and peace will resume." I kissed Pops on the cheek. "I've got to shower."

# Chapter Twenty-Five

By 10:30, we were ready to execute our plan. Haley, Reggie and I snuck out the bedroom passageway and crossed the backyards to Alex's house, hopefully, unseen. It would have been better to take the basement passage, but several of the guys were working out in the gym. *Maybe I should build a trap door to access the mechanical room through my bedroom floor.*

Hattie stayed at the house to work our cover story. She planned on telling the others that we were locked in my bedroom working on a photograph for a new book cover, with Haley and Reggie as the models. Reggie and Haley both thought it was a great idea, and offered to do it for real. I rolled my eyes and encouraged them to stay focused.

We slipped in the back door, and Haley turned off the alarm. We were carrying our gear down the stairs to the basement when I heard a noise, dropped everything, jumped the last two stairs, and pointed my gun that direction.

Sitting on the couch in the basement family room was Donovan, arms crossed, eyebrows raised.

*Damn it.*

"How in the hell did you know we were coming here?" I asked, holstering my gun.

"I had a call that the alarm in Alex's house was turned off and then back on last night. I came down here to check it out and found your special guests," he smirked.

"You have to let me play this out. If the Players know we have them, then they'll just start beating the crap out of them, and we probably won't get any useful information. Besides, this is one of those finder's keeper's things." I insisted.

Donovan snorted. "So you went rogue again and then dragged Reggie and Haley into your games?"

"I played it safe. I didn't go solo. Reggie helped. There was no way I could have dragged all three of them down here by myself. They were heavy," I said.

"So, I was just the dumb muscle?" Reggie asked.

I rolled my eyes and turned back to Donovan.

"Please Donovan, give us a chance," I pleaded.

"They have a good plan," Reggie said. "It's disgusting, but it might work. I know I would talk."

"What's the plan?" Donovan asked.

Reggie offered to fill Donovan in while Haley and I went to set up. We didn't have much time before the last sedative would wear off.

Working quickly, we stripped the men of their underwear and rigged up the ropes to pull each of them about six inches off the floor, hanging by their tied hands. Then Haley and I inspected their junk and selected the man with the most similar size and coloring of our fake penis. Haley taped his privates back and injected a local anesthetic so he wouldn't be able to feel the difference. Meanwhile, I affixed the fake penis with cement glue and proceeded to tie his ankles together.

The fake penis hung limply off to the side and I tied a red elastic band near the base to make it appear that we were partially stopping the blood flow. We had just finished our set-up when the man in the middle started to wake.

When he was aware enough that we were in the room and that they were hanging naked from the ceiling, he started thrashing around, which caused the other two to start waking up. I waited without speaking a word, staring at them, while their panic grew. The one with the fake penis started really flipping out when he saw the elastic band tied around what he thought was his appendage. Haley stepped up onto a stool and cut their gags off.

"Why can't I feel my dick?" he whimpered. "What are you doing to me?"

The other two started to panic even more. All three of them were sweating bullets and stared in horror at his penis with the red rubber band tied around it.

"Here are the rules. I am going to start with you," pointing to the biker with the fake penis. "If you lie to me about anything, withhold any details whatsoever, your favorite body part gets removed." I picked up a large pair of garden clippers and snipped them closed a few times for effect.

"No, No. Please. I'll tell you anything you want!" he cried. "We were sent to follow you." He was sobbing, but I could still make out his words. "We were given your name and address. We came into town about a week and a half ago."

"Follow me?" I questioned.

"Yes! We were to report back anything we could find out: your schedule, your friends, who you slept with, your financials, anything and everything. It sounded like an easy job. But then the Devil's Players were always around. You were never left alone, and we couldn't get inside the house or the store."

"Keep talking. I want to know everything."

"We recognized Anne one day and called it in. Orders were changed to kidnap Anne and the kid, and get them back to the charter in Indiana. While we were waiting to catch them alone, a kill order was issued on you. We figured we could grab them and kill you at the same time."

"Why the dog, then? Why would you tip us off that you were here?"

"You were supposed to run!" he whimpered. "We were waiting to follow you, but then you didn't. No one came out of the store, so we sent the whore in to see what was going on, but she never came back out either." He looked back down at his appendage again and started sobbing. "Please. That's all I know."

"Who hired you to come find me? Who put the contract on my head?"

"They'll kill me. I can't." he sobbed.

"Hold him."

Haley stepped up and grabbed onto his hips while I stepped in front of him and snipped the fake penis in half. Haley at the same time added pressure to the blood bag behind him and blood flowed down his leg and onto the floor. He started thrashing around screaming before he passed out.

The other two bikers were royally flipping out as they stared at the remains on the floor. I walked over to my bag and pulled out another red elastic band. Haley steadied the second man while I tied off his real penis.

"Walter. Walter Hartwood," the second man, confessed without being asked. "We know him through a dealer we work with out of Texas. Walter is one of his customers."

"Drugs?"

"No - women and children. Walter likes his girls young, real young." He had alligator tears streaming down his face and was as white as the basement walls.

"Sex trafficking. So, what, you kidnap random people and then sell them off to this guy? So he can sell them to creeps like Walter?" I was disgusted and furious. My hands tightened on the pair of gardening clippers.

"Yes," he admitted. "I'm sorry! Please! I'm so sorry!" He was sobbing worse than the first guy and staring directly at his penis. He started to piss himself, and I stepped back so my boots didn't get wet.

"Who's the dealer?"

"Ernesto Chaves!" he was panicking and having trouble breathing. I didn't feel sorry for him in the least. Not even a smidgeon.

"Where in Texas can I find him?"

"He's on the Southeast Coast, a town called Fishers Cove," he whimpered. "He has other sellers. The Hounds aren't the only ones he buys from so he has his own security."

"Did your club kidnap Walter's daughter-in-law, Penny?"

"Yeah. Walter tricked her into meeting him. We loaded her into the van and took off. We were supposed to kill her and leave her body somewhere to be found. But she was Ernesto's type, so we sold her to him instead."

"Walter wasn't mad?"

"Furious," he panted. "But Ernesto handled it. Penny's his mistress now. She helps sort the women and children when they are dropped off. Decides which clients get which product. Walter can't touch her."

His oxygen level must have gotten too low from all the panicking because he passed out. I untied the elastic and recycled it on the third biker.

"Tell me every detail of the sex trafficking process."

And, he did.

When he was done, I switched back to the current crisis. "Is your club sending more men?"

"They should be in Indiana by tomorrow night. We were to meet them there."

"How many?"

"Thirty? Forty? I don't know how many made the trip. Plus, they'll have the Indiana charter which is another twenty."

"When were you supposed to call in?"

"This morning. We have to call in every morning with an update. Scar has been livid ever since we found Anne. He's out for blood."

"One last question. Does Ernesto work with any sellers by the name of Max or Nola?"

"I don't know any of the other sellers. We drop off at the side door and then only Scar or Crack would go in to collect our money. I always stayed in the van. I swear it, lady. I swear it."

I threw the shears on the floor, nodding to Haley that it was time to leave. I had had enough.

# Chapter Twenty-Six

Donovan and Reggie were sitting on the couch where we left them. Haley went over to the bar and washed her hands. I took off my leather gloves and threw them in the trash.

"Did it work?" Donovan asked.

"Yeah. It worked."

I sat in the recliner and leaned forward with my head between my knees. I felt queasy from the information overload. When the nausea passed, I explained the details of how many of the Hell Hounds were coming and when. That was the only important matter at the moment. I didn't know what I wanted to do about the rest of it.

"What are you not telling us?" Donovan asked.

"A lot. But let me sort through it a bit."

He must have seen how affected I was by the situation because he let it slide. Reggie went in and gave our guests another generous dosage of sedative and cut them down from the ceiling. When he came back, he looked a little green.

"That looks a whole lot more realistic than I expected it to look," he said.

He threw the bag of supplies, including the garden clippers, into the trash.

"I'm hungry," Haley grinned, winking at me as she walked back into the room. "Do you think there is any leftover sausage at the house?"

Donovan and I laughed, as Reggie vomited in the trash can.

We didn't try to hide our return to the main house but walked across the front yards. I unlocked the atrium door, and we entered through my bedroom. From there, Haley went to find something to eat, Reggie and Donovan went to do whatever guys do, and I went to the basement and retrieved the phones and wallets that we had left in the bag behind the furnace. I took them to Sara's room and handed them to Tech.

"What do you have on Walter Hartwood?" I asked.

"A lot," Sara said.

"He's a snake," Tech said.

"Anything more specific?" I asked.

"He married into money. Bones' grandfather is still the majority shareholder, and the next largest shareholder is his only daughter, Bones' mom. Walter, Bones, and Bones' sister own hefty shares too. Looks like papa Walter though has free reign with the company most days and sits in the CEO chair. Walter's daughter also works there but is one of many VP's. Walter pulls in a heavy middle six figure salary. Most of his financials are sleazy, but nothing surprising. Hiding money in the Caymans, buying a few hookers here and there, but there is one thing that seemed off so we kept digging. Honestly, I don't know what to make of it."

Tech pulled up some documents, and I leaned over to look at them.

"Payments to a title company?" I asked.

"Yeah, he transfers $4,000 a week, the amount never changes, and he has been making the payment for about five years now. We dug further into the title company and found seven other men making the same money transfer every week." Tech said.

"And that's not all. Walter flies to Texas the second weekend of every month like clockwork, but we can't figure out why. His phone records don't show him calling anyone in Texas either," Sara said.

"By chance is he flying in near Fishers Cove?" I asked.

Sara pulled up a map. "Next city over. Fishers Cove doesn't have an airport."

"This weekend is the second weekend. Did he fly in today?"

"He's scheduled to depart this afternoon and arrive by 7:00."

"Check the flights for the other seven men that make the weekly deposits. Are they regulars to Texas too?"

They worked in tandem and ten minutes later looked back at me.

"Three of the seven make the same trip every second weekend of the month and the other four fly on the third weekend of the month," Sara confirmed.

I looked at my watch. I walked back downstairs, and Sara and Tech followed. It was almost noon, and the house was packed with people.

"Is everyone back at the house?" I asked loud enough to get everyone's attention.

"The store is ready for tomorrow, so we called it a day. Everyone's here," Katie answered.

"I have an update. Let's move into the living room, so I only have to say this once," I said.

Everyone except for Hattie started moving to the living room.

"Do I need to hear this dear? If you need me there, then fine. But otherwise, I think I would rather keep myself busy in the kitchen," Hattie admitted.

"You can skip it. Just don't worry if you hear anything breaking. Not everyone is going to like what I have to say," I whispered back to her.

She nodded and hurried off. Hopefully, she would have a very large adult beverage for me when I was done.

The living room was crowded, but it was the biggest space available other than the gym, and I didn't think it would be safe to have the weights available to be thrown if anyone lost their temper. I walked over to the French doors and leaned against the cool glass.

"You shouldn't stand in front of the window, Kelsey. We still haven't located the scouts," Bones said.

Reggie snorted, and Donovan chuckled.

"Actually, I did locate them, and they aren't going anywhere anytime soon," I said. "I dragged Reggie on a kidnapping mission last night. We shot them with tranquilizers and moved them to a secure location." I thought it best not to give up their location just yet.

"So you two thought it was a good idea to go up against three men, by yourselves, no back-up, and no one knowing where you were?" Wild Card asked.

"Haley knew where we were at. She could have raised the alarm if needed," I said.

Haley looked down at the floor smiling but didn't sell me out.

"We went back this morning and encouraged them to confess, *everything*. The Hell Hounds are grouping up at their Indiana chapter by tomorrow night. They should be in Michigan late Saturday, early Sunday. The scouts missed their check-in so the rest of their club will be antsy to try to get to Anne. Scar was leading the charge last they knew."

"How did they find us?" Anne asked.

"They didn't come here looking for you. It wasn't until they were already here that they spotted you and called Scar."

"What the hell were they doing here then?" James asked.

"They were watching me. I've had a few weird phone calls that never made any sense. The caller was warning me to stay away from someone. The second call was a bit more threatening. Apparently that was around the same time a kill contract was put on my head."

"Who is coming after you, Kelsey? Is it Max?" Katie asked.

"No. Walter Hartwood."

Bones stood abruptly, his eyes searing into me as he registered what I said. He walked over to me.

"Why would my father want to kill you? That makes no sense, Kelsey."

"He found out about us somehow, and he doesn't approve. I don't know if this is about money or if he's trying to control you. He's your father so you would have a better idea of how his mind works. And, this wasn't the first time he's interfered in your life. He's the one that paid the Hell Hounds to kidnap Penny."

"What?"

"Walter had Penny meet him so the Hell Hounds could pick her up. They were supposed to kill her, but they sold her instead. She's still alive. I know where she is."

"I'll kill him!" Bones roared.

He upended the coffee table and the glass vase shattered. Grabbing the lamp from the side table, he launched it at the far wall. James and Whiskey barely had time to duck. I stepped up to him blocking his path and laying my hand on his chest. His whole body was trembling, but he looked down at me.

"He's always been a mean fucker, but I never thought he would go this far. I won't let him hurt you."

"He can't hurt me. He can't get near me. But there's more, Bones. There is another horrific layer to this story."

Donovan and Wild Card both moved closer and took positions on both sides of Bones. I kept my hand on his chest, hoping it would keep him centered.

"Tell me," Bones said, between heavily panted breaths. He was struggling to control his rage, but he was at least trying.

"Your father is involved with a sex trafficking ring in Texas. He buys young girls. Once a month he flies down along with several other wealthy men. He flies in tonight. I need to have the place raided by the FBI before any other women and children get hurt. If you alert your father, we might not be able to save the women and children. If you don't alert him, he'll be arrested and go to prison. He will be boarding his flight soon, and I am running out of time to get a raid set up."

"Are you saying my father is a pedophile?" Bones asked.

"I'm saying he's a fucked up bastard, and we need to take him down."

Bones was frozen, seeming far off in thought.

"Do it," Bones growled, after a long moment of silence. "What about Penny?"

"The information I have is that she's acting as mistress and helps with the trafficking business. I don't know if she's being forced to do it or if she is doing it willingly. The FBI will have to sort that out, and you can hire her a lawyer if needed."

He nodded and sat down on the couch.

Everyone exhaled in unison.

"I need to call my sister," Bones said. "I won't give her any of the details, and she won't ask. She can set up something with my mother and grandfather to keep everyone late at the office tonight and then have a surprise board meeting after the raid. We'll need my father voted off the board before this hits the news, or the company will take the hit."

"As long as you protect the raid so Walter isn't tipped off, do what you have to do," I said. "I need to call this into the FBI. Tech, Sara, let's go upstairs so we can email the information that you already have."

Donovan, Wild Card and Philip followed us upstairs. I called Agent Kierson on speaker phone filling him in on what I knew and directing him to his email box. He started shouting orders at people to start running the information and setting up flights.

"I have a couple of guys we subcontract out in Texas," he said. "Hopefully, they can help. It's going to be hard to find enough agents this late in the day to get down there in time."

"Hey, Jimmy," Wild Card hollered toward the phone. "You thinking of Reggie and me? We're in Michigan. We have a job going on here tomorrow night and wouldn't be able to fly home and back in time."

"Cooper, what in Sam hell are you doing in Michigan and how do you know Kelsey?" Kierson asked.

"Long story, brother. Tell you about it some other time," Wild Card winked at me.

"Shit, you know if any of the other guys would be available?" he asked.

"I can make some calls," Wild Card said.

"I have my jet here. If Kelsey's sure we're not needed until tomorrow night, I can fly you down and back," Phillip offered.

"I'm sure. You should go. It's important. There will be a lot of women and children that could get caught in the crossfire if they have to pull the local police into the raid," I said.

"Sounds like it's settled then. I'll grab Reggie and a couple other guys. I should be able to round up about ten, maybe a dozen guys. Text me our meet up location," Wild Card said and walked out.

Phillip followed. Donovan looked upset. I ended the call with Kierson, and Donovan and I went downstairs.

"Go. It's fine. I will watch Lisa," I said.

"What if you're wrong, though, and they get here early?"

"We will have plenty of firepower to handle them. Phillip will be just as eager to get back here. It will be fine."

"She's right," Lisa said coming up and wrapping her arms around his waist. "We will be fine, but those women and children need a few more heroes tonight. You need to go."

Donovan kissed Lisa and left to go pack his supplies.

Within a half an hour, Donovan, Wild Card, Reggie, Phillip, and Bones were ready to leave, along with a handful of the other security guys. The rest of the club was staying behind to keep an eye on us. I went to my room to take a mental minute and pray for their safe return. It was a risky operation, and I knew one of them if not all of them could get seriously hurt.

"Hey," Bones said coming up behind me. "We'll be back." He wrapped his arm around me and turned me to face him. "I love you."

And, then he kissed me.

My heart broke from the overwhelming passion of the kiss. When he stepped away, he left before I could say anything.

I looked up, and Reggie was leaning against the door frame. "I see it now. He makes you want a different life. He makes you feel safe. You never had that with Cooper."

"You need to do me a favor, Reggie," I said, pushing my raw emotions back behind the thin shell of a cover I hide behind.

"I know, I know. Don't let them do anything stupid. Make sure they come back safely. I've heard it all before, little Sis," he chuckled as he came over and hugged me.

"Yes, all that. But when it's over, you need to tell Bones something. Tell him that I know he has to stay. He hasn't digested everything yet. But he'll need to stay for Penny. Tell him that I know, and that I understand."

"Damn, you have the biggest heart," Reggie said as he hugged me again before he left.

# Chapter Twenty-Seven

I stayed in my room while the men said their goodbyes and left. From the atrium, I watched them depart until they turned right at the end of the road and disappeared from my view.

As I turned back into my bedroom, I caught a glimpse of Sam walking away from my doorway. I walked over and looked down the hall, but he was nowhere in sight. He must have just been checking to see where I was at. While Tyler was usually assigned to keep an eye on me, Sam had served plenty of security shifts as well. It was probably second nature now to always know my whereabouts.

Deciding an afternoon cocktail was needed, I went to the kitchen and was greeted by Hattie passing me my already prepared beverage of choice.

"Thank you, Hattie."

"You are welcome, Sunshine. I heard enough that I figured you could use one to help you relax a bit. I also heard the interrogation went well. The fake penis fooled them?"

"Yeah, it was a bit too realistic. I don't think Reggie will be able to see or smell ground sausage for a while."

"Well, I am glad it worked. Sounds like you got a lot of information out of them," she said patting my shoulder. "And, now we have more important things to discuss like these pot roasts that are in slow cookers, everywhere. Should I check them?"

"Nope," I grinned. "They will be done at 2:00 and not a minute before. We need to set one of the cookers aside for the men that went to Texas. I promised Reggie I would save some for him."

"I still can't believe you cook. But they smell amazing."

"She can do more than just cook," Pops said entering the kitchen. "She was a legend in Texas from the first day. There is nothing my baby girl can't do." He kissed my forehead and wrapped an arm around my shoulder.

"Tell us more. Tell us more." Katie pleaded from the dining room doorway with Tech grinning behind her.

Knowing there was nothing Pops liked better than telling stories, I went to the dining room to claim a chair and get comfortable. Everyone else settled nearby as Pops geared up to tell a tale.

"First day I met my baby girl, it was love at first sight," Pops grinned.

I snorted.

"Bullshit," said a voice from the doorway.

"Jackson!" I squealed throwing myself at him.

He spun me around in a hug before setting me back on my feet again.

"Long time, little Sis," he grinned.

"Another brother? How many times were you married?" Katie asked.

"Once. That was enough. Jackson grew up with Reggie and Wild Card. He is a permanent part of the family by association," I explained.

"I was telling a story over here," Pops said.

"Sorry, Pops," I giggled, reclaiming my chair.

"Sounded more like a fairytale the way I heard it. The truth was when you met Kelsey, you were ready to tan Cooper's hide and set Kelsey loose as bait in the wild," Jackson said.

"Why on earth would you not like Kelsey?" Hattie asked.

"It's not every day that your eldest son calls and tells you he married a stripper in Vegas. Can't say I was expecting pleasant company while I waited with my shotgun on his front porch," Pops admitted.

"A stripper?" Whiskey asked looking at me.

I realized everyone was looking at me. Hattie just shook her head and giggled.

"What? I needed a job that would pay really well. I racked up a nice pile of cash before I left, too."

"What is it with you and money?" James laughed.

"Anyway," Pops grumbled. "This Spitfire got out of the car and marched right up to me. She never even flinched at the shotgun but stood her ground while she told me she wasn't going to put up with any judgmental bullshit from some old man that thinks he knows a thing or two. And, then I looked at her, really looked at her. It was in her eyes. The anger, the pain, the *everything*. I set down the gun and folded her into my arms. She's been my baby girl ever since."

"So it was one big happy family?" Katie asked with a suspicious look.

"Not even close!" Jackson said. "Cooper and Kelsey fought whenever they were around each other, which meant Cooper usually took off for several days every week for the first month and a half. The rest of us took turns teaching Kelsey the Texas way of life. But the little shit kept showing us up and was a freaking natural at shooting, riding, gambling, Texas brawling. It was embarrassing."

"Remember that time Kelsey smashed Wild Card's truck windshield out?" Pops asked Jackson.

"Or the time she poisoned his dinner?" Jackson added.

"What about the time she put horseshit in his bed?" Pops laughed. "I could hear the yelling from my ranch."

"Why would you put horseshit in your own bed?" Anne asked.

"We didn't share a bedroom. It wasn't a real marriage. I got myself in a jam in Vegas and Jackson offered Cooper up as a solution to my problem. We agreed I would stay with him for a couple months while the dust settled in Vegas and then we would have the marriage annulled."

"It sure seemed like a real marriage four months later when it all blew up, though," Pops said absentmindedly.

I remembered the day as if it were yesterday, the fight, the divorce papers, packing my SUV and leaving the ranch. It was a hard day to forget. The weeks that followed were just as hard to forget.

"Did you get the photo album?" Jackson asked, breaking my thoughts away.

"Yes. It's great. I am going to get the picture of StarBright enlarged and framed. How's she been? She still winning?"

"She's slowed a bit, but still manages to pull in some purse money," Jackson grinned. "Reggie won't let them race her as often as they want. StarLight, on the other hand, is raking in some serious money. He's really tearing up the tracks."

"Are either of them showing any signs of stress?"

"StarBright still has her moments. That's why Reggie regulated back her schedule. And it's easier with us sharing custody of her. She ranch-hops, spending a week with each of us," Pops said.

Jackson snorted. "She ranch-hops because Cooper and Pops kept stealing her from Reggie's barn. He decided that if he set up a schedule for shared custody, he would at least know where to find her."

"What's so special about this horse?" Lisa asked.

I looked at Jackson and Pops, but they looked away sadly.

"I rescued her when she was about two. Her brother, StarLight was just a foal. They both had been abused by whips and a heavy hand."

"So you adopted them," Sara grinned.

"She did. She also convinced the owner it was in his best interest to sign over their ownership to her," Jackson said.

"Literally, twisted his arm I would say," Pops chuckled.

Katie grabbed the photo album and removed the cover photo to have a closer look.

"I remember the day that picture was taken," Jackson said. "Reggie and I had walked out to watch Kelsey work with the horses. It was the first time in six long weeks that I saw her smile. It about knocked me over. Cooper came up behind us and started snapping photos."

"Cooper was always a good photographer," James said. "Used to carry that camera around wherever we went."

"He does have a talent," I agreed, looking at the picture again.

I checked my watch and declared a pause in story time. It was 2:00 and the pot roasts were done. While everyone lined up to self-serve, I nodded to Tyler toward the balcony. He smiled and followed me out, pulling his cigarettes out from his inside cut pocket.

"It's hard to imagine you living in Texas or being a stripper in Vegas," Tyler chuckled. "I thought you were Michigan born and raised."

"I am. I moved away when I was eighteen and didn't move back until a little over a year ago. I started up the business and met you all shortly after that." I lit up and looked out around the backyard and then to the back of the store on the other side of the field.

Someone was sitting in a truck in the East parking lot facing toward the back of the house.

"Is that Sam's truck?" I asked.

"Looks like it," Tyler agreed after looking where I pointed. "He's supposed to be at the clubhouse, though. Couple guys are getting the clubhouse locked down in case the Hell Hounds decide to hit us there. The women and children are being relocated to either Chops' house or your old house."

We watched Sam's truck pull out, and as it turned around to leave, I could make out enough to confirm it was Sam behind the wheel.

"Not the first time he's been around when he should have been somewhere else," Tyler said in a low voice. "I haven't said anything to the club because I didn't want to be labeled a rat. I'm still just a prospect. But, he disappears a lot."

"When did he prospect in?"

"Shortly after he moved here, I would say about ten months ago."

"Keep an eye on him and let me know if anything else happens. I will check it out, though."

I didn't want to think of Sam as a bad guy. He was barely an adult and always seemed pleasant enough to be around. I honestly never spent the time to get to know him, though. Either way, I would have Tech get me a detailed background. And his ass was on my radar now. He better not be involved with anything from Florida. It could be life threatening, *for him*.

I claimed my share of pot roast and potatoes as everyone declared lunch was cooked to perfection. I barely remembered eating, though as I tried to think of every interaction I had ever had with Sam.

After dinner, several of us pitched in to help clean-up. Whiskey was drying dishes while I washed them.

"Who's Max?" Whiskey asked.

Luckily my back was turned to Whiskey so he didn't catch the surprised look on my face.

"Why do you ask?"

"Katie asked if the person that had put a contract out on you was Max. Is he one of the Hell Hounds?"

"No. He's someone I knew long before I came back to Michigan. He's not a threat," I assured him. "Where did Anne and Katie go?"

"They are hiding in the living room going through your photo album from Texas," he chuckled. "Someday you will have to tell me why there is a wedding reception picture of you smashing the whole top layer of cake in Wild Cards face. That's the picture I want to frame."

"Those were crazy days. Neither one of us wanted that wedding reception, but Pops insisted. I think he regretted the decision after the food fight broke out. Reggie expected it though and had a camera going during the whole event," I laughed.

"So how close are you and Reggie?" Whiskey asked cautiously.

"He's my brother, in every sense. He's the only one in the world that knows all my secrets," I grinned. "And, he supports my decisions no matter how crazy they get."

"Like sneaking out in the middle of the night with tranq-guns?" Whiskey asked with a raised eyebrow.

"They've done worse," Jackson said entering with another stack of plates. "Pops and I had to bail them out of jail three times in one day once. After the third time, Pops asked if they were done for the day, and Kelsey said she had one more stop to make. She handed Pops an envelope of money and Reggie dutifully followed her out the door.

"We waited by the phone for another call from the police, but the next morning they snuck in, covered in mud and scratches. They never did admit what they were up to, but obviously didn't get caught in their fourth round of trouble brewing."

"That was a fun day," I chuckled.

"How do you get arrested three times in one day?" Katie asked joining us in the kitchen.

"Well, the first time, I assaulted a guy in the diner, but he totally deserved it. Reggie was fighting his friend. The second time, we sort of borrowed a golf cart, without asking. And, the third time was totally a misunderstanding. I didn't intend to throw the pie at that cop."

"We are so going to vacation in Texas together," Katie high fived me.

"I don't think so," Tech quipped from behind her.

Katie just laughed.


"Kelsey, your phone was ringing," Hattie said as she passed me my cell phone. I looked at the caller id on the screen and stepped out the front door to speak privately. Tyler was outside but walked closer to the road to give me some space.

"Scott, is everything okay?"

"Carl's still in ICU, but he's doing better. That's not why I called you." Scott spoke in a low tone as if someone was listening. "A cop and another guy I have never seen before tried to gain access to Carl. The nursing staff stopped them, but the only people that know he is here are you and me. Is Carl in some type of trouble with the police?"

"Shit. No, he's not in trouble with the police. But he may be in danger. Scott, don't trust the police. Don't let them near him. I'm going to call in some bodyguards until it's safe to move Carl. Can you watch him until I get help there?"

"What's going on Kelsey?"

"I think Carl witnessed a murder, and they won't want him to talk to me," I answered honestly.

"But even if he witnessed something, he wouldn't be able to testify. Why would they bother to hurt him?"

"They don't keep loose ends around."

"This is about your son, isn't it?"

"Yes."

"I'll keep an eye on Carl. How will I know the good guys from the bad guys?"

"The good guys will know the proper ingredients," I said before disconnecting the call.

Finding Tech and Katie in the family room, I nodded for them to follow me. We went to the basement, down the hall, and into the 'storage room,' that was locked by a keypad entrance that only the three of us had access to. Several club members watched us as we entered and closed the door behind us.

"Shit got real if you are willing to come in here with everyone around," Katie said as she slid on top of one of the eight-foot tables.

Tech went over and started up three of the laptops that never left this room. To us, the room was the War Room. It's where we worked to find Nicholas.

I pulled a box marked phones down from a shelf. I pulled out burner phones for each of us and a few spares.

Handing Tech my day to day phone, I started to explain.

"There's a witness in Miami that tried to get a message to me. I didn't get the message until Tuesday morning, and by then he was hurt and needed medical attention. He's in the hospital, but the bad guys are trying to get to him, which leads me to believe that my phone may have been tapped. It's either that or the store is bugged. I need to get him some protection."

"Stop," Tech said, going over to retrieve another box. "Not another word," he instructed as he pulled out some equipment.

He scanned the room slowly and then went back to my phone and opened the back. Sure enough, a small chip of some kind was between the battery and the sim card. Tech removed it before walking over to the bathroom and throwing it in the toilet.

He then pulled another handheld electronic device from the box and set it on the table.

"This is a scrambler. If I missed a bug, it won't let the signal through. I will get one for each of us to carry around." He dragged both his hands down his face. "Kelsey, this is not good. We can get security for the witness, but someone got too damn close to you to mess with your phone like that. Who the hell would have that kind of access?"

"Maybe it's not that bad," Katie interjected. "I mean, Kelsey leaves her phone lying around all the time. Maybe a customer was able to swipe it and return it unnoticed."

"No. She only leaves it around the house or in the back room of the store. When she's in public, she has it on her."

"I can only think of one person to check into," I said. I paced back and forth, trying to calm my rising fury. "This isn't my Spidey senses – I have nothing to go on but a warning from a friend."

"Just tell me where to look," Tech said.

"Sam." I stopped pacing and looked at Tech. "This afternoon Sam was parked in the side lot of the store when he should have been at the club. Tyler says Sam isn't always where he is supposed to be. Tyler's a prospect, so he didn't want to stir up trouble by ratting Sam out."

"The timing is about right," Tech admitted. "Sam moved here shortly after you moved back. I hate to think the club has put you in danger, but when we look at backgrounds, we are generally looking for clues of undercover cops, not criminals."

"Shit. You mean sexy little Sam might be a dirtbag?" Katie whined.

Tech gave her a stern look before he turned to his laptop.

"Katie, reach out to Donovan's company and get guards for Carl," I said. "They will need to know the security code for Carl and Scott to trust them. Make sure they know that the best French toast is made with cinnamon and honey."

"If that's what you did to the French toast this morning, I completely agree," she said as she started dialing on a burner phone.

By the time Katie had finished setting up security, Tech had enough information on Sam to confirm that he was involved with Max's crew in Miami. We even had a few new financial leads that we could follow that might lead us to Max's location.

"I can make something up, and turn this into a club problem. He'll disappear," Tech said.

"No," I said as thoughts processed at high speed in my head. If Sam did something to jeopardize my son's life, I would kill him with my bare hands. I didn't need the club stepping in to do my dirty work.

"Kelsey, I know you like Sam, but if he's a threat, maybe it's better for everyone to let the club get rid of him," Katie said.

"I'm not positive that he is a threat," I said shaking my head. "He was definitely hired to keep an eye on me, but I don't get the sense that he would actually hurt me or anyone else."

"You can't take that chance," Tech said.

"Yes, I can. But that's not why I am sparing him. Look at the leads we all of a sudden have. What if we use him to find out more information? Bug his phone, his truck, his room. Watch who he talks to and what his habits are. It may help us find Nicholas."

"And, if nothing turns up? How long are you going to let him stick around?" Katie asked.

"Until I have no other choice," I answered. "And, then I'll kill him myself."

# Chapter Twenty-Eight

Katie received confirmation that the security team was in place with Carl and Scott at the hospital. Carl was alert enough to convince Scott that cinnamon and honey were indeed required ingredients in making French toast.

We stayed up working on all the new leads until after 2:00 a.m. We had more research to do, but needed to get some sleep if we were going to survive a busy Saturday at the store, followed by a possible shootout with the Hell Hounds later that same night. It was shaping up to be one hell of a weekend.

When the alarm blared in the morning, I felt as if I hadn't slept at all due to all the tossing and turning I did from several nightmares. I stumbled into the shower which helped to revive me before dressing in some sweats. I wasn't quite awake enough to dress in a slinky silk gown.

In the kitchen, I was greeted by Hattie with an exchange of our good mornings and a hot cup of coffee. In the dining room, I was surprised to see that the guys were back from Texas. I took inventory of everyone. Everyone except Bones was present and seemed as healthy as when they left.

"Not a single scratch on any of us, Sis," Reggie grinned.

"Glad to have you all back," I said, kissing Reggie on the cheek. "How did the raid go?"

"As planned. Nine women and four children were rescued. Sixteen arrests were made including Penny and Walter," Donovan filled me in as he ate his eggs. "One of Kierson's agents asked me to give you this, too."

Donovan slid a flash drive across the table to me.

"Which Agent?" I asked as I pocketed the flash drive.

"Agent Maggie O'Donnell. She's a profiler on Kierson's team," he answered. "Do you know her?"

"I don't think so, but maybe I spoke to her once when I was working with Kierson."

"She's good," Wild Card chimed in. "She saved my ass last night. She sniper shot a guy that was sneaking up behind Reggie and I. He was three feet away from us when she took him out. Of course, all hell broke loose after that, but I still appreciated her covering our six."

Wild Card was always in his element during and after a good adrenaline rush. He was casually leaned back enjoying the morning, looking perfectly content. Reggie was grinning with him as he slapped him on the back.

"Doesn't hurt that she's hot either," Reggie laughed.

The guys all nodded and my curiosity about Agent Maggie O'Donnell went up a notch.

The basement door opened, and Tech and Katie appeared.

"You guys stay up all night?" I asked.

Katie nodded, and Tech yawned.

"Get some sleep. If the store is ready to open, we can wait until 9:30 to go in, so at least you can get a two-hour nap."

"Sounds like a plan," Katie said as she started up the stairs. She was tired enough that she didn't even care that Tech was openly following her upstairs.

"Something going on?" Donovan asked with a raised eyebrow. He knew they had been in the mysterious locked *storage room*.

"Nothing to worry about," I answered, glancing quickly at Reggie.

"Great. More secrets little brother?" Wild Card asked Reggie.

"Nothing to worry about," Reggie echoed my words. "I'll make sure you know if and when that changes, brother. Come on, Sis. Looks like you need a nap before you start the day too. You look like hell."

I slugged him in the shoulder, but the temptation of a possible hour or two of peaceful sleep was too alluring to pass up. I followed him to my room and after resetting the alarm, I fell asleep with Reggie's arm around me.

A half an hour before my alarm would have gone off, Lisa, Anne, Sara and an exhausted looking Katie barged into my bedroom, arms full of cosmetic bags, accessories, and hair care products. Hattie followed caring our gowns.

"Out, Reggie," Anne laughed throwing a decorative pillow at him. "It's girly time."

"I like girly time," Reggie said sitting up and sifting through the cosmetics bag.

"You can come back after we change our clothes. Alex will be coming in anyway. He's already antsy to make sure we do our hair up 'just so'," Lisa added.

"Why don't you go check on Pops and Jackson," I suggested.

"Jackson? When did Jackson get here?" Reggie asked.

"Shortly, after you guys left yesterday. I thought you knew he was here."

"No. Pops must have called him. I haven't talked to Jackson in months."

Hmm. Jackson and Reggie were always close. Closer than most people even knew. I had been so wrapped up in my own drama that I hadn't thought to ask Reggie what was going on in his life.

"It's fine, Sis," Reggie insisted, reading my thoughts. "Get changed. I'm sure Jackson will want to come back too." Reggie kissed my forehead before leaving, and Katie shut the door behind him.

We were barely dressed when Reggie, Jackson, and Alex piled into the room. Alex started helping Anne do everyone's makeup while Reggie and Jackson sorted through purses, scarves, and jewelry to accessorize. Reggie was standoffish with Jackson at first, but they soon fell into old patterns of joking and teasing back and forth.

Alex was throwing a fit that I had napped with my hair wet, and it was now completely out of control. Reggie shooed him out of the way and proceeded to intricately braid my hair back and up off my neck, leaving only a few wispy curls.

"I want him to be my brother, too," Katie insisted as she sat down in my place for Reggie to do her hair.

"He's pretty good at that, isn't he?" Pops agreed, entering and sitting in my desk chair. "He would get so frustrated when Kelsey would go out riding and get her hair all knotted up."

Jackson moved over to hand Reggie a designer clip for Katie's hair. Reggie was careful not to touch Jackson, as he took it. Jackson noticed and left the room.

"I need to go check on some things and get changed. You girls all set?" Reggie asked.

"We're good," Anne answered. "I need to go help Sara get dressed. Lisa and Katie, can you check on the rest of the guys and make sure they are getting in their tuxes?"

Lisa, Anne, and Katie left, and I sat in a guest chair across from Pops.

"What's going on?" I asked concerned.

"I keep waiting for him just to say it out loud. But he won't. I just want him to be happy, and he's only really happy when he's with Jackson. Does he really think I give a shit if he's gay?"

"What are you talking about?" Wild Card asked coming into the room. "Reggie's gay?"

Pops and I both laughed. Wild Card was probably the only person in the world that knew Reggie and hadn't figured out that he was gay. Other people's sexual preferences are something he just didn't care about. The only reason he knew Jackson was gay was because Jackson advertised it.

"Why didn't he just say something? Does he really think we would care?" Wild Card asked.

"Kelsey, you are the only one other than Jackson that Reggie has ever confided in and trusted to be himself. What should we do?"

"He's been scared since puberty of losing the two most important people in his life if he admits to how he feels. If you want to truly help him, you have to just come straight out and tell him that you support him. Then give him time to see that you mean it. Whether his fear is irrational or not, he loves you both and needs you."

Pops got up and took a deep breath.

"I don't know what we would do without you, baby girl," he said before leaving the room to find Reggie. Wild Card followed him out.

A few minutes later, Goat entered.

"Some of us are heading to the store to get last minute stuff set up. You need anything before I leave?"

"Got any suggestions on where I can hide my gun?" I asked looking at myself in the mirror.

The shimmering champagne fabric hugged my curves and exposed the skin above my hips, up to the bottom of my ribs. Alex must have known when he found it that both my tattoo and most of my scars would still somehow be covered. Only the scar at the top of one of my breast was still visible, but it didn't bother me anymore.

"Not in that outfit. Several of us are wearing double holsters, though, so we will have two guns. I'll find out who's carrying double and let you know who they are."

He left the room, and I slipped on my strappy heels.

I had mentally drifted off and didn't notice Wild Card come back until he was standing in front of me.

"You okay?" he asked.

"Yes, just day dreaming. How'd it go with Reggie?"

"Good, I think. Pops talked to him in front of Jackson. He came right out and told him that we didn't give two shakes about his love life other than we wanted him to be happy. Told him to get his head out of his ass and accept that. Then Reggie started to cry, Jackson started to laugh, and Pops gave them both a hug before I hugged them too, and we left them to talk. I'm an idiot for not having known."

"Cooper, you are just not built that way. You didn't know because it's no big deal to you. It's not because you don't care about your brother."

"And, you? What did I miss with you?" he asked. "I know that leaving you that night with the divorce papers was wrong. I have kicked myself every day since. It was a shitty move. But you wouldn't hate me this long for that. What is it, Kelsey? What happened?"

"Not today, Cooper. I will tell you, but not today. I need to focus on the present," I said standing and looking at myself in the mirror again. "And, that includes figuring out how to carry a gun in this outfit."

"You look amazing, Kelsey," Wild Card said.

He looked me up and down and finally noticed my scar. He raised a hand toward it.

I stopped his hand, and he raised his gaze to meet my eyes. He had a concerned look, but when I shook my head no, he nodded. He wouldn't ask any questions.

There was a lot said between the two of us without a single word spoken aloud.

Goat walked back in and rattled off the names of the men wearing two guns. It would help, but if we were hit hard, it wouldn't be enough.

"Where are your holsters?" Cooper asked.

I opened the bottom drawer of my dresser, and he sifted through them. Selecting two, he then asked where my glocks were. I pulled one from my handbag and one from my nightstand.

Cooper was already wearing two holsters but added another shoulder holster and a waistband holster. He was now carrying four glocks under his tux jacket.

"Four guns? Really?" Goat asked.

"Kelsey and I are both dual wielding trained for point shooting. Two guns are for her, and two are for me," Cooper explained as he loaded his belt with additional clips. "When she trained with Pops on shooting, she thought she had me beat until I showed her I could shoot with both hands simultaneously. Then it was just another challenge for her to learn. She's almost as good as me at it."

"She drops her left a bit on the third round, but she's still pretty damn accurate at it," Donovan said as he entered. "It's time to go."

# Chapter Twenty-Nine

It took a few yelling matches and a couple of bribes, but I finally convinced Alex that he needed to stay home and rest. Pops and a few of the others were also staying at the house with Hattie and Alex. They would be watching the back of the store from the back balcony, ready with sniper rifles if needed.

As a precaution, I showed them the tunnel access in the mechanical room in case they needed to escape unseen. Passing the War Room, Pops inquired about the security panel. I answered it was a storage room, and the subject was dropped.

Being in the last group to rush out the front door, I was surprised by the limo waiting in the driveway. James and Wild Card helped me inside, and we were driven to the front entrance of the store. Outside, a dozen Players dressed in black tuxes lined the sides of a red carpet leading to the front doors. The crowd started cheering as the limo pulled up and James exited, offering his hand to assist me out.

The crowd screamed louder when I exited in my shimmering gown, but when Wild Card exited the car with all his massive muscles, the women's piercing screams forced me to cover my ears as I laughed.

Wild Card offered me his arm, escorting me to the doors as I waved at a few familiar faces. More than half the customers were dressed up for the occasion. While many wore simple dresses, some were dressed in elegant gowns or party dresses.

The entrance door was opened to allow us to pass through, then closed hurriedly. I rushed around rechecking the registers, the office, and the backroom doors, before taking the time to appreciate my surroundings. White lights were strung throughout the store, and the manikins were dressed in beautiful gowns. Silk flower arrangements were elegantly placed about, and the ends of clothes racks were streamed with tulle. The store looked beautiful.

"Wow, everybody. I am in awe."

"Finally, we have impressed you!" Lisa smiled. "And, Katie and I didn't fight once getting all this together."

"I think I like pregnant Lisa better than regular Lisa," Katie muttered.

"I like the fact that you are less likely to become violent with pregnant Lisa than regular Lisa," Lisa replied.

"You should get married here," I said interrupting their bickering. "After today, we are closed for several weeks. The walls need fresh paint, but we can move the racks out and bring in some trees and such to finish decorating the room. The register counters are on casters so we can move them out as well. What do you think?" I asked Lisa.

"It's perfect, but are you sure you don't care? My family will be invited, and they are all, well, *the Mafia*. They will be armed and in your personal space."

"Bahh. I don't have an issue with that. If anyone gets out of hand, your father or Phillip will handle it. So, you going to talk to Donovan?"

"He said it's up to me, so what about Christmas Eve?"

"People may not want to be away from their family Christmas Eve, and I won't be home for Christmas, but what about New Year's Eve? That would be pretty spectacular," I suggested.

"New Year's Eve sounds perfect. You can explain later why you won't be here for Christmas though because James is about to start his behavioral modification speech," Lisa grinned.

As James stepped on top of a nearby planter, to give his mind your manners or you will be forcibly removed speech, a quintet started playing jazz music in the center of the store on a raised stage. Moments later, the doors were opened, and the crowds were guided forward into the store. By the looks of the parking lot, we would have another sellout day before closing for the holidays.

Wild Card stayed by my side as I walked the store checking to make sure all the staff was where they needed to be. Katie was in charge of the registers today so that I could monitor the rest of the store as needed. In the backroom, they were checking in a drop-off. After they had finished, I instructed that the overhead doors and back door be locked. I also instructed the laundry employees that smoked to make sure they had escorts if they went out. Wild Card nodded his approval along the way as he listened to his earpiece of other activity in the store. He chuckled a few times, and I was sure it was customer related. Our Saturday shoppers were an odd breed.

I saw Tech motioned me up to his loft office, and I asked Wild Card to wait at the bottom of the stairs.

"What's up?" I asked after I had finally made it up the steep staircase in my tight dress and excessively high heels.

"Sorry," Tech chuckled. "It would have been easier if I would have just come down the stairs, but I don't like to leave the monitors on Saturdays."

"It's good exercise for my calves," I grinned. "You got something to update me on?"

"I have the devices to bug Sam's truck, room, and phone. I just don't know the best way to go about it. I've never been tight with Sam. He'll be suspicious if I try to get too close."

I walked over to the window overlooking the sales floor and spotted Tyler. He looked up, sensing eyes on him. I pointed to him and then to James and motioned for them to come upstairs. Tyler nodded and was approaching James when I stepped away from the window.

"I'm still working on tracking the money being deposited in Sam's account. And, I hope to have a copy of his phone bill later today."

"Sounds good. I was passed a flash drive this morning from the FBI. I haven't had a chance to look at it yet. If you get to it before I do, it's in my top dresser drawer tucked inside of a pink sock."

"You hate pink. Why would you have pink socks?"

"Sara thought they would look cute on me," I grinned.

The door opened, and James and Tyler walked in followed by Wild Card.

"Problem?" James asked.

"No. But I need a big favor, and it involves trust, James. I need Tyler to plant some bugs for me. It doesn't have anything to do with the Hell Hounds, and your club is not in any danger. I can't tell you more than that, other than we will be listening to one of your guys. I need you to trust me that I will protect your club and that only Tech, Katie and I will have access to the recordings."

"Why can't you give me the whole story?" James asked.

"She just can't, Prez," Tech answered. "The fewer people that know, the safer everyone is. We even have scramblers running every time we talk. You have to trust us."

James reluctantly nodded his approval.

"James, I need your word that you won't press Tyler with questions. I will explain more when I can, but he's only a prospect, and I am putting him in a bad situation between his club and me."

"You have my word. Tyler, you have a green light to help Kelsey and Tech with whatever is going on. Consider it club sanctioned." James turned and walked down the stairs.

Wild Card stood in ready position without any indication of leaving.

"Out, now," I ordered.

He smirked and descended the stairs.

Tech quickly explained to Tyler how the bugs worked and how best to install them. I offered Tyler the storyline of flirting with Katie and Tech banishing him back to the club to use as an excuse for his return. Both Tech and Tyler smiled in agreement.

"Is this all because I said Sam was acting suspiciously?" Tyler asked.

"No, it's because I took that information to Tech and he found out why Sam is acting suspiciously. He's involved with some very bad people from my past, and I plan on using him to learn the whereabouts of certain individuals."

"So, we are spying on the spy? Awesome," Tyler nodded as he gathered everything and left grinning.

"May the Force be with you, Brother," Tech grinned.

The next few hours were a nightmare. In less than two hours I had replaced the strappy heels with a pair of tennis shoes. Most of the other girls that were working the clothes racks did the same. By 1:00 we had cleared half our inventory. We pooled resources, and in assembly line fashion, including some of the Players, moved the racks from the sales room to the back room, passing them to the next person.

I stepped out of the assembly line and walked another circuit around the store. Wild Card remained at my side, and Donovan and James joined us when we were near the registers.

"What's wrong?" Donovan asked.

"Fricken-spidey-senses," I grumbled, continuing to scan the store. The hairs on my arm had been pointed upward for the last hour. I shook my hands as they were sweaty and shaky.

"What should we do?" James asked.

"Close laundry services. Get all non-essential employees out of here. As soon as the last full rack crosses the threshold, send the sales floor staff out the door too. Spread the word for everyone to stay alert."

James and Donovan took off in opposite directions in a rush. My stomach was knotted as I called the main house.

"Hello, Sunshine. For the third time, we are just fine," Hattie answered.

"Hattie, I need to talk to Pops."

The other line was silent as Hattie handed off the phone.

"Hey, baby girl. What do you need?"

"I need you to trust me that something is wrong. Get Hattie and Alex in the furnace room. Get ready with sniper rifles. Something's coming."

"Consider it handled," Pops said as he hung up.

Turning around, I caught the end of Wild Card's phone conversation questioning what my spidey senses were. He must not have liked the answer, as he turned a shade whiter and looked back at me with widened eyes. He ended the call promising to keep me safe, so I assumed he was talking to Bones.

"Bones says your gut instincts are more honed than our friend Grady from the service. That man saved our lives more times than I could count," Wild Card said as he looked around the store.

"Grady? I don't remember that name ever being mentioned. Did he make it out?"

"Yeah, barely. He lives in Montana now but works some of the security gigs with us on occasion," Wild Card answered while he looked around the store.

I watched several players push a half a dozen full racks onto the sales floor, before promptly shutting the overhead doors. They were closing down the back room and clearing out the floor staff. My stomach tightened again. I called Whiskey and told him to prevent new customers from coming inside and that we would soon be out of inventory. The message was followed by loud complaints as the Players moved the frozen crowd back to their cars and blocked the entrance doors off for the day.

The remaining customers already inside, sensing the end of the stock was coming, started panicking and grabbing clothes in a mad rush. I added to the frenzy by announcing over the PA that the store would be closing in ten minutes. It was pushing the crowd a little faster than what the inventory required, but my head was screaming we were in danger, and I needed to get these people out.

Several Players stepped in and formed more cash only checkout lanes with me. Wild Card watched my back as I worked. We had two-thirds of the crowd checked out when my phone rang from the dainty shoulder purse that I had strapped over my head and shoulder.

It was Tyler.

I stepped away to take the call.

"This call may be monitored. You okay?" I asked.

"I was coming back to the store and passed a shit load of bikes on the other side of the highway. There here. It's at least forty, probably closer to fifty guys. They were getting on their bikes as I passed," Tyler reported in a rush.

"Tyler, if you don't have time to get here, pullover and stay out of it. Don't get between them and us, that's an order. Otherwise, come in through the front doors." I disconnected the call and reached for the PA system.

"Attention Everyone. Red Alert. All customers and employees evacuate the store and leave the premises immediately. I repeat, *Get-Out-Now*."

I hung up the PA and started ushering customers out, with unpaid clothes in hand. They could take all the money too as far as I was concerned. We were sitting ducks unless we could clear the store. All the customers except three senior ladies that were regulars were out by the time Tyler came squealing tires to a stop in front of the store. He jumped out and ran inside.

"They're coming! I can hear the bikes!" he yelled for all to hear.

"Sorry ladies, but you will have to come with me, and we have to hurry." I gathered the remaining cashiers and other staffers and led them along with the senior ladies into my office. Sara had already opened the access under my desk into a hidden panic room. She led the way, and the rest of the women followed, crawling inside.

"Lisa, get inside the panic room," I ordered by the doorway.

"No, I should stay out here," she answered.

"Damn it, Lisa. I promised you that if you pissed me off, I would yell at you. This is me, treating you like family—*get in the fucking panic room*!"

Lisa huffed loudly and stomped her foot in protest before she spun on her heel and crawled inside. I closed and latched the hidden compartment.

"Damn. I have never seen my sister follow orders before," Phillip grinned.

The Players had moved the register counters to use as a half barrier in the center of the store, near the office. We all started prepping for war as we checked magazines and turned safety switches off. I had my two glocks and several spare clips.

The sound of bikes vibrated around the building. They were circling and parking away from the glass windows. The few customers that were still in the parking lot must have finally sensed the danger and screeched their tires making a fast exit. I looked at Tyler's truck sitting dead center in front of the store with the door still open on the driver's side.

"So, Tyler, you aren't especially fond of your truck, are you?" I asked.

Several of the Players and security guys laughed.

"Um, sort of. It's a nice truck. Has low miles. Why?"

"Because, in about five minutes, it will be so shot full of bullet holes, you aren't going to recognize it," Whiskey laughed.

"Damn it," Tyler groaned as the first round of gunfire shattered the windows in the front of the store. We all took cover behind the counters until we could hear the Hounds feet crunching on the glass.

Then, as one, we opened fire.

# Chapter Thirty

It was crowded behind the counters, so I stayed low, firing dual handed as Wild Card shot over my head. Reggie and Anne followed my lead and positioned themselves low on both sides of me in front of Jackson and Whiskey.

I could hear rifle shots behind the building and knew that Pops was in control of securing the back entrances. If Sara had to evacuate the women, he would ensure they had safe passage out the back escape route.

Bullets flew in both direction as both sides volleyed for the win over life and death.

A scream from Anne turned my attention her way.

Whiskey dropped behind her as Anne turned wildly with a gun aimed to the right. Scar stepped out from behind a shelf to shoot again, aiming for Anne.

Dropping one of my guns to the counter, I positioned both hands on the other, stood, aimed and pulled the trigger.

I fired at the same moment that Scar's shotgun fired.

Wild Card grabbed my waist and spun me behind him. It wasn't until his body was thrown into mine that

I understood. The shotgun fired to the right. And, Wild Card just took the bullet meant for me.

"NOO!!!" I screamed as I lowered him to the floor.

"NOOO!!!!" I screamed again, tears streaming down my face.

I wiped the tears to clear my vision and saw Wild Card was passed out. I inhaled deeply, standing and welcoming the rage that filled me.

I reloaded my guns.

I would not watch any more of my friends get shot today.

Throwing myself over the counter, I charged forward, both guns firing, blowing holes in anyone I spotted.

More shots fired beside me as we moved forward in a V-formation, ending the life of anyone who dared to step inside the building.

Police cars roared into the parking lot from every direction. Officers bellowed for the Hell Hounds to drop their weapons. I could see a dozen Hounds drop to the ground with their hands behind their head. Several dozen bodies were scattered inside either bleeding or dead.

It was over.

It was really over.

*God, please help Whiskey and Cooper.*

"Dave? Steve? You out there?" I yelled out the front windows.

Dave and Steve came around the corner, stepping cautiously through the broken floor to ceiling windows.

"All the bad guys in here are down but need to be secured. We need to move two of our own out the back and get them to the hospital."

"Move in, use caution and bring a box of flex cuffs," Steve called out to his fellow officers.

"Who's down?" Dave asked, kicking some guns away from some of the Hounds.

"Whiskey and my ex-husband," I answered as I turned away back to the group.

I ordered the hired security to assist the police, and Tyler, Phillip, and Donovan were put in charge of Sara and the women in the safe room. The rest of us quickly carried Whiskey and Cooper out the back doors and loaded them into SUVs. We didn't wait for permission to leave but cut the corner of the field and bounced off the curb into the road, driving at full speed to the hospital.

I leaned over Cooper holding pressure on his wound. He still had a pulse, but he had lost a lot of blood. The shot could have destroyed any number of vital organs in his lower left side. I couldn't think of what organs were even in that area of the body, as my mind spun with hopeless thoughts.

"I can't lose you too. Please, Cooper. Please don't leave me," I whispered leaning over him.

We were greeted outside the emergency room by a full staff and gurneys. Someone must have called and told them we were on our way. The medical staff rushed them inside and behind closed doors as we all gathered in the waiting room. A nurse approached and gently held my arm.

"Miss, are you injured?" she asked.

I looked down at myself and saw that the once beautiful satin dress was shredded and covered in blood.

"It's not my blood," I answered as a shiver racked my body.

James stepped up behind me, bracing me, as he took his tuxedo jacket off, and draped it over my shoulders. I tucked my arms into the sleeves and wrapped myself up tighter.

I don't know how long I had been sitting in the surgical waiting room, watching the memories play out inside my head. I finally came out of my stupor when Tech was squatted in front of me talking to me. I focused and finally his voice was audible.

"You with me now?" Tech asked.

I nodded.

"Doc says both Whiskey and Wild Card are in surgery. Whiskey should be fine. The bullet didn't appear to hit anything vital. Wild Card lost a lot of blood, but they say that the bullet exited straight through the body, which can be a good sign that it didn't do too much damage. Do you understand?"

"Yes," I slowly nodded. "Whiskey is going to make it. They are hopeful about Cooper," I responded to assure him I was mentally present.

"Good. Now how about we get you cleaned up? Hattie brought some clothes. Maybe we should wash up a bit and put them on. It will help you warm up. You're still shaking."

"I'm cold, Tech."

"I know, Kelsey. Let's get you changed," Tech said as he guided me up from the chair. I swayed, and he reached his arm behind me to support me as he grabbed my hand with the other.

"Doc-," Tech called out. "She's ice cold and dizzy."

"The bullet went straight through Wild Card?" Anne asked walking over to us.

"Clean exit, straight through," Doc answered as he stepped up to check on me.

Anne pushed him back as she helped me back in the chair.

"Wild Card blocked Kelsey from being shot. She was standing behind him," she said as she pulled the tuxedo jacket back.

I looked down and saw the blood on my dress had expanded, but that didn't make any sense. Nothing was making any sense. The room spun and then everything went dark.

# Chapter Thirty-One

A bag of blood, a dozen or so stitches, and a warm blanket and I was feeling much better.

"When you are on your feet again, I am going to kick your ass," James said from beside me.

"You'll have to get in line," Tech added.

"Gentlemen, it's very likely that Kelsey wasn't even aware she was injured. I talked to Anne, and when Kelsey was shot, her first concern was for Mr. Wesley followed by an adrenaline rush of charging head first into a gun fight," Doc defended me.

"Yeah," I added sarcastically.

"You're not helping your cause my dear, but I am glad you are feeling spunky again." Doc chuckled.

"Me too. Can I get up now? I want to check on Whiskey and Cooper," I asked.

"Whiskey is good. He should be out of the recovery room soon. Last I heard they were finishing up surgery on Cooper, and then the surgeon would update us," Tech said.

"Yes, you can go, but take it easy for the next few days. You will have to shelve kicking anybody's ass for awhile," Doc said.

"Can I keep the blanket?" I asked.

Even dressed in warmer, more comfortable clothes, I was still chilly.

"I won't tell," Doc winked. The nurse grinned on her way out, and we followed turning toward the surgical wing elevators.


Exiting the elevators, a crowd of Players, staff from the store, friends, and police officers crowded the halls. Because of my friendship with Dave and Steve, we were on a first name basis with most of the city and county officers.

By the looks of his expression, Detective Atwood wasn't there in friendly support, though. Half the officers tensed as Atwood turned my direction to cut off my path.

"About time, you made yourself present for an interview, *Officer Harrison*," Detective Atwood sneered.

Dave and Steve looked to the floor. Several Players shot their heads up with questioning looks. Tech and Katie stepped closer to my side, protectively.

"Sorry to have inconvenienced you by being shot, *Detective*. And, for clarity, it's *former* Officer Harrison. I resigned my position almost three years ago."

"From what I've gathered, it was more of a mandatory medical leave for mental issues," he sneered.

He was determined to gain the upper hand, but it had been a long day – I wasn't in the mood. On a good day, I didn't like bullies.

I stepped forward, our faces inches from each other.

"You should know better than to believe everything you hear, *Detective*. I mean if I believed everything I heard, then that would mean I believe the rumors are true that you are cheating on your wife with twenty-two-year-old Jenny from the grocery mart. And, that you have a certain fetish that involves wearing silk panties."

Detective Atwood's face turned bright red as laughter broke out around us. I watched the pulse quicken in his swollen neck veins. He grabbed me roughly by the arm and the room went instantly silent.

"You'll need to come with me to the station for a formal statement," he said as he tried to steer me toward the elevators.

"That won't be necessary, Detective," a male voice behind me said.

I turned to see Agent Kierson holding his badge up for inspection. Two other women flashed their badges behind him.

"This is now an FBI case. If you can copy us on any statements and prepare the evidence to be turned over to our custody, I would appreciate it. I already spoke with your chief," Agent Kierson said.

Detective Atwood was beyond pissed, but he knew better than to argue. He turned toward the elevators without another word.

"And, Detective?" one of the female Agents called out, stepping up beside me. "Just for the record, former Officer Harrison was a well-decorated officer of a specialized, high-risk squad. She is very much wanted back by her old department and has turned down several solicitations from other agencies, including the FBI. Quit being pissed at her for being a better cop than you, even after she gave up her badge."

I looked back at the woman as Detective Atwood, not waiting for the elevator, opted to take the stairs.

"You must be Agent Maggie O'Donnell," I grinned.

"At your service, Harrison," she grinned back.

The guys were right, she was gorgeous. Her bright green eyes sparkled playfully. She was of medium height, medium build, and had thick wavy dark brown hair cascading down her back that most women would pay the big bucks to have. But it was the way she scanned the room and summed up everyone in sight with a quick glance that intrigued me.

The surgeon appeared through the double doors, and immediately all interest shifted his way. Reggie came up beside me and held my hand. Pops came up to my other side and secured my other hand.

"Doctor," I greeted.

"You're the wife?" the doctor asked.

"Sort of. Is Cooper going to be okay?"

"We think so. We will have to keep him in ICU for a few days and monitor him, but as long as he doesn't get an infection or start internally bleeding again, he should pull through and be back to normal in a couple weeks."

I exhaled slowly, steadying my next breath.

"Thank you," I said.

"I heard the bullet clipped you after it exited Mr. Wesley," the Doctor said. "You got lucky that you only needed stitches."

"I did. But I'm still going to kick Cooper's ass for my tattoo getting messed up with a scar going through it."

The doctor looked a little shocked until several of the Players started to laugh. Even then, he didn't stick around after giving us some recovery information.

"I do need to take your statement if that's okay," Agent O'Donnell said when conversations had lulled.

"Sure. Let's take a walk and see if we can find a quiet area," I said.

"Maybe you should get an attorney," Katie said.

"No. I'm fine," I assured Katie as I followed Agent O'Donnell.

"So, where do you want me to begin?" I asked as we found an empty waiting room down the hall.

"Go ahead and read this typed statement and tell me if anything needs to be changed," she grinned.

The statement was pretty vague, but covered the basics of good guys versus bad guys and read like your typical self-defense in a war zone situation. It was a no-brainer to sign it.

"Agent O'Donnell, I see you like to cut corners and get straight to the point."

"It's Maggie. And, I hate wasting time on bullshit," she grinned. "You should know that three of the men arrested today insisted they had been captured days ago and that one of them had his manhood cut off. The police didn't want to check for any missing ding-a-lings, so they brought him to the hospital. He was declared to have all body parts intact and returned to a cell."

Maggie was full out smiling.

"How strange," I smirked.

"I honestly don't want to know the details, but off the record, I approve of whatever transpired to shut down that trafficking cell in Texas. We owe you."

"I haven't had a chance between gun fights to look at that flash drive you sent my way. Can you give me the cliff notes?"

Maggie stood and walked over to the doorway, double checking to make sure no one was within hearing distance. I pulled a scrambler from my fancy purse and turned it on.

"Some of it, you may already know. I read the case on your son. And, before you freak out, I didn't contact anyone. I picked up on the fact that it was dangerous to even make inquiries. I did, however, do some deep digging into some of the staff with the Miami PD, the ME's office, and the DA's office."

She checked the hallway again, before returning to sit next to me.

"I didn't like how neatly the case was tied up and shelved. The file I sent contains information on some very corrupt individuals. There is enough there, that if you want, I can get the FBI and State police to step in. I will wait for you to decide after you have a chance to look at it all."

"Thank you," I said sincerely. "But, I don't want you to act on the information right now. I probably know the people on the list but seeing some proof to back up my suspicions will ease my mind. Right now, though, I'm focused on a local mole and am working that angle to see where it leads."

"I'm sure you are working a lot of angles. Anything I can do to help?"

"I have a friend in the hospital in Miami. I have protection on him at the moment, but those same corrupt individuals are already trying to get to him. I need help getting him out quickly and quietly, as soon as he's stable enough to be moved."

"Give me the info and consider it done. Do you have a location in mind or do you want us to put him in a safe house?"

"He's a bit eccentric. A safe house won't work, but if you can get him to Michigan, I can take care of him from here."

"That won't be a problem," she assured me.

"You will need a passcode. Better go with the best pizza has burger, green peppers, and onions. Make sure

Carl hears that or he won't go willingly," I said as we walked back to the group.

"I'll do better than that and personally deliver one to him," Maggie said.

It was impossible not to like Agent Maggie O'Donnell.

# Chapter Thirty-Two

Hours later, the doctors finally approved visitation for Cooper, as long as it was one visitor at a time. I kept skipping my turn until everyone else had visited him first. When I finally passed through the double doors into ICU, I had tears streaming down my face. By the time I opened Cooper's door, I could only make out a blurry version of him.

"Ah, Kel, I'm okay," he assured me as he held his right arm out.

I folded into his shoulder as his arm wrapped around me.

"I'm so tired, Cooper," I cried. "I can't take much more."

"Yes, you can, Kelsey. You are the strongest person I know, man or woman." He rubbed my back comforting me. "You can handle this. You have too. You haven't fought your demons yet."

"What do you know about my demons?" I curled tighter to his good side, sliding myself into the bed to lie next to him.

"You've been gone a year, and I still hear your screams in the middle of the night. You scream for

Nicholas." He pushed my hair out of my face and brushed away some tears. "Since the day I met you, I've watched you religiously looking over your shoulder. You spend countless hours tucked away on the phone or computer. I may not know what your demons are, but I know they are chasing you. And, I get the feeling you are waiting for them."

He leaned his head down and kissed my forehead.

"And, as many times as I begged you to tell me what haunted you, you couldn't let me in. No matter how close we got, you still couldn't open up to me. Did you love him so much that you will never love another man?"

"Yes, I love him more than I will ever love anyone else, but not the way you think. I have my reasons for not telling anyone. People I love will die if I do, Cooper. I trusted the wrong people once, and the cost was too high. I can't take that risk again until he's safe."

"Until who's safe, Kelsey?"

"Nicholas."

"I'm sorry. I thought he died." He kissed my forehead again "Your tattoo, I thought it was a mark of vengeance. No wonder you couldn't commit to telling me anything. You are still loyal to him."

"I've already said too much. Please don't ask me any more questions I can't answer."

"You don't have to tell me anything else except why you hated me for so long. Why wouldn't you take my calls or answer my letters, Kelsey?"

PAST HAUNTS – Kelsey's Burden Series

"I don't have the energy to explain it tonight, Cooper. Just know that I'm not angry anymore. Almost losing you put a few things from the past in perspective. I'm just so glad you are going to be okay," I cried.

"I can wait then," he said as he continued to rub my back.

It felt good to be close to Cooper again. We had started our fake marriage under protest and continued to fight for weeks. Then the fighting turned into pranks. The pranks turned into getting to know each other better and becoming friends. And that eventually led to comforting each other sexually. We never defined our relationship back then, but seeing it now, we both just needed someone to lean on for a while.

As my mind continued to recall all the good memories, I drifted off to sleep.


Several hours later a nurse gently woke me and helped me crawl out of bed without disturbing Cooper. Exiting the ICU, Jackson, Reggie, and James stood talking in the hallway.

"You okay, Sis?" Reggie asked.

"Yeah. Fell asleep," I yawned.

"We know. The nurses agreed to let you stay for a couple hours after I told them that you were also shot earlier tonight," Jackson said.

"Everybody else go home?" I asked.

"Some club members are stationed outside Whiskey's room, and Anne is inside with him," James said. "She wants to spend the night. Reggie and Jackson are staying on this floor to guard the ICU entrance. Everyone else called it a night, and I'm here to escort you home."

"I need to check on Anne and Whiskey, and then I will be ready to leave," I answered giving Reggie and Jackson both hugs before James escorted me down the hall to the elevator.

"I called Bones and told him Whiskey was out of commission for a few weeks, and I needed my Sergeant back while the VP was down," James said. "He told me to fuck off. I then told him you were shot, and he said he would be on the next flight home."

"James, sometimes you can be such a dickhead."

"I know," he grinned.

"He has to deal with his wife and the attorneys. Not to mention his family may need him to step in with the company problems regarding his father's arrest."

"This is where he needs to be. You keep Bones centered. He's never had that before. Even if you aren't ready to talk to him yet, just being near you is good for him."

"So, what's next, James? You want me to coach him through his marital problems?"

"No. I'm hoping he gets his head out of his ass all by himself regarding that bitch."

"You can't judge someone so blindly. You have no idea what she went through to put her in that position."

"I might not know what she went through, but I would stake my life on the fact that you would never assist with selling women and children to the highest bidder. No matter how much torture you endured, you would fight for them until you drew your last breath."

I knew what he was saying was the truth. Even if my own family was threatened, I couldn't turn a blind eye and allow others to be hurt in their place or mine.

My phone rang, and I reached into my pocket to answer it. I realized it was the burner cell. Only Scott and now Maggie had this number.

"Hello," I answered.

I moved away from James as we exited the elevator.

"It's Maggie. I got a call requesting to release Penny Hartwood into her husband Declan's custody pending further investigation. It sounds like they want permission to fly to Michigan. I wanted to check with you before she was released."

I thought about what James had said about never being capable of doing what this woman did. I wondered if she was more involved in the operation than anyone knew. If she was, I could use that to gain more information.

"Let her come."

"What about Carl? Should I change the destination for him?"

"No. I can work that in my favor too. If Penny is more involved than we know, I can easily convince her that Carl isn't a threat, and she can pass that information along. If she isn't involved, then it won't hurt either way."

"I'll make it happen, but watch your back. You're walking down a dangerous path and your son needs you."

"I know."

I walked over to where James was talking to two other club members. I nodded a greeting as I entered Whiskey's room. Anne slept curled into Whiskey's side, much like I had been for the last few hours with Cooper. She looked peaceful.

Whiskey stirred and turned my way.

"I finally got the girl," he grinned, looking down at Anne.

"That you did, my friend." I kissed his cheek. "Next time let's leave the getting shot part out of the equation."

I told him I would be back soon to visit. He drifted back to sleep before I was out the door.

# Chapter Thirty-Three

By the time we arrived at the house, I was beyond exhausted and went directly to bed. I didn't wake up until early afternoon. I showered, grabbed a carafe of coffee and went to the War Room to work.

I found the audio surveillance of Sam was already set up on one of the laptops. I hit play so I could listen as I worked through the flash drive that Maggie sent me. Maggie's research confirmed my suspicions for three of the guilty parties: my old boss in Vice - Trevor Zamlock, my friend and renowned Medical Examiner - Feona Hughes, and an internal affairs officer by the name of Simpson that was also friends with Trevor. The fourth was the missing link, an administrative clerk in the DA's office.

I filled my coffee cup and dug deeper into the files while listening to Sam do the wild thing on the speaker next to me.

Hours later, Tech and Katie joined me. I took the opportunity to stand and stretch. Katie had brought sandwiches with her, and based on the caffeine shakes my hands were making, I was well past time for needing nourishment.

"Anything interesting on the audio?" Tech asked.

"Just that if Sam doesn't slow down with his sexual conquests, his favorite body part is likely to fall off," I answered.

"Eww. You listened to that?" Katie asked.

"Never skip the bedroom conversations when listening in on someone. You would be surprised what people say right before the finale," I laughed.

"I'll take your word for it and leave those sections for you," Tech smirked.

"What about the files Maggie sent?" Katie asked.

"There is enough dirt to prove a cover up and that they are on the take, but nothing directly linking them to Max or Nola. They are definitely involved, though. We need to have my old boss and the ME traced and tracked. I can sneak into Miami, tag their cars, and sneak out before anyone notices."

"No way. If you are spotted, they could punish Nicholas. I will go," Katie said.

"Hell no," Tech said. "With your temper, you might do something stupid while you're there and get arrested. Then the gig is up."

"Did you just say I'm stupid?" Katie's voice was a bit pitched, and this wasn't going anywhere pleasant.

"Stop. You are both right, neither Katie nor I can go. It's too risky. I will find someone else. Just get me some good equipment."

"I can pick everything up tomorrow morning. What's next?" Tech asked.

"Food, a strong drink, and I want to check on Sara. Has Anne come back from the hospital yet?"

"No," Katie answered. "She's going to stay the night again, but it looks like they are releasing Whiskey in the morning. Reggie and Jackson came back to get some sleep and said Cooper is doing well today too."

"Can you get with Donovan and figure out the best way to pay everyone? I also want sizeable bonuses for everyone that participated in the shootout. That was insane."

"What was insane was watching you turn into Wyatt Earp, jump the counter and go toe-to-toe with a dozen-and-a-half men on your own," Katie said. "It's a good thing that Reggie, Jackson, Tech and James followed you over the insanity line or more than just your tat would have been shot up."

"It all worked out," I shrugged.

"It was totally badass," Tech grinned.

I found Sara with Hattie in the kitchen cutting apples.

"What are we making?" I asked pulling a knife out of the drawer to help them peel and cut.

Hattie and Sara looked at each other and then back at me.

"So, we are making apple pies, huh?" I said.

"Pops asked if we had any of your apple pies. We didn't know what to say, so we said no. And, then he said maybe he would get lucky, and you would make some before he leaves on Tuesday," Hattie said.

"Why did you used to make apple pies if you don't like them, Aunt Kelsey?" Sara asked.

"Once upon a time, I did like them," I answered. "And, it's fine. I'll help you whip up a couple in no time."

After the apples had been cut and peeled, I started working on the pie crusts, while I gave them instructions on the filling ingredients.

"The contractors are supposed to start Tuesday on remodeling the kitchen. Should I try to reschedule them?" Hattie asked.

"No, it will be fine. I have a house guest coming later this week, too. I will move Alex out of the guest room so Carl can use it. I wanted to talk to both of you about Carl before he gets here, though."

"Is he another bodyguard?" Sara asked.

"No, little-bug, we don't need another bodyguard. Carl is an old friend of mine that needs a place to stay for a while. He's just a bit odd. He's super smart but doesn't understand rules or laws very well. We can't let him on a computer without supervision, and sometimes he forgets to put clothes on. I will do my best to keep him under control, but I wanted to warn both of you."

"Kelsey Harrison, are you telling me that you have some crazy loon moving in with us that is likely to run around the house naked?" Hattie said. "What if Sara sees him naked?"

"I'll just close my eyes," Sara said.

I couldn't help but grin at Sara.

Hattie huffed and puffed.

"Look, Hattie, I get it. But wait until you meet Carl. Sometimes he's scary smart, like smarter than Sara and other times it's like having a two-year-old running around. I think once you get used to him, you will agree he is completely harmless."

"A harmless naked man sitting on the furniture, I can't wait," Hattie mumbled as she smoothed the pie filling on top of the lower crusts.

I winked at Sara, and we left the kitchen together to give Hattie some time to adjust.

"Is Carl really smarter than me?" Sara asked curiously.

"In science and mathematics, yes. He just doesn't understand social behavior or consequences if he breaks the law, so we have to keep an eye on him."

"Do you think he will like me?" she asked.

"Yes," I smiled down at Sara, brushing her hair back with my hand. "Carl is going to love hanging out with you. And, you can make him feel welcome by getting a

Kindle set up for him to read his newspapers on. He will like that."

"Which papers?"

"Pick the top eleven newspapers in the world and add in the Miami Post, and he will be happy."

"Should I get the English versions?"

"No. Carl can read any modern language and some ancient languages."

Her eyes got huge, and I laughed.

"Ok then," she said as she skipped away to work on her new assignment.

Haley, Bridget, and Alex were in the living room when I entered. I went to the bar and made myself a drink before joining them.

"How are you feeling, Alex?" I asked.

"Right as rain, Luv. Ready to move back home."

"Good, because in a couple of days, I have someone else moving into the guest room," I grinned. "Oh, but don't go in your basement storage room until I have a chance to clean in there."

Alex raised an eyebrow and was about to say something when Bridget interrupted.

"Already cleaned, and talk about nasty. I would have loved to have seen you take the clippers to that dude's manhood, though. That must have been epic!" Bridget bounced in excitement as she talked.

"Clippers? To his manhood? In my basement?" Alex exclaimed.

"Relax. It was a fake penis that Hattie made for us," Haley said, patting his knee trying to sooth him.

"Hattie made a fake penis?" Alex looked at me in confusion. "I think I hit my head harder than the doctors even know. None of this is making any sense."

"It's been a busy couple of days," I said as I got up to leave the room. I had a thought before I made it to the doorway and turned back around.

"Haley, Bridget, how would you two like to do me a favor? The reward is a paid vacation in Florida?"

"Hell yes," Haley answered while Bridget jumped up and down clapping.

"I'll get the details set up and get back with you both," I grinned.

They would not only make sure the tracking devices were installed, but both of them deserved a good old fashion girls' beach vacation. It made perfect sense.

Pops was in the dining room, drinking coffee with Goat and James.

"There's my baby girl," Pops grinned.

"Hey, Pops. You getting along okay? I know I have been pretty absent today," I said kissing him on the cheek.

"I'm just fine, baby girl. I dropped Harold and Kevin off at the airport earlier with a few of the other security guys. I booked a return flight for Tuesday for Reggie and me. But, Wild Card is going to need a place to stay for a couple weeks. The doctors don't want him flying, and it's a long drive. Reggie and I need to get back to the horses and cattle."

Pops gave me 'the look'. It was the one that was halfway between applying enough guilt to the other person to make them submit and threatening them into cooperating. I laughed.

"It's all good. I'll either take care of his ass or kick it, whichever is needed."

"I'm sure you will. You going to get things straightened out between the two of you at the same time?"

"I promised him he would hear the rest of the story about what happened in Texas. You know I keep my promises."

"I'm proud of you, baby girl," Pop grinned.

"Well, somebody should be. I worked damn hard to get this close to perfection. I deserve the praise," I grinned.

"Hear, hear," Pops toasted.


It was still early when I turned in, but the lack of sleep over the last few days was kicking my butt. Reggie was asleep in my bed already. I changed into stretch shorts and a comfy MSU t-shirt and tucked in beside him.

"Hmmm. Hey, Sis," Reggie mumbled.

It wasn't long before I drifted off.

# Chapter Thirty-Four

Sleeping peacefully, I was subconsciously aware of the sound of a familiar motorcycle nearby. Feeling warm and safe, I cuddled deeper into the blankets until I noted a rigid person next to me. Forcing myself to wake up, I yelled just in time.

"No, hold your fire, Reggie. It's just Bones," I said reaching over him and forcing his gun to point to the floor. "Damn it. Next time wake me up if you think someone is breaking in."

I leaned over to the lamp on my side of the bed and flipped the switch. The light was bright enough to verify to Reggie that the man standing in the atrium was in fact, Bones.

"What do you mean *if* I think someone is breaking in? He *was* breaking in. I heard him pick the lock. Why does he pick the lock? Why doesn't he have a key? Why doesn't he enter through the front door like everyone else?" Reggie was clearly still tired and a bit cranky.

"None of your business, to any of those questions. Now, scat. Go find Jackson and curl up with him," I said pushing him out of the bed. He stole a pillow and my favorite blanket and stomped out as I donned a robe and walked out to the atrium.

"Sorry, I forgot about your bunkmate," Bones grinned.

"You're lucky he didn't shoot your ass. What are you doing here so late? Where's Penny?" I asked while curling up at the end of one of the couches and discretely turning on a scrambler in my robe pocket.

"I waited for her to fall asleep before coming over. Tyler is at the club house, keeping an eye out in case she wakes up."

"So, only home for a day and already sneaking out behind her back? That doesn't bode well for your marriage vows, Mr. Hartwood."

"The hell with my marriage," Bones said while dragging his hand over the back of his neck. "I never loved her, Kelsey. We knew each other growing up, and I married her on a whim when I was on leave. I was back overseas when her last letter said she talked to her father about filing for divorce. I was all for the plan but didn't want to sound like a douche bag if I wrote that as a reply, so I just never wrote her back. I figured she would get the picture and the divorce would be done before I ever shipped home."

Bones sat next to me and reached out to hold my face in his hands.

"Kelsey, pure guilt was my only motivation for looking for her, especially after I met you. It didn't feel right to divorce her when she was missing, so I had to find her. It was the honorable thing to do."

"Why didn't you tell the club? Why the big secret?"

"I didn't hide it because I was emotionally distraught over some lost love. I hid it because I didn't want Whiskey and Tech and the other guys to find out that I was raised with a silver spoon in my mouth. My parents might suck, but my grandparents were the ones that raised me for the most part. I went to the best schools, drove the best cars, and had the nicest clothes. That's not your average biker background. I didn't want them to treat me different."

I pulled away from him, leaning forward, resting my head in my hands. We sat in silence for a long moment. I knew he was waiting to hear what I had to say, but my feelings were all clouded by my past.

"What now? What's the plan?" I asked.

"You tell me. I'm was ready to send Penny back to her family and wash my hands of her, but Tech said I should check with you first. He wouldn't explain why."

"You aren't going to like what I have to say, Bones."

"Talk to me, Kelsey. What's going on?"

"The FBI can't prove that she wasn't helping under duress. They are going to officially cut her loose, but there is a good chance she was a willing participant. If she was willingly in the business, she might know where some key players are at. We need that intel," I admitted.

"What do you need me to do?"

"Be a doting, loving husband for a couple of weeks. Whatever it takes, Bones. I need her to buy it."

Bones jumped off the couch.

"You want me to sleep with her? Do you hear how crazy that sounds?"

"I know you don't understand, but I need you to do this." I stood and walked toward him. "If I could do the deed myself, I would. But, you're her husband. It has to be you or she will leave. And we will miss our chance. I just need her to be around for a week or two to set her up. Please, Bones."

"Tell me why. Why is this so important?" he gritted the words between his teeth.

"I can't."

"Fuck you, Kelsey!" he roared.

Bones stormed out slamming the atrium door.

He yelled into the dark night before starting his bike and tearing up part of the stone walkway in his hasty retreat. I walked further into the atrium, pulling my robe tighter around myself as I watched him drive wildly down the slippery road to the end. Turning back, I saw Donovan in his bedroom window looking the same direction. He turned and looked over at me. I shook my head and walked back into my bedroom.

*What have I done?*

I laid awake in bed for hours before it was light out enough to drag myself up. I skipped the shower and went in search of coffee.

"Good morning, Hattie," I said planting a kiss on her cheek and retrieving my cup.

"Good morning, Sunshine," she replied. "Any idea what I should make for breakfast this morning? I'm finally at a loss. I'm not used to cooking for this many people every day."

"We'll make Reggie and Jackson bake some casseroles," I grinned. "We can sit back and tell them they are doing it wrong to rile them up."

I sat at the small kitchen table, and Hattie joined me.

"It won't work to rile us up since we know your game plan. But we will cook the casseroles," Jackson announced coming into the kitchen.

"Speak for yourself. I am still mad at Kelsey for kicking me out of her bed last night," Reggie grumbled following him in.

"But if she wouldn't have kicked you out, then we wouldn't have had the chance to spend time together before I leave today," Jackson teased.

"Since I fly out tomorrow, I think we would have made it one more day until we were both back in Texas. Besides, you agreed to move in with me so we will see plenty of each other."

"You are such a delight when you're tired, Reg," I laughed.

"Watch it, sister," Reggie scolded.

He began helping Jackson gather the food and dishes to make the casseroles. Jackson winked at me and then slapped Reggie on the ass.

"So, I take it the visit last night with Bones didn't go well," Hattie said.

"No. He's really pissed at me. I don't blame him either."

"Do you regret whatever it is that you did?" Reggie asked.

"No. I can't," I answered truthfully.

"Then give him time to sort it out. Have faith, Sis."

An hour later, our group in the kitchen had expanded to include Katie, Lisa, and Donovan.

"What? Seriously? You guys want to have a potluck tonight?" I asked again. I couldn't fathom throwing a party right now.

"We have a lot to be thankful for right now," Katie said. "Whiskey and Wild Card are both on the mend. Your Texas family is here visiting. The bad bikers are all dead, in the hospital or in jail. The FBI has cleared us of any wrong-doing. And, we are officially closed for the holiday season. Let's celebrate!"

"I think it's a great idea other than I can't drink," Lisa added.

"Anne's bringing Whiskey back today so they both will be here," Donovan added.

"I could make a couple batches of soups, and bake the pies we prepped yesterday," Hattie added. "And, I could invite Henry over. He's been calling asking when he can see me again."

Sara came stumbling in half asleep and crawled up onto my lap.

"What are they talking about?" she asked.

"They want to have a potluck party tonight. What do you think?"

"Will mom be home?" she asked curling into me.

"Your mom will be home, with Whiskey, in a few hours."

"Can Amanda come over tonight too?"

"Sure. Why don't you give her a call and see if it's okay with Goat? It appears we are throwing a party."

Sara was suddenly wide awake and ran for the house phone to call Amanda. I looked at my watch and noted that it was only 7:00 am. Poor Goat, I laughed, hoping he was already up and getting ready for work.

By 11:00 a.m. the house was swarming with people. Anne had Whiskey settled in the family room. Several club members were removing the bunk beds that we no longer needed. They promised to come back the next week to remove the rest. They were going to store them at the clubhouse until the next time they were needed. I hoped that would be never.

Jackson cleaned up the yard damage from Bones' bike. Reggie helped Hattie plan and prep the day's menu. Haley and Bridget helped Alex move back to his own house and set the guest bedroom up for Carl. They were having fun making reminder signs to post in the room. "Brush your teeth" was noted on the mirror. "Lock window before bed" was on the nightstand. "Put pants on before exiting" was noted on the inside of the bedroom door.

Goat dropped Amanda off to play while he supervised the contractors at the store. They were nice enough to start over the weekend to help secure the windows and doors. There was going to be a lot more work to do than a fresh coat of paint with all the new bullet holes to fix. Goat assured me though that it was manageable to get done before the wedding on New Year's Eve.

Donovan had already called Lisa's father and received his blessing. Of course, he downed a shot of Jack Daniels after he hung up the phone.

I was in the living room dusting when Tyler and Tech entered. Tyler came over and picked me up in a bear hug and swung me around.

"Thank you!" he grinned. He must have received his 'replacement' truck.

"You deserve it. If not for you, we would have had a store full of customers when the bullets started flying."

"Still, I was the idiot that parked in front of the line of fire," he grinned. "That truck has more holes than a strainer. We parked it in front of the clubhouse as a warning to anyone that wants to start trouble."

"Should work better than your average sign," I laughed. "You boys have time for a smoke break? I have a few thoughts I want to run by you both."

I pulled a pack of smokes and lighter from a side stand drawer, and they followed me out on the deck. Tech pulled a scrambler from his pocket, and after knocking the snow off the railing, he set it down and turned it on.

"I know the club comes first, but I was wondering if you were interested in a full-time job watching out for my family," I asked Tyler.

"Like a bodyguard?"

"No, you're not trained to be a bodyguard, though if you want, we can teach you. But you're observant. You have good gut instincts. We get distracted and are not always paying close attention to what is going on around us. That's what I would hire you to do. Watch for anything suspicious and report it to Katie, Tech or myself. I have some traveling to do in the next couple weeks, and would feel better if someone was watching their backs."

"Sure. I'm usually assigned to you anyway so it would be cool to get paid for it. And, I would like to learn to fight like you guys. It looks like fun. You really think I have good instincts?" he grinned.

"I do. What you told me about Sam was important. Then you giving us the quick warning on the Hounds, was a cherry on top. I won't involve you further into some of the other things going on, but just let us know if you see anything that looks off."

"Will do boss. Better get going. I said I would relieve Bones at the hospital to cover Wild Card. He was moved to a regular room, and they want protection for him."

Tyler left via the back porch steps and Tech waited until he was out of earshot before speaking his mind.

"Bones was a mess last night. You should explain."

"I can't. You know I can't."

"He didn't tell me everything that was said, only that you told him to get back together with his wife. Then he hit the Jack Daniels bottle pretty damn hard. He's really torn up, Kelsey."

"I know, Tech. And, believe me, I don't want to hurt him. But if the choice is Nicholas or Bones, I will always choose Nicholas."

I stepped on my cigarette and walked back into the house.

Lisa was carrying tote bags through the front door as I entered the back door. I motioned for the other girls to follow us into my bedroom where I quickly explained my plan. Everyone agreed to help without asking any questions.

By 6:00 the party was already in full swing. Dallas walked in like she was the queen of the world followed by Dave and Tammy. She spotted Goat and crossed the room with lightning speed. Goat barely registered her presence before she locked lips with him.

"Mom, behave yourself!" Dave yelled at her.

"That's nothing. You should have seen what she did to the mailman last week," Tammy giggled.

Dave shook his head and grabbed a beer.

Dallas crawled up Goats body like a monkey and strapped her legs around his hips. He turned her back into the wall to press against her. Dave stomped the opposite direction into the living room.

"That's what she did to the mailman," Tammy giggled, and we all laughed.

"Can I get some help here?" Tyler called from the kitchen doorway.

James, Tech, and I jumped up and moved that direction. Tyler was half carrying a pale but grinning Wild Card through the door.

"What the hell?" I asked.

"My guard shift was over, and I was pulling out of the hospital parking lot when I spotted him sneaking out the hospital door. He refused to go back inside. He wanted to come to the party."

Tyler readily gave up control of Cooper to James and Tech. They led him into the dining room and settled him next to Whiskey. Cooper didn't waste any time reaching for a beer and cracking it open. I walked over and took the beer away, along with Whiskey's. Hattie followed behind me and handed them each a glass of water.

I had just sat again when Bones strolled in holding Penny's hand.

She was beautiful. Her long white-blonde hair ran in a sleek river down her back. She was dressed as expected, in high tailored fashion, down to the tips of her peep toe shoes. Her makeup looked professional and accented her shrewd eyes, as she scanned the room and tried not to display her distaste for the blue-collar crowd.

"Welcome," I said standing to greet them. "Bones, it's good to see you made it back to town. You will need to be sure to take your turn giving us a break from Wild Card and Whiskey while they recover from their injuries." I turned to Penny. "And, you must be Penny. You are just as beautiful as Bones described. I'm glad you could make it. Can I get you something to drink?"

"Yes, please. Do you have any decent wine?"

"Red or white, dear?" Hattie asked, stepping in to offer assistance.

"White, thank you," she answered dismissively, turning her back to Hattie as Bones helped relieve her of her coat.

"Here, let me take that for you. I can put it in the guest bedroom with the others," I offered as the coat was handed to me.

When I arrived in the guest bedroom, Tech was already waiting for the coat. He started inserting his equipment in the seam, while Anne was waiting to sew the lining back into place. I rejoined the guests.

An hour later, my poor acting skills were fully used up. We all struggled to continue being nice to Penny as she made rude comments repeatedly and intentionally. Lisa finally saved the day, by turning the conversation.

"Kelsey, did you sort your purses today? I want to have a look at what you are giving away before you drop them off at the mission. Some of them are very high end, and I might steal them from you," she grinned.

"I need a new purse," Anne whined.

"Me too," Hattie chimed in. "Do you have any red ones? I just bought a new black coat that has a fancy red scarf."

"They're all still on my bed. Go help yourselves to whatever you want," I offered.

The girls all drifted that direction, pulling Penny along for the ride. I leaned back and exhaled. Pretending to be nice was exhausting. Bones chuckled from behind me.

"Suck it up, Kelsey. Your role is nothing compared to what you sentenced me to," he whispered before he wandered off.

Wild Card still sat in his chair, slightly away from the table. He had been intently watching and listening the entire time.

I nodded my head toward the living room. "Was that you that convinced him to help?" I asked quietly.

"He's not happy about it, but I told him that there was no way in hell you would go along with something like this if it weren't necessary."

"Thank you," I whispered, hearing the girls coming back.

"So, did everyone find something they wanted?" I asked.

"Yes, we all found the perfect new bag. Penny even found one that she likes. Hattie found one that will work with her new coat. And, I got the baby blue one that will go with that dress that I bought," Lisa said.

"What about you, Anne?" I leaned forward to see Anne still staring at the purse she selected.

"I'm in love," she said as she gently stroked the purse.

"Well, that's nice, dear," Hattie laughed.

I decided it was time to make a toast, and James whistled loudly to gain everyone's attention.

"When Katie asked this morning if we could throw a party tonight, I wasn't in the mood. It's been a long couple of days, and I just wanted to crawl in my bed and disappear. But I'm glad everyone convinced me otherwise. I want to thank all of you, for coming to our rescue. There is no way we would have survived if we didn't have the support of the club, friends, and family.

I look around tonight and see a lot of reasons to celebrate.

"To my Friends and Family!" I yelled.

I lifted my drink and cheers were bellowed around the house. I downed the rest of my drink before hugs started circulating.

It was late before I turned in for the night. Earlier, I had Wild Card sent to my room, figuring we would share the bed tonight and plan more permanent sleeping quarters tomorrow.

"You must be b_____ oper said as I entered and turned on the small lamp on the dresser.

"Completely wiped. You going to behave if we share the bed tonight?" I asked.

"As much as I love that body of yours, even the thought of moving evokes muscle spasms and not the good kind."

"Good. I wouldn't want to blur the lines."

"The lines are clear, Kelsey. You are in love with Bones. Once upon a time, you cared about me, but you never fell in love with me. I knew that even back then."

"I promised you the truth, Cooper. I owe it to you. You're right, neither one of us fell for the other, but we did become closer than either one of us intended. And, then shit got real," I said stealing one of Katie's familiar lines.

I sat on the side of the bed, convincing myself to tell him the rest. "Cooper, the night you came home and asked for a divorce was the same day I found out I was pregnant."

Cooper reached for my face, lifting my chin so I would look him in the eyes. He saw the truth of what I was saying, as my eyes began to pool with tears.

"Kelsey, I didn't know-," he started.

"It's not your fault. And the divorce wasn't the problem. I just wasn't ready to leave you guys. And, the pregnancy had me freaked. I was in no position to raise a baby. Neither one of us were."

"Did you have an abortion?" he closed his eyes as he asked the question, dreading the answer.

"No, Cooper," I assured him and reached out to place my hand on top of his. "I needed time to figure things out, so I moved over near the racetracks and took a job as a groomer. The next week, Pops showed up at the track to convince me to move in with him. We were in the middle of arguing when a runaway horse barreled our way. It was heading straight for a group of kids on a field trip. I didn't even think. I just reacted. I ran out in front of the stallion and grabbed his reins. The horse reared and kicked me."

In my head, I saw it all happening again in slow motion. The screams of the kids as the horse kicked me and threw me into the fence. The look of panic on Pops' face as he tried to separate the horse from where I was pinned.

"Luckily, Pops and some other men were able to pull the horse away and secure it. But, I lost the baby."

"Pops knew you were pregnant?"

"I never told him, but he suspected. All those fricken apple pies I kept eating," I groaned. "I just couldn't stop craving apple pie!"

Wild Card nodded, as we both remembered the strange obsession I had with keeping the house stocked with fresh apple pie.

"When I started bleeding, Pops knew for sure."

"And, you blamed me. If I hadn't asked for the divorce none of it would have happened," he leaned back and looked up at the ceiling. "God, we would have a child by now."

"It wasn't your fault, Cooper. I think I really blamed myself, but I couldn't handle the guilt, so I redirected it to you. And, as horrible as it sounds, I think it was for the best. Neither one of us were prepared to raise a child. I wasn't the only one having nightmares back then."

"We would have found a way to make it work, Kelsey. We could have been a family."

"No, Cooper, I couldn't have. I could not have raised that baby with my past still unsettled," I shook my head. "I know you don't understand, but for me, it would have been choosing one child for another. I was not prepared to make that choice."

He looked at me, really looked at me, for the first time in all the days that I had known him. And, he finally saw it all, the pain, the loss, the fear, the anger.

"I don't know what to say."

"You are still my friend, Cooper. I'm sorry that I blamed you."

"You and I," he said while grasping my hand tightly, "we might be the worst married couple in the world, but you will always have me in your life."

As fresh tears fell, I leaned in and kissed his cheek.

He reached up and wiped the tears away.

"You need some sleep. We can talk more tomorrow," he comforted me.

I nodded and rose to move to the bathroom when there was a light knock on the door. I opened it to find an agitated Tech on the other side.

"Meet me downstairs," he said. "*Now.*"

I turned to Cooper and asked, "Can you make it down the stairs without assistance? I think it's time I explained a few more things. The demons are getting closer."

Cooper carefully exited the bed and followed me down to the War Room. He watched carefully as I entered the security code, and nodded indicating that he would remember the code. Inside, Tech and Katie waited for us.

"About time you are adding troops to the army," Tech commented. "I was scanning through tonight's audio tapes and Sam made the call we were waiting to hear. It's fucked up, so be prepared."

"Prospect Sam?" Cooper asked.

"Yeah, we'll catch you up on the rest later, but Nicholas wasn't a man I was in love with. Nicholas is my son. And, he was kidnapped a few years ago. Sam was sent to spy on me and report back to the same people that took Nicholas."

"Holy shit. The nightmares – he's your son?" Cooper appeared completely shocked. I pulled a stool out for him to sit, afraid he would topple over otherwise.

"We are now listening in on Penny as well. The coat, the purse, they have been accessorized with our listening and tracking devices. We think she may reach out to the human trafficking world. We want to see if her connections lead back to the same group."

Tech started the audio of Sam's phone conversation:

Female: You're late. I've been standing here for 10 minutes.

Sam: Sorry to have inconvenienced you. This assignment isn't exactly a cake walk.

Female: Stop whining. What have you found out?

Sam: Nothing new. I haven't heard a word about Florida or any names mentioned. As far as I can tell, Kelsey is just running her business. It's her friends that have trouble always following them.

Female: What about Penny Hartwood?

Sam: Why do you want to know about Bones' wife? Kelsey didn't even know her until tonight.

Female: So she's there?

Sam: Yeah. She's with Bones staying at the clubhouse. They were all cozy and kissy face tonight. Personally, I can't stand her.

Female: Shut up

Sam: Look, let me talk to my sister. It's been two months. Either you let me talk to her, or we're done.

Female: I will tell you when we are done. And, I will decide when you talk to her again. If you challenge me, I will just kill her. Understood?

Female: Understood?

Sam: *YES*! I understand.

Female: Good. Report in on Thursday, on time.


The call was disconnected.

"That's Nola," I confirmed.

"You sure? It's been years, Kelsey," Tech questioned.

"It's Nola. I'm sure."

I sat on the closest stool and rested my head in my shaking hands.


"I looked it up. Sam has a twelve-year-old sister named Bianca that went missing about eleven months ago. They have different fathers and different last names, so I didn't see it in his background check. He's from a poor neighborhood where kids run away all the time, so the police never made it a priority case."

"Obviously, I have a lot of catching up to do," Wild Card said. "But, can you trace the location of the phone calls for this Nola person?"

"Yeah. The number traces back to a pay phone in Miami. But as smart as this chick is, she probably rotates call locations."

"So we find her next location and have someone pick her up."

"No," I interrupted. "Look, I know you are trying to help, and we need it, but as you said, you have a lot of catching up to do. Nola is deadly. And, she's the only one that knows where Nicholas and now Sam's sister, Bianca, are."

I got up and rubbed my neck.

"We need sleep. We will meet up in the morning with fresh minds."

I walked out alone.

Tears flowed down my face as I walked through the dark house to my bedroom. Once there, I curled up on my bed and cried myself to sleep.

*I'll find you, Nicholas. Stay alive. I'll be there soon.*

Thank you for reading Kelsey's Burden: Past Haunts. I hope you are enjoying the series, but if you've come this far, I'm sure you're feeling the itch to find out more about Kelsey's past.

Well, hold on to your hats, here comes Book Three: Friends and Foes!

# FRIENDS and FOES

The story continues as darkness surrounds Kelsey and her friends. After years of research, she is finally making progress with her investigation. The odds are stacked against her and time is running out.

Will her friends step up to help her fight her enemies? Will she win or lose the second war against her foes? And, if she succeeds, what will the final price for her victory be?

Be sure to stay in touch to receive book release information. Updates will be provided through my Facebook page: Author Kaylie Hunter or if you would like to join my email list for book release announcements simply send me an email request at AuthorKaylieHunter@gmail.com.

## Kelsey's Burden Series:

LAYERED LIES

PAST HAUNTS

FRIENDS and FOES

BLOOD and TEARS

LOVE and RAGE

If you are a fan of this series – don't forget to tell others about them by leaving a review on one of the distributors/store sites. Thank You!

At five-years-old, I stood in the far corner of the playground looking through the chain-link fence down the long residential street. I wasn't seeing the neighborhood that stretched in front of me though. I had once again drifted off inside my head, where the people were adventurous, funny, and brave. And while I don't remember what tale I was daydreaming of — I remember my mother calling to me about twenty feet away on the other side of the fence. I snapped out of the trance and focused on her, but she pointed behind me.

Turning, I was surprised to see that the playground was empty. The security guard stood patiently waiting for me at the far away school's doors. I ran as quickly as my little legs could carry me, fearing I was in trouble. The security guard grinned kindly down at me as she opened the door to grant me access.

Racing down two halls, I entered my assigned kindergarten room. The other kids were working on drawings, and my teacher was walking around spraying her plants with the water bottle. She turned when she heard me enter, as I quickly raced to my desk.

"I called for you three times," my teacher smiled, referring to her usual bellow of olly-olly-oxen-free. "You must've been far away." She tapped the side of her head and nodded at me before turning back to continue watering her plants.

And, that was it. That was all she said. She wasn't mad. I wasn't in trouble. She understood. But, she was a rare gem. As I progressed through the grade levels, it became less and less acceptable to 'space-out' and other adults were not so accepting of my lack of attention. I worked diligently to stay in the here and now. And, slowly my daydreaming worlds slipped away.

Until now. Now I schedule time to drift off into these other worlds and am blessed to be able to show my readers a glimpse of them. Imagine that.

Best Wishes to All! I look forward to hearing from you!
*Kaylie Hunter*

41141175R00215

Made in the USA
Middletown, DE
04 March 2017